"I'm not accustomed to arguing with a woman."

She sighed. "Then please don't."

"Look. Only a small percentage who attempt to make it to the Klondike actually get there."

She fingered the wool threads of her shawl. "I'm aware of the challenges."

"A woman as delicate as yourself can hardly keep up—"

"Why does everyone use that word around me? Delicate."

He planted a hand on his hips. "Don't make me tell you."

"Why not?"

"You couldn't take my exp‌l⸻

"Then it's all ⸻

"You're incon‌⸻

Dumbfounded, ⸻ up at him. "Incompetent? ⸻ugh medical college to be told by *you* that I'm incompetent!"

The cool lines of his face remained impassive. "We'll see if you can handle life outside the walls of your mansion."

"How dare you!" Her chin trembled. "I'll show you what I can and can't handle...!"

* * *

Klondike Doctor
Harlequin® Historical #848—May 2007

KATE BRIDGES

KLONDIKE DOCTOR

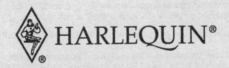

HARLEQUIN®

TORONTO • NEW YORK • LONDON
AMSTERDAM • PARIS • SYDNEY • HAMBURG
STOCKHOLM • ATHENS • TOKYO • MILAN • MADRID
PRAGUE • WARSAW • BUDAPEST • AUCKLAND

ISBN-13: 978-0-373-29448-0
ISBN-10:   0-373-29448-4

KLONDIKE DOCTOR

Author Note

The height of the Klondike Gold Rush occurred between 1897 and 1899. For Americans and Canadians, the Yukon was one of the last frontiers.

The border between Alaska and Yukon Territory had never been clearly defined. It came into dispute between the Americans and Canadians when the massive goldstrike was discovered in Canada along the Klondike River close to Dawson City. The dispute was settled peacefully, and the border was defined and guarded at the top of the mountain peaks by the North-West Mounted Police.

I had the privilege of traveling to the Yukon and Alaska to research this book, savor the wild beauty, touch the ice-cold rivers and inhale pure, fresh air. I was stunned by the jagged terrain and rough waters the stampeders had to cross to get from Alaska to the Yukon, and I tried to capture some of that difficulty in this novel. Only one of every three stampeders who set out for the Yukon made it and many of these hardy people were eccentric characters. I hope you enjoy *Klondike Doctor,* the first novel in my new series about the Klondike Gold Rush. To see photographs of the area, please visit my Web site at www.katebridges.com.

This book is dedicated to my friend and fellow writer,
Kathleen Davies.

Thank you for your kindness, support and the endless
information on living in the Yukon.

Available from Harlequin® Historical and
KATE BRIDGES

The Doctor's Homecoming #597
Luke's Runaway Bride #626
The Midwife's Secret #644
The Surgeon #685
The Engagement #704
The Proposition #719
The Bachelor #743
A Season of the Heart #771
"The Christmas Gifts"
The Commander #810
Klondike Doctor #848

Other works include
Harlequin Books

Frontier Christmas
"The Long Journey Home"

DON'T MISS THESE OTHER
NOVELS AVAILABLE NOW:

#847 HIGH PLAINS BRIDE
Jenna Kernan

#849 A MOST UNCONVENTIONAL COURTSHIP
Louise Allen

#850 HER IRISH WARRIOR
Michelle Willingham

Chapter One

British Columbia, late May 1898

"All you have to do is pretend I'm your sister," she said.

Frustrated, Sergeant Colton Hunter of the North-West Mounted Police stared at the bold young woman sitting across from him in the first-class compartment of the train. Her posture stiffened. Colt pressed his shoulder to the velvet drapes of the rumbling window and assessed her money-bought looks.

"Miss, I can no more pretend you're my sister than I can pretend you're my maid."

"Try harder. You can start with the name. It's not Miss. It's not Doctor. It's Elizabeth. Just plain Elizabeth."

There was nothing plain about her, yet there was no way on earth he wanted to be stuck with Dr. Elizabeth Langley. She might seem harmless, but Colt, as private bodyguard to her father, knew otherwise. He would never trust her again. What she'd done to him in his personal life had been reckless. Maybe accidental, but reckless nonetheless.

And now *this*.

The morning sun billowed over the Coast Mountains of British Columbia, through their window, and lit the red sleeve of his Mountie uniform. They'd only been riding east for fifteen minutes and were still making stops on the outskirts of Vancouver when Colt stood up and slid the aisle door closed to prevent anyone from overhearing.

He had one last chance at trying to convince her.

"Listen, miss, I don't know why you think I'm supposed to be your savior. Take this train across the country like you planned. Take that ship to England. They're expecting you." He tossed his Mountie Stetson to the seat and eased in beside it.

"I have no intention of doing that," said the young doctor. "I'm getting out at the next stop with you and your men. Furthermore—"

"Why do you always make things difficult?"

"They don't have to be. Just escort me to the Klondike. You're going anyway—"

"Sh." Exasperated, he leaned forward on the cushion. His long legs, straining beneath dark breeches, penetrated the swirl of her gray satin skirts. "Miss, I beg of you, lower your voice. Or better yet, pinch your lips together. You're jeopardizing my mission and the safety of my men. Surely even you can understand *that*."

Her face colored as ripe as a berry.

Her dark blond hair, pulled tight above her ears, exposed flushed cheeks and searching brown eyes. Soft amber stones dangled off her ears.

It was hard to believe she was a newly graduated doctor. Her youth—midtwenties—and her gender contrasted sharply with the gray-haired doctors most folks were accustomed to seeing. Dressed from head to toe in shiny gray satin, she looked untouchable. But then, she'd always been above his station. Lace and satin were buttoned up to her throat. They might rouse another man's curiosity as to the spoils that lay beneath, but Colt would be damned if he'd give in to those thoughts.

Nonetheless, he tugged at his hot collar.

A small gray hat, adorned with a burgundy feather that plucked the air as she spoke, topped the blond curls pinned on her head. A highly ridiculous outfit for traveling.

"My father doesn't think I'm jeopardizing your mission." Elizabeth straightened her spine again on the red velvet seat. "When you get to the Yukon border where the crimes are occurring, you're to escort me to my grandfather's door while the rest of your men finish the investigation."

"Perfect," he said with sarcasm. "Just what every officer wants to hear. To be on the brink of adventure and freedom. To head the team directly into the heart of danger, only to be cut short and forced to escort a…" His gaze swept over her.

Her lips pressed together. Her cheeks grew taut. "A *what?*"

"A coddled young woman to Dawson City."

She gasped. "I'm a doctor."

"Of what?"

The light in her eyes flared. "I beg your pardon?"

"You're a doctor of rashes and fevers…or whatever else ails the female population of high society Vancouver." He wondered what else she spent her time on, when privately summoned by a lady's maid. Childbirth? The menstrual cycle? "You've no business interfering in the lives of working men. Hardworking men you don't understand."

"I'm not here for your insults. I know all about the differences between men and women."

Elizabeth reeled to the window, but not before he saw the dewy sheen that sprang to her eyes.

He fought the urge to feel sorry for her.

She would *have* to come to terms with her father's limitations on what she could and couldn't practice in medicine. Her father, the Finance Minister of Canada, liked to call himself a champion for women's education, but there were natural limits to his generosity.

Folks weren't comfortable with female doctors. It was said they took business away from men, that women didn't have the constitution needed to handle gruesome illness or surgery. Being the Minister's daughter put her in an awkward social situation, as well. She couldn't very well work beneath her.

And her father had forbidden her to practice medicine on men. She was forbidden to touch male strangers, and forbidden to have a man "drop his drawers" in front of her. It was indecent, Colt agreed.

"I know what your anger stems from." She turned stiffly toward him, the ruffles on her bosom fluttering. "And I can't seem to apologize enough for the heartache I caused you at Christmas—"

"Perhaps you did me a favor."

"I did you *no* favor. Please, let's not pretend. And you're doing me no favor in taking me north. You're doing your duty."

Who the hell was she, telling him what his duties

were? Perhaps this quality of hers was why her own engagement had fallen apart.

His muscles flexed beneath his uniform. It was no use fighting her. Her father was too powerful. "I shall *do* my duty, miss, as promised."

The train screeched around a curve. Sunlight slanted across her cheekbones. "Why do you insist on calling me *miss?* One would think that after eight years' time—"

"It's my *duty.*"

She groaned.

"I'll escort you to the Klondike." He shifted his legs in the tight space between them. "But first we've got to go over the rules."

She leaned back. "All right. I'll listen to your rules. *Colt.*"

He hated when she used his first name. He hated her ability to weave in and out of his private life. For the next five weeks, she'd be doing exactly that.

His plan had been simple until two days ago, when she'd confided to her father that she wanted to join her grandfather in the Klondike for the summer. Apparently, she preferred to practice medicine on the hundreds of migrating women instead of touring England.

Gold had recently been discovered in Dawson City, Yukon. The gold rush was creating a frantic pitch heard around the world. Most stampeders were American, but the Klondike belonged to Canada and was policed by the Mounties. With a population that'd swelled overnight to thirty-five thousand, the area had an overabundance of gold but few resources to feed, clothe and house the miners.

Food items that sold for pennies in Vancouver sold for one hundred times their value in gold dust in Dawson City. Criminals infested the trails. A Klondike crime ring was targeting incoming food supplies. Since the Finance Minister was responsible for some of those supply lines getting through, he was sending Colt as part of a team of six Mounties to infiltrate the ring. They would travel in disguise as a group of brothers. They'd be hauling a ton of sausages to exchange for a fortune.

What better way to attract thieves than with a cache of goods literally worth its weight in gold?

But *she* wanted to be their sister. Colt pressed his hand to his thigh. "You're not a doctor."

She smiled in disbelief. "Pardon me?"

"Rule number one—on this journey, forget you're a doctor."

Her smile faded. "What on earth for?"

"We're supposed to be a modest family of ranchers seeking a great fortune. We don't want anyone thinking you're educated. Or wealthy."

An artery at the base of her throat pulsed. "But the whole purpose of my going is to treat women when I get there."

"I understand that, but I'll need to get you there without compromising *my* duties." He glanced at the suede bag by her feet. "Since you're not a doctor, you've got to leave your medical bag behind."

"But the patients when I get there—"

"You can borrow supplies. From the two or three doctors already at the hospital—"

"That hospital is nothing more than two log huts. They don't have enough—"

"If you can't abide by the first rule, then you can't—"

"What if someone falls ills on the journey? Someone in distress—"

"You'll ignore them."

Elizabeth stared at him in dismay. The train careened around a corner and they braced themselves. She looked, quite simply, as though she wanted to throttle him.

"We'll be traveling in the wilderness. No help, no towns, no shops to buy supplies. Nothing but the wind and sun around us. What about wild animals and accidents that might befall us? What if someone on the team gets ill? One of your men? Maybe you."

"We can take care of our own bruises."

"*Bruises?* Is that what you think I do?"

"Look, we can't risk you taking the bag. Some folks might have heard of your father. Or maybe his unusual daughter."

"But I've got a whole trunk of badly needed gauze and tonics—"

"Sorry. Not on this trip."

She snapped to the window and stared at the passing shanties. The woods were getting thicker. They were leaving Vancouver behind.

Her cap and feather shifted on her head. "What if I take some essential supplies and tuck them into my clothing bag, but leave the medical bag behind?"

Colt leaned back into the plush upholstery. "That might work. But you can only lend *us* the supplies. No strangers. You can't let on you're a doctor."

She pressed her mouth closed and yanked off her hat.

"Rule number two," he continued. "We're changing our names."

"Yes, of course. But how am I to—"

"I'll make it as simple as possible. Our surname will be Blade. Your first name will be Liza. It's close enough to Elizabeth so if your real name slips out, no one will blink. I'll keep mine as Colt, Tommy will remain Tommy. As for the other four men you haven't met yet, I'll introduce you by their new names so it won't confuse you. You think you can heed that?"

She nodded. "The Blade family. From where?"

"Ottawa. We sold our ten acres of farmland to buy supplies for the trip and payment on a gold claim. You know the Ottawa area from your travels with your father almost as well as we do, so picture it in your mind if someone asks."

"And our parents? Where are they?"

"They died in a terrible fire."

"How awful." She sniffed. "How old were we?"

"No one's going to ask that."

She surveyed him. "They might."

"You were the youngest at six, okay?"

He watched her lashes flicker. "That's so tragic."

Colt sighed. "I'm the oldest. Ten years older than you. I'm bossy, okay? I boss everyone around and you all listen." He *was* the commanding officer on the team, so this would make sense.

"I bet you're the least liked."

Colt scowled. "The final rule. Number three. You've got to look and act the part of my obedient sister. You're not above my station. You're not an eyelash better than me. Got that?"

"Huh," she moaned softly. She wove her satin-gloved fingers together, looked down at her lap and fingered her cap. Sunlight streaked the blond hair amassed on top of her head.

With a swoop of his broad Stetson, Colt rose. He

glanced through the window at the jagged mountains. "We're almost there. Twenty more minutes."

She had bought tickets to London months ago to visit friends. Colt was supposed to escort her partway by train, so they were still using the story as a cover to hide their new trip to the Klondike. Everyone in Vancouver would think she was spending the summer in London. When she didn't arrive in London, everyone there would think she'd changed her mind and was remaining back home. But her real journey was about to start.

He opened the door that led to a private bath and sleeping quarters. "It's time for you to change. I'll change out here and then flag Tommy back in."

She rose, and by the color in her cheeks, was finally catching on that he was boss here. She brushed by him in a womanly sway, a bundle of satin and feathers. Colt inhaled her fresh scent and observed how the delicate fabric fell against her ample curves.

She had a hell of a walk—a way of penetrating into a man's private thoughts, making him imagine all sorts of things and lingering in his imagination when she wasn't welcome.

Abruptly, he turned away.

He'd never confess it aloud, but rule number three would be the most difficult one for him. He swallowed hard.

Sister. Elizabeth was his devoted *sister*.

Why did he provoke her at every opportunity?

Alone and half-naked in the private quarters of the train, Elizabeth tugged a chemise over her corset, shoved her bare arms into a simple white blouse, then fastened the multitude of buttons, silently criticizing Colt.

What could be wrong with a woman wanting adventure and freedom, the very things he'd mentioned?

Men and women were similar in many regards. Weren't they equally cheered at seeing the sun rise on a warm spring day? Didn't they both enjoy the taste of a strong cup of coffee? Weren't they equally touched by the sad tales of the weary traveler?

Her enthusiasm for adventure didn't mean she didn't want home and family, too. When Elizabeth had ventured to tell someone—her dear Gerard—about her bigger dreams, he had been dismayed.

Gerard. Her stomach fluttered at the thought of seeing him in the Klondike. A twinge of guilt followed, at how he must have felt reading her goodbye letter. How sad that in six months' time, he hadn't written back. Was he that angry with her?

It seemed anger was the only sentiment she was able to evoke in men. First her father. Then Gerard. Now Colt.

With a sigh, Elizabeth stepped into a brown muslin skirt. Cool mountain air whisked up her bare thighs. She pulled the skirt over her hips and clasped the buttons.

She'd prove that her abilities as a doctor were equal to any man's. That no one could bar her from treating male patients. If she could ease someone's discomfort in sickness or injury, no matter what their sex, then why should it matter to a bunch of other healthy men who ran the country?

And there was her other personal dilemma, her uncle's secret whispered on his deathbed…she'd see to that in the Klondike, too. Gerard would have to answer directly to her.

She thought she knew Gerard, yet if he was involved in the theft with her uncle…

Elizabeth rummaged through her bags and repacked necessities. After changing into more sensible boots, she burst out of the private quarters and back into Colt's so quickly that he hadn't finished changing.

He was buttoning a fresh blue shirt and tucking it into faded denim jeans, the rugged ones miners and drovers usually wore. He had a forceful stance, and it contrasted with the intimate nature of his buttoning. The muscles of his chest rippled beneath his undershirt, and slivers of smooth tanned skin, bronzed by the sun and hammered by the wind, slid in and out of view. She was frozen by the sight.

Eyes as gray as gunmetal held hers.

Her heart seemed to beat at a hummingbird's pace. "I'm sorry, I—I didn't realize…"

She glanced away.

"It's okay. I'm almost done."

She looked back to see him buttoning his sleeves.

"You seem accustomed to women watching you dress."

He raised his eyebrows, smiling gently, and she blushed. She always managed to blurt the most inappropriate comments to this man.

A brown cowboy hat, black leather belt and silver buckle completed the striking picture. His cowboy boots were well worn-in the toe and heels, the creases along the tan leather softened from years of wear.

When he gave her a slow gaze up the length of her body, she shifted with discomfort.

Gerard had never looked at her like this. Even when…even when she'd been with him…in their most intimate time, he'd been a gentleman. She reminded herself Colt was a Mountie, sworn to uphold the law, and one of her father's most trusted guards.

Rubbing her face to mask her unease, Elizabeth stepped to her medical bag. She brought out the few items she needed most—stethoscope, scissors, sutures and gauze— and tucked them into her two other bags. She plopped her gray satin skirt and blouse onto a discarded pile. Next to the red leather trunk she was forced to leave behind.

"Two bags?" Colt declared. "You've whittled your things to two bags already?"

Elizabeth hid a satisfied smile. "You wanted me to pack lightly."

"But I didn't think…well…*good*." Colt tucked his uniform into a leather bag of his own. "This will stay behind."

For some inexplicable reason, she regretted that she wouldn't be able to see him in uniform on this journey. She'd never seen him *out* of uniform before, not once in eight years, and this casual look held a new fascination. But not for her. She tore her gaze away from his denim-clad figure.

Colt, a block of muscle, tugged on the door and leaned into the aisle. "Tommy, we're ready."

Tommy St. James—now Tommy Blade—a slightly younger and shorter Mountie with similar brown hair to Colt's, sometimes served as her father's replacement bodyguard. He, too, was dressed in rancher's clothes. She didn't know him well, but his build and the agile way he moved reminded Elizabeth of a boxer. Behind him came another Mountie, a skinnier man dressed in full uniform.

"Miss," said Tommy, "this constable will tend to your extra luggage. He'll make sure your bags arrive safely at their secret location for the summer. He'll also pretend you're still on board and going all the way to Montreal."

"Thank you." She reached into her skirt pocket and handed him a parchment envelope. "When you get to Montreal, could you please deliver this letter to the ship bound for England?"

"Yes, miss."

Her hosts, Lord and Lady Abercrombie in London, wouldn't receive the letter for another month. It stated that with much regret, Elizabeth had decided to stay in Canada for the summer. By the time she and her *brothers* reached the Klondike, the secrecy of their mission would no longer have to be guarded.

"Get ready," said Colt, causing her pulse to jump. "Wait for my command. We'll disembark after everyone else."

The train hissed through the forest, causing blackbirds in the cedars to flee for their lives. Timber shacks appeared in clusters. Their chimneys spewed smoke, laden with the heavy scent of peat moss. Then their train left the houses behind as it chugged and bellowed into the iron-vaulted ceiling of Whippoorwill Station, like a man chugging on his last breath.

"Gracious," whispered Elizabeth, peering at the packed platforms. "I've never seen so many people."

"They're heading to the coast," said Colt. "To board the ships for the Klondike." In the same direction they should be headed, except they were still pretending to be going to England. Soon they'd be traveling incognito and turn west again.

"I've read about gold rush fever in the papers, but this is incredible," she said.

Their train rolled past lineups a quarter-mile long and six people deep. Some travelers were dressed in rags. Others in expensive suits. Some were accompanied by women. There wouldn't be enough trains to seat them. And when they reached the coast, Elizabeth knew there wouldn't be enough ships to carry them.

Goats, donkeys and horses lined the far platforms, waiting to board the boxcars. The smell of animals cloistered with their sweaty owners drifted through her window.

A toothless man, wearing a potato sack as a shirt, sold lettuce and peas in one corner. Beside him, a fishmonger weighed salmon on a scale. The earthy smells of vegetables and fish drifted into the car as the train came to its final stop.

"Stay put," Colt said to Elizabeth. "But you go, Tommy. Find the others and we'll meet you someplace outside the north entry."

Tommy scooted down the aisle and with duffel bag in hand, jumped to the platform. He got lost in the crowd. Colt nudged Elizabeth to the side door. They waited in the aisle, watching for the perfect moment to disappear into an ocean of bodies.

Her dear brother, she reminded herself, aware of Colt's shirtsleeve brushing her own, his solid stance and the breadth of his shoulders as he tried to fit into the cramped space.

"Now," he said.

Elizabeth gripped her handbag, shawl and umbrella and bounded down the steps onto the stone platform.

Colt lugged her two carpetbags as well as his own duffel. The dark brown hair at his temples glistened beneath his cowboy hat, moist from the heat.

They headed toward the merchant stalls and ticket vendors.

Panic quelled in her throat. What if she couldn't get their story straight? She leaned in toward his tall frame and kept her voice low so others couldn't overhear. Her lips were an inch away from his shaven cheek. "Do any of us have family of our own? Wives or husbands?"

He turned his smooth dark face toward her and she realized she was standing much too close. His eyes flickered and her stomach tugged in response.

"I suppose some of us should. Let's say you and Tommy have never been married. Let's say I was married once."

Her voice strained. "What happened to her?"

A muscle flexed in his jaw. "She ran off with the head butler from the mayor's house."

Elizabeth didn't miss the slight. "Are you trying to make me feel terrible about your fiancée again? Rosalyn was the best kitchen maid we ever had and I truly enjoyed her company. She was the one who came to *me* for advice."

His gaze riveted on her face. "Why exactly do you suppose that was?" he asked with the same disgust as when he'd first confronted Elizabeth, two days after Christmas when she was home for the holidays. Why couldn't the man lighten up?

"I don't know. Maybe Rosalyn trusted me because I'm a doctor. A female one, as you and my father insist on reminding me. The only advice I ever gave Rosalyn was to follow her heart. To choose love over what others expected of her."

"Love?" His voice was tempered restraint. "Then you

might be happy to know she married that butler. He's a lot older, but he's the man she wanted, with money in the pot and required love in his heart. I hear their first child is on the way."

Elizabeth groaned, feeling sympathetic and wishing he'd accept her explanation. "When I advised her on how to choose between two men, I had no idea you were one of them. How could I know you were courting, let alone engaged? You kept it to yourselves."

His cowboy hat drew hard shadows on his cheeks. "It's called being discreet. A skill you are sorely lacking, otherwise you never would have put your nose where it didn't belong."

The man's arrogance was too much. He'd never accept her apology, no matter how hard she tried.

She snapped. "I think I did Rosalyn a favor."

His gray eyes narrowed. He lowered his bags to the platform. "How's that?"

"You're driven by your duties and inflexible when it comes to women. Good qualities in a bodyguard. Poor in a husband."

His voice came as low as a growl, as if he were uttering a threat. "What makes you think you know what drives me? Don't you have enough romantic woes of your own?"

She detected pity, and flung her bags to the ground. "I did her a favor…because now she won't be saddled with you for life."

"The same might be said for your poor Gerard. He'll no longer be saddled with a mouthy wench. Congratulations. You've managed to ruin two engagements in one winter."

Elizabeth gasped. *"You…I…ahh…"*

"Do you finally understand what you're getting your-self into?" And suddenly his dark and dangerous face was a blink away from hers.

Chapter Two

Colt's breath was hot on Elizabeth's neck, but she didn't dare flinch. A wave of heat pounded up her skin.

"I repeat," she said, damned if she'd cut and run from this man. Instead, she'd ignore his outburst. "Are any of us married?"

He stared at her for a moment and she braced herself for what he might do next.

"Let's just say I'm a widower. No kids."

Elizabeth glared at his tight expression, then yanked her bag off the ground and huffed past the folks streaming around them. Tommy flagged them from the corner a hundred yards away, then disappeared outside.

The tension between them as they stalked in silence toward the north entry gripped her stomach. "At least this journey will provide me with one satisfaction. You'll finally have to address me by a Christian name, and not lord your position over me. How many brothers do you know who address their sisters as *miss?* Honestly, you work for my father, yet you act higher and mightier than us all!"

Colt stepped around a donkey and backed away from an approaching ticket vendor. "There'll be one satisfaction in it for me, too." With an ease that infuriated her, he whipped their bags around as if they were as light as pillows. "You'll finally have to help with your own blasted luggage, and help yourself up and down the buckboard. I mean, how many brothers do you know who treat their sisters like royalty?"

A preacher and his wife passed by, frowning at them. Elizabeth flushed. She and Colt were acting like…like *siblings.* "I guess I'm getting what I asked for, aren't I?"

Colt was not amused.

She needed to do something to salvage this situation, to make their journey tolerable. People were staring.

Be pleasant and compatible, she told herself.

The silence coming from Colt indicated he was re-thinking his approach, too. He stacked the bags on the platform, removed his hat and tossed it to the pile. Running his fingers through his dark hair, he swiveled toward her, his manner somewhat calmer.

"Listen, are you hungry? We may not eat for hours."

Elizabeth pressed her bag against her swirling skirts. The hum of voices inside the station echoed off the vaulted ceiling. She craned her head upward, forcing herself to face him.

"I'd appreciate a bite to eat." She'd accept his invitation if only to demonstrate how pleasant and compatible she could be.

That would be her new goal. She felt ten pounds lighter with relief already.

Besides, something warm in Colt's stomach might calm him. Maybe his behavior was similar to a bull's, a restless and combative beast who hadn't eaten for days.

That's what she'd do on this trip. She'd treat him like livestock, ensuring he was properly fed and watered and comfortable in his stall…um, surroundings. Some men were like that, very simple in their needs. He looked the simple sort.

The wonderful aroma of grilled fish, sausages and roast chestnuts drifted around them. Colt moved their bags to a stone wall, twelve feet away from the crowd and potential listeners.

Here was her opening.

"Perhaps if we discuss this rationally, we can tolerate each other without resorting to poison. I won't get in your way. I promise."

"You're already in my way." The heavy outline of his shoulders strained against his shirt. "I hesitate to tell my men about you. They might jump ship—"

"Then you don't have a good grip on your men. You're the sergeant, you give the orders and they follow."

"I'm not accustomed to arguing with a woman."

She sighed. "Then please don't."

"Look. Only a third of the people who attempt to make it to the Klondike actually get there. Some of them die on the rocky trails. Most turn back because they can't get over the mountains and rivers. The gnats and mosquitoes swarm around your mouth till they drive you mad." He scuffed his big boot along the platform. "And that's not even counting the scum who'd slit your throat for any sign of gold."

She fingered the wool threads on her shawl. "I'm…I'm aware of the challenges."

"A woman as delicate as yourself can hardly keep up with six tough men who've seen more wicked stuff in one year than you'll ever see in a lifetime."

"Why does everyone use that word around me? Delicate?"

He planted a rough hand on his hips. "Don't make me tell you."

"Why not?"

"Because you'd be insulted. Let's just say in my police experience, you don't have the stuff it takes."

"If you can't be specific, then how can I address the problem, which means it's your personal pride—"

"You couldn't take my explanation—"

"Then it's all in your mind—"

"You're incompetent!"

Dumbfounded, she took a step back and gaped up at him. "Incompetent?"

"Yes," he whispered hoarsely. "Incompetent when it comes to the outdoors. I've watched you. A tiny speck of mud on your boots drives you insane. Too many bugs make you run for the house. You've never saddled a horse in your life and you need two maids to run your bath. How are you going to survive on the trail? Do you think *I'm* going to run your bath?"

She took a moment to calm her breathing.

Pleasant and compatible.

"Most doctors I know don't like dirt. And I don't need to saddle a horse right off because there'll be six men with me. If you show me, I'm a fast learner." Unable to hide her temper, she flung her shawl over her arm so fast the beaded ends flicked against her hips. "I don't need any maids to help me bathe, and I didn't get through five years of medical college to be told by the likes of you that I'm incompetent."

The cool lines of his face remained impassive.

"We'll see if you can handle life outside the walls of your mansion."

"How *dare* you." Her chin trembled.

"Tell me the real reason you want to go. Not the one you gave your father."

She fingered the beads on the edge of her shawl. "I—I don't know what you mean."

"Everybody's got a secret. Some people have more than one. Tell me yours."

Could she?

Elizabeth slowly raised her head and stared at the set lines of his mouth, the rigid jaw, the unyielding forehead. No. Not yet. "I've already told you. I haven't seen my grandfather for well over a year. And I'd like to practice medicine on…the women arriving in the Klondike." And the men, but she wouldn't press her intentions to do that yet. "They're short of doctors and…and…"

Colt puckered his lips with irritation and she knew very well he didn't believe her. Not fully.

"So that's how it's going to be, is it?" With a sharp breath, he turned away and stalked off toward the food vendors.

He didn't even ask what she preferred to eat!

Muttering, she leaned against the rough stone wall and yanked at her shawl.

He'd left her alone to guard the luggage. She heard a whimper. A huge dog brushed by her, his head at her waist level. She jumped back in fright. He was one of those dogs called…a Saint Bernard. But so skinny that his fur hung off him like a saddle.

"Shoo," said Elizabeth. "Go on, now. Shoo!"

The dog circled her bags and sniffed along the edges. She trembled slightly and waited. She'd had a fear of dogs ever since grade school when she'd been bitten hard on the arm, straight through to the bone.

The Saint Bernard lost interest in her bags and went off to scout for other treasures. Elizabeth followed his movements through the travelers. Her wandering gaze settled on the train she'd disembarked from, still sitting in the station. The Mountie who'd been assigned to take care of her luggage opened a window. Leaning through it, he peered up and down the tracks as if he were bored.

An idea flashed through her mind.

It was brilliant. What's more, it was something the obnoxious Colton Hunter would never have to know. With a hesitant gulp, she hastened toward the constable, searching for a pencil and piece of parchment in her handbag.

So much for pleasant and compatible. She'd be selfish and direct.

Colt's experience as a pickpocket and thief during his adolescence, a time he wasn't proud of, had honed him into an excellent liar. It had been years, however, since he'd had to practice. Everything in this mission hinged again on his ability to lie.

He wondered how good a liar Elizabeth would make.

Carrying foodstuffs wrapped in brown paper, he wove his way back to where he'd left her on the platform.

To Colt, it was annoying having to pretend. Pretend she was going to England, pretend he was joining her, pretend he liked her. At least he could stay his distance as he pretended to be her brother. There'd be no need to get on her good side, for many siblings he knew squabbled like hens and roosters.

Yes, that was it. Elizabeth was a spoiled hen who

needed attention, clucking at everyone and everything around her.

"Pardon me," he said, weaving around an elderly couple.

His acuity sharpened as he noticed a commotion along the far wall where he'd left Elizabeth. A small crowd was forming. Elizabeth whipped her handbag through the air, fighting two ruffians. A rise of panic hit Colt. He raced toward her.

The young men didn't see him rushing through the observers. Colt tossed the foodstuff, grabbed one man by the scruff of the neck while the other kicked him in the shin.

"Dammit!" Colt swung around, and still gripping one man, clasped the neck of the other.

"Leave my brother alone!" Elizabeth lifted her heavy bag and clobbered the dirty culprit who'd kicked Colt.

"Easy does it, Liza. I've got them."

She glowered at the two idiots. Her hair spilled from the top of her head. "How dare you presume to steal our bags."

Colt surveyed the pile of luggage. "Did they get anything?"

"No."

"Are there any more of them?"

"No." Elizabeth lunged toward the burly one Colt was holding steady. "If we ever see you around here again, my brother will box your ears."

"Problems here?" asked a man from behind.

They turned to see a constable, a member of the British Columbia police force, standing among the spectators. Colt would let him handle the situation, for he wished to remain incognito. Besides, Mounties didn't have the jurisdiction to practice as police in this province. As a federal agent, Colt had been hired to protect the federal Finance Minister of Canada as he crisscrossed the country. Colt *would* have jurisdiction in the Yukon, though, where the Mounties were the only police.

"We need your help, sir." Colt explained what had happened to his sister and the constable took over. He handcuffed the two men and dragged them away.

"The judge won't have any mercy on you this time," Colt heard the man say through a crowd.

A train whistled and the crowd dispersed.

He faced Elizabeth, trying to catch his breath. His shin was still pounding from the hit. "Are you all right, Liza?"

"Yes, I—I'm fine." She stooped down to the strewn pile of bags and lifted one to its rightful place in the stack. "They almost got your duffel bag."

"You were protecting *my* bag?"

"I couldn't very well let them get away with it."

"You surprise me."

"Really? How—" Elizabeth glanced toward his legs, her demeanor shifting to annoyance. "Shoo! I told you, shoo!"

The monstrous brown-and-white Saint Bernard, as who was as thin as a book, gobbled the grilled chicken Colt had bought for Elizabeth. Colt lunged to save it but was too late. When he raced to protect the beef he'd bought for himself, the dog beat him to it, as well.

"Get out of here, you blasted thing!"

Elizabeth groaned. "It seems a thief got the best of us anyway." She glanced around the station. "He doesn't seem to belong to anyone. I think he's homeless."

Colt picked up a packet of dried apricots that had

fallen onto the luggage. "Here," he told her. "The mutt left us something."

She gripped the packet with smooth hands. "I didn't know you paid attention...I mean...that you'd ever noticed apricots are my favorite."

He cleared his throat. "It was convenient to buy."

"I apologize for the trouble. I wanted to prove how competent I am...and I guess I proved the opposite."

Colt straightened his shirt and appraised the way her shawl had shifted around her bosom, the way she tried to tuck the fallen strands of hair back into her bun. When she swayed, the fabric on her blouse stretched over the outline of a hidden corset and accentuated her waistline. His pulse quickened in response. Glancing away, he told himself he was noticing only because he was trying to get a feel for how other men—scoundrels—might look at her.

"You might be the cause of a lot of things," he said, "but you weren't the cause of this. The main thing is you're unharmed."

He was impressed with her ability to fight back, despite being a doctor. But he reminded himself not to leave her alone again. With her attractive figure and pretty face, she was a magnet for trouble. The trails would be filled with men who would gladly pounce on a beautiful woman.

Which was exactly why Colt had objected to taking her in the first place. He knew her stunning good looks would be a big problem, but he'd be damned if he admitted to her just how pleasing she was to his eyes. With a groan of apprehension for the days ahead, he lifted their bags. This journey would be a hell of lot harder than he'd originally thought. The energy required to guard her would be draining.

"Come, I'll buy you some more food. Our *brothers* are waiting for us outside." He added under his breath, "A meeting I've been dreading for forty-eight hours."

"What the devil do you have there? A *woman?*"

Twenty minutes later, Elizabeth cringed at the manner in which the tall, auburn-haired fellow—she assumed another disguised Mountie—was gaping at her as she and Colt made their way outside to the wagon. Another man sat beside him in the front seat while Tommy stood beside a cluster of pines.

Colt clenched his jaw and hurled their bags to the pile of straw in the back of the buckboard. Far behind them, a steady stream of people and horses moved into and out of Whippoorwill Station.

"That's what she looks like, doesn't she?" Colt snarled. "A woman. You remember those."

The fellow was as tall as a giraffe, his shaggy dark hair tinted by the sun with streaks of red. On the seat beside him, another auburn-haired fellow, with dark muttonchop whiskers, eyed her from head to toe. They'd had time to grow beards and allow their hair to grow unkempt for their cover, she assumed, whereas Colt and Tommy were still neatly cropped from coming off their duties.

Elizabeth squirmed beneath their stare. The two men had such similar square faces that she swore they must truly *be* brothers.

The taller one rubbed his nose and repositioned himself. "Then you must have found her stranded at the depot. Are we droppin' her off somewhere?"

"Yeah," Tommy muttered with objection, the first

word she'd heard him say that indicated he, too, didn't approve of her. "Dawson City."

"What?" The tall one hitched the reins of their two mares to the side of the buckboard and jumped off. The bearded man hopped off, too, and bounced over to join them.

The first man chomped on a piece of grass. He peered down at Tommy. "You've been standing here for half an hour eating jerky with us and you didn't say a word."

"I thought I'd give Colt that pleasure."

"What's this all about?" the fellow asked.

Elizabeth adjusted the brown felt cowboy hat Colt had given her over her tumbling hair, but couldn't seem to catch the entire spill. "Good afternoon, sir."

"Afternoon, miss." Narrowing his eyes as if not knowing what to make of her, he held out his hand in greeting. "What's your name?"

She took his hand and shook. "Elizabeth Lang—"

Colt clicked his tongue. "You failed on the first attempt."

"Oh," stammered Elizabeth. "I thought maybe this gentleman was with...sorry."

"He *is* with us. But I didn't tell you that, so you're not supposed to assume it."

"Wilfred and Edward, meet Miss Liza Blade. Your sister."

Wilfred, the tall shaggy one, choked on his blade of grass. The man with the muttonchop whiskers scowled. Colt had said she wouldn't learn their true names, that their new identities would already be in effect. The men glared from her to Colt to Tommy.

Tommy flung his hands in the air and jumped onto the back of the wagon. "I didn't have anything to do with it."

"Well," said Elizabeth awkwardly, "I...I guess we'll have some time to get acquainted. I'll jump up here and we can all get moving." Not waiting for assistance, she hopped onto the wagon with her handbag.

She watched with mounting embarrassment as Colt led the two hairy men to the cedars. After five minutes of vigorous arm-waving and an exchange of heated words, they returned.

"Are they truly brothers?" she asked.

Colt sat beside her on the opened tailgate, looking out the back. "Yeah. Will and Ed will be our cooks."

The wagon jerked forward. Elizabeth rocked on the boards. The ratty old Saint Bernard came out of nowhere and jogged behind them in the ruts, nipping at her dangling boots.

"Shoo! Go away, shoo!"

Two minutes later when the dog licked her boot for the tenth time, she sighed and lowered her legs. He hadn't bitten anyone yet and seemed more interested in food than aggression. Frankly, the muscles in her legs were screaming from being held up so long.

"Go ahead. Bite my legs off. I can't fight you anymore." She *could* say the same to Colt.

The dog sniffed and, losing interest, fell behind.

The wagon hit a bump in the road and the two of them flew into the air. Colt muttered, "Whoa."

A funny thing happened. The dog stopped altogether. Didn't budge, even though the wagon kept rolling.

Colt noticed, too. "Gee," he called out.

The dog turned to his right and went in that direction.

"Haw," said Colt.

The dog responded by turning to his left.

"Whoa," Colt repeated. The dog halted again.

"Mush!"

The dog bounded toward the wagon.

Colt grinned. "Wow."

"What's going on?" asked Elizabeth.

"Those are the top four commands of dog mushers. He's been trained for a dogsled. What's more, he was a lead."

The dog reached them. "Good boy," said Colt, summoning a happy growl from the Saint Bernard. "We can use him as a pack dog through the mountains. He's all ours for the mere cost of food."

Elizabeth peered at the beast, stunned.

Colt whistled. "Who on earth would leave a gorgeous dog like this behind?"

She peered at the dirty fur. "He could use a bath.... I thought only huskies were used for dogsleds."

"The gold rush changed all that. Stampeders from Europe are bringing all kinds of breeds with them. This poor guy's been to Chilkoot once already."

"How do you figure?"

"He's emaciated. No food. That's what the trail is like. Just as hard on animals as it is on humans. Harder. Because most newcomers don't know how to handle animals."

Elizabeth shuddered. "Why do you think someone left him behind?"

"Two out of three people attempting to make it to the Klondike wind up turning back. I guess his former owner was one of those."

She had anticipated the trail would be difficult. Everything she'd read about and all the stories her uncle had told had led her to believe it would be the most physical challenge she'd ever attempt. But seeing this dog…the sad condition he was in…brought it home like no amount of talking could.

"Shouldn't you give him a name?" she asked.

"He's a Saint Bernard. How about Bernie?"

"How about Saint?"

"Yeah, Saint. A guardian angel. I like it."

"Would that be his real name, or a masked identity?" Elizabeth laughed softly.

She didn't think Colt would smile at her attempt at humor, but his lips turned upward. His smile spread, softening his mouth and warming his complexion. Watching it made her insides bounce.

Or, more likely, her insides were bouncing due to the hard ride.

"He just needs one name," said Colt.

They continued in silence for ten minutes, Saint lopping behind them, obviously accustomed to running great distances, paws as big as a bear's, Colt brushing up against her every time the wheels hit a rut.

"I don't mean to complain," she said to Colt, thinking of the journey that awaited them. "But…"

"But what?"

"The cooks have auburn hair. Yours is brown and so is Tommy's. Mine is blond. We hardly look like a family."

"I bought a tin of shoe polish at the station. We'll need to dye someone's hair."

She moaned out loud. That meant it was either hers or theirs. With a sinking feeling, she knew who they'd pick. What a sticky mess.

What really stung was that the gentle moment she'd just shared with Colt over the dog had vanished.

Colt turned, assessing the condition of her tangled hair, his muscled thigh brushing her loose skirts. The sun burst from the clouds at that moment and heated her skin. Blazes. She yanked her cowboy hat low over her brow. How was she going to get through five weeks of being this close to someone she preferred to avoid?

Five miserable weeks.

Heading toward certain impending doom, she prayed that one of her brothers would volunteer to dye their hair. And leave hers alone.

Chapter Three

"She's too damn skinny and too damn frail." Hours after they'd arrived at the cabin, Colt's most trusted man on the team, newly christened Buxton Blade, was still complaining. "She can't carry a heavy pack through the wilderness. She's scared just being here. Look at her, *Sergeant.*"

Springtime air chilled the back of Colt's neck. He was tired of complaints, and decided to try humor to thwart them.

"First off, don't call me Sergeant. It's not *brotherly.*"

Buxton finally grinned. A jagged scar beneath his left eye gave him a rugged look. Dark-haired like Colt, the man was three years older and his specialty was taking care of horses. Colt had expected the least amount of flak from this brother, but Buxton was raising the most objection. If Colt could get him to lighten up, the rest of the team would follow.

It was close to seven o'clock and the sun was setting. Although the days were warm, the evenings cooled quickly when the light left. And that, good grief, meant an influx of blackflies. Brushing them away while sorting through their gear alongside five other Mounties, Colt mustered his patience and glanced at Elizabeth.

She sat alone by the campfire, awkwardly balancing a book on her lap and not reacting to the comments. She tucked her skirt beneath her and adjusted her posture under a pressed white blouse, as if she were seated in a church pew instead of a gritty log in the woods, as if she didn't expect a fleck of dirt to come her way.

The six Mountie brothers were packing supplies in preparation for a morning departure. Saint was off chasing groundhogs. The men, dressed in cowboy clothes, looked the part of drovers and ranchers.

A thick growth of red cedars surrounded them, individual trees so thick a man couldn't put his arms around half the trunk. Ferns and shrubs teemed with butterflies, chipmunks and gray speckled birds. Loons called from the nearby river.

In other circumstances, Colt might have sympathy for Elizabeth, but she'd brought this on herself. He could order his men to be polite, but he couldn't order how they should feel.

Hell, he couldn't order himself to enjoy her company.

Colt rolled his hunting knife into a suede cloth. He reached for a tin of salmon, opened it and mixed it with a batch of hard biscuit.

He didn't even have to call out the dog's name. Saint was already panting beside him.

"You're feeding him again?" asked Will.

"He's hungry."

"How are we going to feed him the amount he needs?"

"Alistair Langley is financing this trip. He gave me more than enough to buy whatever supplies we need at the market tomorrow."

The Saint Bernard almost snorted down the food. After he'd licked the tin bowl clean, he tilted his head at Colt and whined.

"Take it slow. You'll get what you need, but not too fast or you'll get sick." Colt rose and addressed his men. "You're all to call me Colt from now on. We're using our new names. Right, Buxton?"

"Right, Colt." Crouched on his knees in the dry grass, Buxton rolled up a canvas tarp five yards away from Elizabeth.

An owl hooted from the trees. Elizabeth jumped an inch off her log.

"See that?" said Buxton. He shooed flies away from his shoulders.

"Ease up, will ya?" Colt asked. He was close to Buxton, but there was only so much of his needling Colt could take. "You have a point, but Langley has given his orders. We're to take his daughter to the Klondike." Colt slid his knife into his saddlebag.

"Can't we convince her it's in her best interest to stay behind?"

"She doesn't see it that way. Personally, I wonder why she doesn't prefer to stay at home as wife and mother, as nature intended."

Elizabeth looked up from her reading and Colt wondered if she'd overheard.

Buxton lowered his voice. "I've been in the force for fifteen years. Now I've gotta take a goddamn woman with me?" He removed his hat and swatted at the tiny flies.

"These dang gnats! How come they're not bothering any-one but me?"

Will and Ed, smoking cigarillos as they packed pots and pans, smirked.

Tommy, sorting through a pile of axes and shovels, chuckled.

The remaining man, Anderson, was oiling his gun in the friendly and mellow way he did everything. He was skilled in bartering and would be good in negotiating the price of food supplies tomorrow. Tall and lean, he'd grown his sandy-brown hair over his ears, similar to the other men, but had added a handlebar mustache.

Anderson called out, "The flies like you best, Buxton."

"Ha," said Buxton, getting back to his tarp. He focused on Elizabeth. "I went back and forth to the Klondike last year. Two of our men didn't make it. One of 'em died of exhaustion. A good number of horses can't even get through."

"I know the stakes," said Colt. "And your experience is why I brought you. But there are six men here and we'll carry what needs to be carried. We can all hunt and fish. We'll have enough to eat."

"What the hell can she do?" asked Buxton.

"Look pretty." Tommy sharpened an ax.

The men laughed.

"What's that book she keeps pulling out?" Anderson asked.

"*A Medical Guide to Diseases,*" said Colt.

"Havin' a woman doctor look at me would be racy," said Anderson. "But I wouldn't mind."

The other men grinned.

In a cloud of gnats, Buxton leaped to his feet. He

clawed at his neckerchief. "They're going to eat me alive." The group laughed as he pulled off his cowboy scarf. With a dawning realization, he fingered the sticky goo on it, then swore. "Is this honey? Who the hell smeared honey on it?"

Anderson remained cool while the others laughed. Colt bit back a smile. Anderson was the practical joker in the group, but the man was always so calm and friendly, no one could hold a grudge against him for long.

Buxton flung his neckerchief to the dirt. "I'm going to kill you, Anderson. Now I've gotta wash the blasted thing. Just for that, you're going to help me lift this tarp and carry it to the wagon." He retrieved something from his saddlebags as Anderson rose to join him.

Anderson leaned over, scooped his fingers beneath the edge of the canvas and let out a large yelp just as Colt heard a tiny snap.

"You son of a—" Anderson jerked his right hand into the air, trying to shake off a mousetrap Buxton had just planted.

Buxton reeled away and lifted the tarp to his shoulders, laughing. Will, Ed and Tommy joined in.

Amused, Colt peered at Elizabeth. She gazed at them without expression, listened to Anderson curse as he removed his fingers from the trap, rolled her eyes and went back to reading.

"Liza," shouted Buxton to louder laughter, "We might need your assistance to bandage some fingers."

"Bandage them yourselves. I've no time for your silly games!"

She sounded convincing as a frustrated sister.

"And if anyone puts honey on my things," she added, "I shall pour a special elixir in your coffee!"

The fear of what a medical potion might do quieted the men.

Round one went to Liza, thought Colt.

When things calmed down again, he whispered, "Tommy, did you find the shoe polish?"

"Yeah."

"Good. Could you…?" Colt motioned in her direction.

Tommy narrowed his eyes as he stared at the woman. He spoke low so she couldn't overhear. "Colt, there are many things I'm good at. I can hurl an arrow through the air for a hundred feet and hit a pheasant. I can work like a mule without complaint. But I'm not going to dye the hair on some female."

Colt looked to the others, hoping for a volunteer.

The men scattered in all directions. Will and Ed snuffed out their cigarillos and hopped away with the canteens. "We're going to the river for water."

Anderson leaped toward the wagon. "The horses need exercising."

When Colt turned his attention to brother Buxton, the traitor coughed. "I'm likely to pull her hair *out*."

With a scowl, Colt snatched the tin of shoe polish from Tommy and trudged toward the fire and Elizabeth.

He was interrupted by the sound of snapping twigs coming from behind the cabin. And a dog's growl.

Footsteps.

Instinctively, Colt slid his gun from his holster and dived toward Elizabeth. She yelped, but seemed to understand his meaning as he pushed her to the grass.

"Don't move," he whispered in her ear.

Just as quickly as his men had disappeared, they all reappeared, guns drawn and ready. The two cooks on the other side of the aspens; Anderson rolling through the grass toward the cabin; Tommy with an ax, stalking silently around back; and hardheaded Buxton with his gun trained in the opposite direction, in case someone was sneaking up from behind.

"It's just a raccoon." Tommy's voice echoed from the treetops behind the cabin. "A whole family of 'em going out for a nighttime stroll!"

Colt relaxed his grip on Elizabeth. "You all right?"

"Yeah," she murmured.

She shifted under him, soft and slender beneath his firm body. He was pressed up against her in all the right spots, and his body responded with a rush of excitement. With a catch at his throat, he rolled off her onto lush grass. Looking for anything to offset the moment, he spotted the tin he'd tossed to the ground, reached for it and held it above her. With a reluctant hand, she reached up and took it.

"Here's the shoe polish. There's a mirror inside the cabin. If you need help, holler."

He had no further business lying here in this position with the Finance Minister's daughter. Trying to mask his discomfort, Colt leaped to his feet. She rose and dusted off her pristine blouse.

Still indisposed, he brushed grass off his thighs, silently ordering his body to behave. Then he stomped away toward the river, unwilling to look back at any of them. Especially the cause of his arousal, Elizabeth.

"Ugh." Bathed in candlelight, Elizabeth stood alone in the cabin and stared at her reflection in the cracked mirror. Logs sizzled in the fireplace and warmed her bones.

She tilted her head. When her loose blond hair fell forward, she pressed another glob of shoe polish into her roots. She'd been at it for twenty minutes. Colt had heated a pot of water and provided a basin and soap. The soapy water rested on the rotted pine table in front of her.

Someone knocked on the door. Her fingers slid from her hair.

"How's it going in there?" Colt hollered through the pine slab.

She slapped at blackflies. "I'm having the time of my life."

Silence.

"Need any help?" he asked.

"I think it's pretty well covered, but it doesn't look appealing."

"Let me see. Can I come in?"

"Not really, I—"

"Are you decent?"

"Yes, but—"

The door burst open to reveal a looming figure silhouetted by the moonlit forest. Colt paused for a moment, likely to adjust his vision. She'd found several discarded pieces of flannel in the cupboards, and, to protect her blouse, had rolled one under her collar. Consequently, the collar gaped open at her throat, exposing more skin than she cared for Colt to see.

When she brought her hand up to conceal her chest, his eyes moved there.

Removing his hat, he strode past the flames in the fireplace. When he reached her, he gripped her arm and sleeve to lean her toward the light so he could get a good look at her hair. His touch was firm, and she couldn't concentrate on anything except the manner in which he was handling her.

Candlelight flickered over the bridge of his nose. It warmed the dark hollows of his cheeks. Slivers of light glistened over his thick hair and met with the wide angle of his jaw. He smelled like wood smoke and cedar. And biscuits.

"Have you been feeding the dog again?"

"There's no need to be scared of him."

"I didn't say I was."

"You didn't need to."

She nervously studied the rotted planks of the table as he examined her hair.

"You didn't need to use so much polish," he said. "Just a pinch would've done your whole head."

"Why didn't you tell me that before?"

"I thought you'd see by experiment. Your hair is light and doesn't need much dye. The clumps in there will ruin your night clothing. It'll stain your blankets."

His voice was gentle and mingled with the soft hiss of burning wood.

"Should I wash it out and start again?" she asked.

"I think I can rub some of it out." He reached for a piece of discarded flannel. "Lean over this way."

Swallowing hard, Elizabeth did as she was told. Her hair streamed over her body. Colt took the flannel and rubbed the strands. His touch was brisk but careful.

A few blackflies scattered around her face. She fanned them away. At least there weren't as many inside as out.

Being here felt wrong. She was far from home and everything she was accustomed to. She wasn't homesick for the luxuries, but for the people and the comfort of familiar surroundings. What hurt most was that the men here didn't want her. She saw it in every cool stare and heard it in every whispered complaint to Colt. Even though Colt was with her, his presence made her feel more isolated than if he'd stayed away like the others. She tried to fathom why. Perhaps because she knew he didn't want her here, either. He was tolerating her because he had to.

Duty and all that.

Well, the good thing about being surrounded by six Mounties was that she might possibly confide in one. Sooner or later, she would need the help of a police officer to right the wrong that her late uncle had begged of her.

Colt rubbed her head. "Okay, let's see now."

Elizabeth flung her hair back over her shoulders. Her collar gaped open again but she snatched it before it revealed too much. When she caught Colt looking at her bosom, she flushed and he hastily shifted his gaze back to her head.

"I think it's almost right." He reached above her shoulders and pressed the flannel into her roots.

"Colt, tell me why you're going to the Klondike. You said most people have a secret. Tell me…what's yours?"

The creases around his eyes deepened. He kept rubbing her head. "My father died for gold. I've always wanted to see what a gold rush looks like."

"Your father was a stampeder?"

"In California. He was a miner who tore off for every vein of precious metal that anyone ever struck. Copper in the Rockies. Nickel in the north. Silver in the west. He'd leave for months but always came back broke, except that last time."

"How old were you when he died?"

"Fourteen."

That was so young. Elizabeth still had both her parents, and a younger sister.

"He had a nugget of gold in his pocket. Biggest he ever found." Colt quieted. "Someone shot him in the back for it."

"I'm sorry…. Is that why you became a Mountie?"

He shuffled his weight. His boots scuffed the boards. "It's why I became a lot of things."

"What do you mean?"

His eyes shimmered. "Nothing. Forget I said that."

How could she? "Your father is your secret."

"What's yours, Elizabeth?"

Elizabeth. He said her name. For the first time in eight years, Colt said her name. He caused an unexpected shiver and a racing in her bloodstream.

The fire crackled with heat. Bristles on his shaven jaw stopped moving. He stilled, completely attentive. The soft pulsing in his throat matched her own. If he leaned over and dipped his face by mere inches, his lips could lightly brush hers.

Her heart beat faster.

It was mad to think of this.

Colt blinked and turned his attention back to her hair. He rubbed the ends a little too briskly. "Why do you want to go to the Klondike so badly?"

She felt a blessed relief being released from the imaginary kiss. She could breathe again.

Colt's interest in her this evening was the first glimmer of sympathy she'd ever gotten from him. Perhaps he'd show even more compassion if she confided her other problem. "I promised my uncle."

"Your late uncle? Sebastian Langley?"

"Yes."

Colt lowered the flannel rag. "I imagine he felt very lucky to have you in the last weeks of his life. As an extra set of hands to help his real doctor."

"Real doctor?"

"His regular doctor. Stewart McFadden." Colt tossed the flannel to the table and stepped back.

Elizabeth shook her head and pressed her fingers to the table. Although she had been capable of so much more as a medical doctor herself, she hadn't been allowed to do more than fill basins, handle towels and change bedsheets. But she had been able to listen in the middle of the night when the other doctor had gone home and her uncle needed to speak.

"Fortunately, he got to live a good, long life." She removed the flannel from around her collar. "But last year during his trip to the Klondike…my uncle…"

When she hesitated, Colt filled the silence. "He struck it rich."

She nodded, unsure of how much to say, but knowing she needed the Mounties' help to fix this legal problem and search for the remaining parties involved. Maybe she should rephrase things and start with what she knew, in a manner that wouldn't reveal how Gerard was involved, that wouldn't incriminate him.

"On his deathbed, my uncle confessed to a crime." The words stuck in her throat like a hard biscuit. "It's one of the reasons I need to get to the Klondike. It's why I need to go with you."

Colt struggled, but was unable to hide the shock on

his face. He leaned back against the wall, looming above her. His superior position made her feel his power.

Perhaps this wasn't the proper time to reveal this.

She gripped the flannel between her fingers. The fabric of her skirt pressed against her bare trembling thighs; her corset wound tight against her aching ribs.

His voice rumbled through the heated air and straight through her chest.

"What crime, Elizabeth, did your uncle commit?"

Chapter Four

Colt scrutinized Elizabeth and tried to control his desire for an immediate response. Dammit, his gut had been right. There *was* more to her reason for wanting to get to the Klondike.

He had enough experience as a Mountie to know when it was better to push hard and when it was better to tread gently. When he was a younger man, he'd once let a murderer slip through his fingers because he'd been so eager in pursuit that, at first, he'd missed the subtleties. Elizabeth's response needed careful extraction.

Although every hair on her head was tousled out of place, its warm brunette hue contrasted with the golden tones of her skin. Her blouse kept parting open, revealing a slender throat and alluring cleavage. She seemed to be aware of it, for every now and again, she clasped the buttons closed and fought with her towel. Right now, it gaped open and he stopped short of staring.

The richness of her lips tugged upward with feeling. She looked so innocent. But her uncle. Hell, her uncle.

Colt steeled himself and repeated, "What crime?"

"I'm no longer sure I should tell you."

"Why not?"

"You're looking at me as though…as though you don't have a compassionate bone in your body."

"I'm listening, Elizabeth, and that's what you wanted, isn't it?"

A dimple in her chin flicked. Saying her name aloud was more intimate to him than he'd imagined. He took a moment to savor how the word felt.

Elizabeth. Warm and feeling, like the woman.

Ultimately, he told himself, he hoped that being this casual would melt her resistance.

She went to the roaring fire, securing the towel beneath her damp hair, then perched on a ripped sofa. They were borrowing this cabin from someone her father knew, a confidential government official, who used it as a fishing hut.

Reaching for her hairbrush, Elizabeth tugged it through her strands.

"My uncle staked his claim dishonestly."

She startled Colt.

"The one he got rich from in the Klondike?"

"That's the one."

"Why?"

She raised her finely arched brows. "Obviously not for good intentions."

Colt would take his time. He eased in next to the fireplace, pulled the poker from its stand and stoked the flames. "So he took another man's claim."

Her hands lingered on her hairbrush. "It sounds so…awful…doesn't it?"

The fire blazed, radiating heat across his face. "I haven't heard the full story yet, so I can't judge."

"Maybe my father was right."

"Your father knew about this?"

"Not when it happened. He had *nothing* to do—"

"I didn't accuse him—"

"Nonetheless, I assure you my father knew none of this."

"All right. That's what you were told."

"You said you weren't going to judge."

"I'm not."

"Then don't get my father involved."

"I'm not getting anyone involved. I'm listening, and I'd like to hear the whole story." He sank into an upholstered chair, its cushion shredded along the seams. Horsehair stuffing spilled out.

"Uncle Sebastian was a good man."

Colt didn't comment.

"He'd never done anything like this before."

"What exactly did he say?"

Nervously, Elizabeth pulled her hair into a bundle and stared at the ends. "That his claim wasn't truly his and that I should…should return the claim to the rightful owner."

"Who would that be?"

"I'm not sure. The rightful owner was killed."

Now she really held his attention.

"Explain that."

She looked up at him. "My uncle said Ivan Mishenko was killed in a hotel brawl shortly after my uncle staked his claim. Mishenko left behind a widow, apparently."

Slowly, with great deliberation, Colt added another

log to the fire. He had her near the brink of disclosure, and he had to coax her over. The sound of scraping wood occupied the dead silence. Still balancing on his haunches, he turned to look at her.

"Who killed Mishenko?"

Words seemed to clump in her throat. "He died in a fight of some sort. It was difficult to understand everything my uncle was saying...the coughing in the end made it hard for him to talk." She shivered and rubbed her arms. "I should have listened to my father."

"What exactly did the Minister have to say about all this?"

"That no good would come if I pursued it."

"Let me get this straight. You told Alistair Langley, Finance Minister of our country, that his brother took another man's claim and he simply told you to keep quiet?"

"Of course not. My father checked into the accusations. He spoke with his brother directly and with my Aunt Rose, Uncle Sebastian's wife. My father had his lawyers check into the legitimacy of the claim and all appears intact."

From his crouched position, Colt rose to full height. The back of his cramped knees thanked him. Elizabeth swatted at the blackflies humming around her face.

"That makes more sense. Alistair Langley, the man I know, wouldn't try anything underhanded."

"Well, thank you for that. The story did change a bit when my uncle retold it and that's why my father doubts him."

"Go on."

"Uncle Sebastian said at first that he alone staked the claim, and then—"

"Yes?"

"Then he trailed off. My father insists Uncle Sebastian was delirious in his illness. That he concocted the story."

Colt had never seen Elizabeth like this, anxiously fingering her hairbrush, unable to meet his eyes, frowning with every word she spoke. What was she concealing?

"Did your uncle tell you the name of the second person?"

Elizabeth furrowed her forehead. She pursed her lips. Then, maybe realizing he was waiting for an answer, she slid the towel over her head and patted her damp hair. The towel conveniently concealed her face.

"In the end, it was difficult to understand what he was saying."

He waited until she dried off and put the towel down. "And what of Mishenko's death?" He scrutinized her soft round eyes. "Did your father look into that?"

She flinched as though Colt had hit a raw spot. "There was no need."

There was most definitely a need, he thought.

This was where his questioning had to be subtle. "Why are you telling me this about your uncle if your father told you to keep it quiet?"

"Because I believe my father is wrong." She fanned her face to keep away the blackflies. "I believe Uncle Sebastian does own another man's gold, and I promised him on his deathbed that I'd return it to the rightful owner."

"What makes you so sure your uncle wasn't delirious?"

"Because he's not the first person I've attended to as they lay dying. Dying people tend to be truthful."

Again, she surprised Colt. She'd already seen an awful lot of life in her short years of study. Maybe she was less delicate than she seemed.

"Who, then, is the rightful owner of the claim?" he asked.

"I believe Mrs. Mishenko. His young widow." Elizabeth lowered her lashes.

"Any children?"

"None as far as I know. There was some talk about… about the widow leaving the Klondike after her husband died. My father was unable to locate her. Some say she went back to San Francisco. Others claim she moved to Alaska. I was hoping I'd find out when I get to Dawson City."

Colt slid his hand into his jean pocket, swatting a blackfly with his other. They didn't bother him as much as they did her. "Why do you want to do it?"

Elizabeth rose from her chair and joined him at the fireplace. Her skirt swirled about her hips. Again, he noticed that great walk of hers, the proud way she carried herself even when she was dressed in farming clothes.

"Because this is *my* duty, Colt. You have yours. This is mine. A dying man asked me."

She turned to him and he felt that ripple in his gut, that awareness that she was a lone woman in this cabin, that they were standing ten feet away from the bed where she would be sleeping. How quickly could he have her flat on that bed and doing what came to his mind?

"What do you think? What's the best direction to take from here?"

Reaching for the mantel, he gripped it and forced himself to think clearly. "I'm going to check into this myself."

"You'll help me find Mishenko's widow?"

"And we'll find out who murdered Mishenko."

She paused. "Murdered? I think he died from an accident stemming from the brawl."

Colt nodded slowly. "What did your uncle have to do with Mishenko's death?"

Elizabeth put a hand to her throat. "I beg your pardon?"

He kept his voice calm. Matter-of-fact. "What did Sebastian Langley have to do with Ivan Mishenko's death?"

Her eyes flashed at him with suspicion. "Absolutely nothing."

"Did he say that?"

"He didn't have to."

"Not in words, maybe, but you said it was difficult to hear him."

Her temper flared in her voice. "He did *not* murder anyone."

"In my line of work, just like yours, we call them deathbed confessions. Lots of folks like to cleanse their souls before they leave the earth and meet their maker. Maybe your uncle was giving you a deathbed confession."

She stumbled backward in disbelief. "What?" she asked softly. "What are you saying?"

Colt was already moving toward the door. He knew she didn't really expect him to answer, for by the alarmed expression on her face, she'd definitely understood every word he'd said.

Elizabeth was still outraged at Colt's absurd accusation at ten o'clock the following morning, when they arrived at the farmers' market on the coast. They were here to buy supplies and she'd do her best to avoid the scoundrel she'd made the mistake of trusting last night. She'd gone to him for help and instead of helping, he was now investigating her uncle.

For murder!

Unfortunately, it was difficult to keep out of Colt's path. In the heat of the midmorning sun, Elizabeth wove her way into the throng, behind a line of six burly Mounties and one hungry Saint Bernard sniffing everything in his path.

Even the darned dog was male.

Her eyebrow itched again. She rubbed it and tried to enjoy the view.

The Pacific Ocean, as blue as her mother's sapphire ring but much more beautiful and tempting than any jewelry, sparkled through the thatched roofs of the crowded stalls. Sunlight bouncing off the water twinkled around haggling customers who were intent on buying the freshest clams and greenest shoots of vegetables.

Elizabeth inhaled the delicate scents of wild berries, smoked sausages and beef, and salmon and bass from the middle of the ocean. She wished she knew how to cook.

When the Mountie cooks stopped to speak to a vendor, Elizabeth scooted to the edge of the mountainside to relish the view of the ocean valley below. A kaleidoscope of colors enchanted her—purples and blues of the water, rich forest greens that were dotted with yellow flowers.

And the people. People everywhere. They crowded the docks below and the paths to the ships. They jammed the ticket booths scattered along the shore whose banners advertised the great wealth of the Klondike.

Wrens flapped their wings in the trees around her. Standing in the heat, Elizabeth pulled off her cowboy scarf and rubbed her neck.

Suddenly, Colt inhaled beside her. Startled by his presence, she drew her skirts in hand and swiveled away, hoping he wouldn't notice—

"What happened to your eyelids?" Colt grabbed her arm and trapped her. Heaven help her, his touch sent a wave of excitement down her arm.

She tilted her cowboy hat lower to conceal the marks. "Blackflies."

"They got you while you were sleeping?"

"Indeed." It was stupid of her to have been so unprepared and she felt stupid having to admit it. She'd drawn the covers tightly over her body but it'd left her head exposed.

"That would explain the swelling. What's the white stuff?"

"A paste made of cornstarch and zinc."

"No matter how much of that stuff you brought along, you'll run out fast. I'll show you how to make a paste of bark and plants that'll get rid of the itch."

"*Fine.*" Lord, his appeal was devastating. The dark looks, the manly way about him, the manner in which he claimed her arm.

She yanked herself out of his hold, located the other men and stomped behind them. They'd sold their wagon, but were taking the two mares with them on the trip. The horses were hitched and waiting by the skinny path leading to the docks.

There was nothing here to warrant a murder investigation. She knew in her heart Uncle Sebastian wasn't that type of man. But some part of her brain made her think differently. He had surprised her with his confession of theft. Just what type of man *was* her uncle?

He hadn't done it on purpose, he'd said. The stolen claim had originally occurred by accident. And he was trying to return it, even upon his death.

To think Gerard may have been involved…if Uncle Sebastian was capable of killing a man, then what of Gerard?

No.

Wasn't it Uncle Sebastian who had three grown sons, and several grandchildren whom he sat upon his lap every Christmas Eve to read them stories?

And wasn't Gerard the one to encourage her in her studies as he finished his own medical degree at the Toronto university? His college hadn't allowed women into their medical program—still didn't—so women had united and formed their own school where Elizabeth had received her education—The Ontario Medical College for Women. Gerard had once visited on a speaking engagement as a newly graduating surgeon, and that's how they'd met. He'd exhibited a kindness and a belief in equality that few men had shown her, and that was the reason she'd fallen in love.

In the end, though, he wasn't the man she'd thought. He'd traveled to the Klondike with her granddad and her Uncle Sebastian, working as a surgeon. Gerard had written home about how badly they needed doctors, but instead of asking her to join him as she'd begged, Gerard had asked if she could stay put for another year or two to be married upon his return.

The answer in her heart had simply been no.

If he wouldn't help her get to the Klondike and practice medicine however she saw fit, she'd get there on her own. It had been her dream to go in the first place, as a married team, but he'd taken her place with her granddad and left her behind.

She wasn't an idiot who would protect Gerard blindly

if he'd committed a crime. But she did believe in justice for all parties, and a false rumor could damage his reputation forever. It was enough for Colt to know only about her uncle's confession until they reached Dawson City where she could speak to Gerard himself. Then she'd disclose whatever she knew, if appropriate, to Colt.

Theft perhaps. Murder no.

"What's happening?" Elizabeth peered behind Colt's arm to watch as Anderson negotiated and then paid a sausage-maker and his wife for their entire stock.

"Why smoked sausages?" she asked.

Colt's shoulder bumped her cheek. "They're a good source of sustenance. Won't spoil on the trip."

"So are beans." Blazes, why did she have to be so conscious of his every movement?

"Yeah, but everyone's carrying beans. The sausages will be worth a fortune. It's for luxury items—in food as well as incidentals—that folks are doling out their gold."

"Hmm," she said, thinking about the possibilities.

"There are two types of men who hit it rich in the Klondike. The ones who strike gold, and the ones who serve the men who've struck it."

"I see. Well, then, I have a suggestion of my own for you and…and our brothers."

Colt appraised her, and she fought that invisible current tugging between them. What *was* that? That electrifying charge he solicited from her body whenever he glanced her way.

"What's your suggestion?" he asked.

Elizabeth looked to the stall across from them and nodded at the dried fruit. "Apricots. Dried apricots."

"Your favorite food is hardly our priority."

"Not because they're my favorite, but because you said luxury items—"

"We'll decide what we take and don't take—"

"You'll need them to survive."

"Survive?" Colt laughed, vexing her. "How do you figure that?"

"In Gerard's letters, he wrote of the scurvy he was seeing. Some of the men are holed up in the mountains for months, eating only the game they hunt. It's their bleeding mouths and loose teeth—"

"I saw a lot of it when I worked in Alberta district."

"Well, not only are apricots a luxury item, but they fight scurvy, too. Wouldn't that make them almost priceless? They're dried, so they wouldn't spoil. Easy to transport. No preparation needed to eat them."

"They'd cost us a bloody fortune to begin with. They're imported from California."

"Didn't my father give you enough cash? Fruit is necessary for our own survival. What'll *we* eat to prevent scurvy?"

"Same thing the Indians used to prevent it. Tea. Boiling the bark and needles of the white cedar tree."

"Why don't the mountain men drink this tea?" She watched him search for an answer. "Tastes awful, I'll bet. Folks would prefer apricots and you know it. My idea would bring in tons more money than sausages would. We *are* supposed to be smart businessmen. And woman."

After a second of thought, Colt shouted over the heads of folks bustling in the aisles. "Hey, Will. Hold on a minute."

And Elizabeth knew she'd won. Apricots it was.

While the men worked out the details, Elizabeth

stopped to buy a dozen packets of vegetable seeds. They were light as air to carry, and would hopefully grow in the Yukon district.

Two passing men stared her up and down. Heat prickled her cheeks. So many men. So few women.

She did spot two ladies headed toward the docks. The younger one, an adolescent girl, looked pale and leaned against the older one. Was she ill? Maybe Elizabeth was imagining it, for the young lady seemed to pull herself together when an older gent—likely her father—nudged her.

Someone touched Elizabeth's arm. A greasy-haired, middle-aged man in bad need of a shave and haircut, leered at her. "You two married?"

"I beg your pardon?"

"You his wife?" He nodded toward Colt.

"Most definitely not."

"You were arguin' like you are."

"He's my brother." For the first time, the words came smoothly.

The man laughed. "I see. That's good."

There seemed to be a commotion where Colt was standing. Before she realized what was happening, Colt had a complete stranger by the wrists and was twisting them behind the fellow's back. After growling something in the man's ear, Colt slowly released him. The man slid a money belt out of his jacket and returned it to the appalled gentleman standing next to him.

What sort of place was this?

It didn't deter the stranger gawking rudely at her. "Would you like to get hitched? I'm a man who's got a great future ahead of him."

Appalled, she stepped back. "No thank you. And my brothers had better not hear you say that. They've all got quick tempers."

He grinned, revealing a stained set of teeth. "Just like you?"

"Yes."

He stepped closer. "What happened to your eyes?"

She pulled away. "Nothing!"

"How many brothers have you got?" He stared at her chest.

"Six big ones!" She rushed past him toward Colt. This was getting dangerous. She tried to push through the crowd but couldn't get anywhere. Her breathing grew rapid and she turned to her filthy suitor when as he spoke.

"Whoa. Got any more sisters? Someone younger than you, and a tad more receptive to a gentleman who—" he straightened his dirty tie "—is willing to make an offer?"

"An offer? *No,* no sisters."

"Pity. Then I still say you and me were made for each other."

She dusted off her skirt with great ceremony. "How on earth do you figure that?"

"We're both so damn fine looking."

Colt reached her. "Liza, what did I say about talking to strange men?"

For a change, standing next to Colt was a relief. He would save her, come to her rescue in some dashing, heroic manner. She gloated at the stranger, waiting for it.

Colt addressed the man. "Sorry, my sister tends to wander off sometimes."

The man leaned in. "Wander off?"

Colt rolled his eyes, as if to explain she was a little dim-witted. "When she smears that mud on her eyes."

Elizabeth rallied. "How dare you imply—"

"Come along, Liza." Colt grabbed her wrist and spoke slowly as if she were simpleminded. "We're going for a nice boat ride. You know. Water. Floating."

She gasped as Colt marched her toward the docks. "Dim-witted?" She huffed under her breath. "I just multiplied our fortune tenfold by suggesting apricots."

"And I just saved your behind."

"I could outwit all six of you."

"There won't be a lot of time for outwitting." He reached the narrow path that headed to the ships. People rushed by. There seemed to be a frantic race for who would board first. She ignored the mule and six mares hitched by the path, as well as a heated skirmish taking place between two men arguing about tickets.

"Pipe down, fellas," Colt snarled. Something in Colt's tone caught the men's attention, for they listened. What was it with Colt's inexplicable power? Well, he didn't have the same control over her.

"The livestock," he told her, "now belongs to us. In addition to the crates and sacks we're hauling to the ships."

The enormous pile reached over her head. How on earth would they get this down the rocky path?

"What we're looking for," said Colt, "is someone who can handle a mule. Here." He thrust the reins of the small brown beast at Elizabeth. "Take Amelia and try and outwit her, will ya?"

Elizabeth fumed. All right, then. This was all-out war.

"May I remind you, you are nothing more than a servant."

"Oh, yeah? A servant?" He gently slapped the rear end of her mule, causing Elizabeth to lurch forward. Colt's smile spread slowly across his dark, sculpted face. "Who's holding the ass?"

Chapter Five

"Some of these ships are in no condition to sail." Colt slid in at the railing beside Elizabeth.

Still annoyed with him three hours later, she stared out at the blue Pacific. When he pressed his forearms onto the wood rail, she begrudgingly moved over to make room for the massive size of him.

"I'm not talking to you."

"Delightful," said the scoundrel. "I'll be able to get a word in edgewise."

She stewed in silence while he seemed to be content watching a school of swordfish diving below them. Saint panted at his master's feet.

Along the mountainous coastline, a golden eagle soared above the firs. A hot, crisp summer wind brought the smells of sea salt and spruce. She stood at the stern, not far from Amelia in her stall, a dozen passengers in between. Steam billowed from the stacks above. Elizabeth steadied herself against the power of the engines churning them through the water.

"That captain—" Colt pointed to a ship on her left "—should be shot for allowing any human to board that vessel."

The wooden monster heaved over the waves, creaking and straining, barely enduring slap after slap. Overloaded with people and livestock, it groaned with every splash.

"They'll be all right…won't they?"

"Maybe. At least the captain's wise enough to stick close to shore. He probably won't make it halfway to Skagway before calling it quits."

"That's horrible."

"It's hunger for gold is what it is. The demand for voyage is so high they're using abandoned vessels. It's not just the captain's fault. Some of these passengers haven't bothered to consult a map. They don't know the difference between Skagway, Alaska or Dawson City, Yukon."

"How long before we reach Skagway?"

"Five days."

There were a dozen land routes to the Klondike, but their sea voyage was the quickest, therefore, by far the most crowded. This pleased the Mounties, Elizabeth had discovered, for men of crime were more likely, due to sheer numbers, to follow them from here onto Canadian soil. It was unnerving if she allowed herself to think of the dangers.

It took the average man three months to reach the Klondike, but there was nothing average about these hard and muscled Mounties. They were aiming for five weeks.

The men had already carried seven tons of supplies on board. One ton per person was required by Canadian law for all who entered the Klondike, roughly what they'd each consume in a year. Since there was nothing at the other end, no form of civilization before the gold rush had started, folks had to bring all supplies with them.

Of course, over one-half of their crates—a huge percentage—contained apricots and sausages. The Mounties were excellent survivors, hunters and fishers, so they weren't concerned about the high ratio. Nor of keeping their cargo secret. They wanted passengers to discover the bait.

Colt bumped his powerful shoulder against her slight one. She swayed at the contact.

"How's that mule of yours doing?"

Elizabeth pulled out a fan she'd tucked into her waistband and fanned her face. "She seems to adore the fresh air."

Colt's laughter was deep and rich. "Is that so?"

The shadow of an impending beard darkened his face, giving him a criminal air. She hated to admit it, but the look was enthralling.

"Where'd you get the fan?"

"A small luxury I brought with me. It's hot. Surely you have no objection to a lady's fan."

"Not a one. Funny what some people choose to pack." His hands, big and square, pushed against the rail. "I better go check on the other animals."

Colt left, just like that, leaving her slightly at a loss at how fast he'd fled.

It took but two shakes of her fan before another man stepped into his place.

"Miss, are you betrothed to that fine gentleman?"

Without even looking at the well-mannered stranger, Elizabeth knew he'd be someone of substance by the distinguished charm of his British accent.

Behind her rose-colored fan, she peered up at him and wasn't disappointed. He looked lovely in his suit jacket. As fair and charming as a professor. Or perhaps a member of the British parliament.

"That man who just left?" she asked. "Heavens, no. He's my brother." The lying *was* getting easier.

The gentleman held out his hand. "Dr. Donovan Wellsley."

"My. You're a physician. From England, no less." She increased her fanning.

"London, to be precise. I'm not a general practitioner. I'm an ophthalmologist, which is—"

"Eyes. An eye surgeon."

Even his grin was lovely. "How did you know? Most folks can't even pronounce the word."

"I—I needed an examination—I mean my folks had bad eyes—and they…" *Gather your wits.*

"Sorry to hear. Did they receive help?"

"Yes, thank you. It was a while ago. I was quite young. Not sure what the problem was exactly. My mother had a problem with her right eye and my father with his left."

She puckered her lips tightly behind her fan, willing herself to shut up. Dr. Wellsley stared, unsure what to make of her.

"I see."

Elizabeth lowered her fan and smiled.

"What's it like in England to study medicine? Did you study at Oxford? Or perhaps the British Medical Academy? Or the Royal Military—"

He laughed. "You are exceptionally educated."

"I—I've heard people talk about it."

"It was Oxford."

Elizabeth sighed with great pleasure.

"And it was grueling."

"Yes, the testing and the board examinations—"

"Liza," Colt cut in rudely. Where on earth did he come from? "I checked on your mule. She's fine."

The blasted man with his blasted mule.

"Thank you," she said. "May I suggest you remain with her?"

Colt shot her a grumpy look, then turned and held out his hand to the doctor. Colt towered over him by a good six inches, but brawn wasn't always the more attractive.

"Colton Blade. And you are?"

"Dr. Donovan Wellsley."

"A doctor, huh?"

Elizabeth glared at her uncouth brother. "We've just been through this. We were having a charming conversation."

"Your sister's very bright," said the doctor, making Elizabeth squirm with delight. He turned his exceptionally handsome face to her again. "Liza, what a pretty name."

"Thank you."

"I named her myself," said Colt.

Aghast, Elizabeth lowered her fan and eyed him.

"I'm ten years older," he said, "so our folks let me name her."

"You made the perfect choice. I bet you didn't know she'd grow into such an outstanding woman. She takes a man's breath away." The doctor took her hand, brought it to his lips and kissed it.

Elizabeth tried to conceal her smile of pleasure, she really did, but Colt snatched her out of there so fast she nearly lost her balance.

"Good day," Colt yelled to the doctor, who seemed equally dismayed by their abrupt departure. The Saint Bernard loped behind them.

"I shall look for you later," the doctor called to her. "Please call me Donovan!"

"Close your mouth," Colt whispered in her ear. "You're drooling."

Elizabeth snatched herself from his arms and tugged her blouse. "I am *not* drooling," she said through gritted teeth.

"It's not safe for you to talk to him."

Her whisper came out as a blast against his cheek. "He's innocuous."

Colt grabbed her again and pulled her toward the animals. "I overheard part of your conversation and you're not a very good liar."

"I am so."

"Your mother had a problem with her left eye and your father with his right?"

"No. My mother had a problem with her right eye and my father with his left. You, see, I can keep track of all the details."

"Please, let's not start the game of one-upmanship."

"You have no patience with people. You'd make a...a terrible doctor."

Colt finally released her beside the row of horses, penned up in stalls lining the deck.

"And you'd make a terrible..."

Her eyes narrowed. She flicked her fan in outrage. "Terrible what?"

"Doctor's wife."

Elizabeth took a step closer, inches away from his

face. "Just because I was speaking to him doesn't mean I'm hoping for marriage."

"Yes, it does. It always does with women."

She waved her fan. "Let's get something straight. You don't know anything about women!"

And with that, she tugged her skirts in hand, flounced her fan for effect and left her dumbfounded brother on the deck.

Theirs was a war of silence, and Colt didn't wish to continue for one more day.

"As it turns out, I *do* know something about women."

He surprised Elizabeth the following evening while she stood alone gazing at the setting sun, in the same spot on the rolling stern where he'd found her the day before.

He watched Elizabeth turn toward him, her chest heaving in a big sigh, and prayed she'd bite her tongue. He didn't have the energy to fight her all the way to the Klondike.

"What is it that you know?"

He took a deep breath of salty air and rested his elbow on the railing. "I knew I'd find you here. Women love to admire a gorgeous sunset."

"You're right…and…I'm sorry about my comments yesterday. I really don't wish to argue."

Well, thank the Lord for that.

She settled back into her spot against the railing, slender and feminine. The sun caressed her cheeks and lashes, and painted her lips the color of burgundy wine.

The sunset was a sinking red ball. Clouds partially occluded the horizon, giving the sky a mystic rose quality, as though a magician were responsible.

"Dr. Wellsley, and that other man who preyed upon

you on shore, have one thing in common. They're both in search of Almighty Gold."

"I don't believe that. The former gentleman, certainly, but not Donovan. He's an ophthalmologist."

Colt looked at her blankly.

"An eye specialist," she explained. And then added with pride, "He likely wants to practice in the north."

"He's a man like any other. He's going for gold."

"Why must you always assume the worst in folks?"

He spread his hands and shrugged. "Because maybe then I'll never be disappointed."

His gaze dropped from her eyes to her shoulders and the way the soft cotton fabric clung to her breast.

"You say that as though you've been disappointed a lot. Have you?"

Always. "Some."

Rosalyn had disappointed him.

In the beginning, he'd been drawn to the lively redhead because of her smile and the way her eyes had followed him around the kitchen whenever he came in for a bite to eat. Later, he'd enjoyed Rosalyn's stories of growing up on a dairy farm, the camaraderie between her and her ten brothers and sisters.

He'd believed Rosalyn's warmth for him was genuine; that her tender words of love held as much meaning when they left her lips as when they reached his ears. On that final evening, when she'd left him the note and asked to meet him, well, it was obvious her words had been meaningless.

The perception that he would protect and love Rosalyn for the rest of his days had been completely wrong. As well as the perception that someone had loved him through all his flaws.

Hell, even Elizabeth had failed him, and he barely knew her. The way she'd meddled in his private affairs was unacceptable. She'd done it by accident, she kept explaining, but didn't that make it worse? What doctor, what woman, had the right to poke her nose into anyone's affairs before fully grasping the situation and all it might entail? She'd sent Rosalyn into the arms of another man without a thought.

"Do you ever give them a second chance?"

This time, her question surprised him.

Her murmurs echoed against the hidden alcove behind her. "The ones who disappoint you…do they ever get to explain…and do you listen if they do?"

He was silent. She continued.

"Let me guess who tops your list…."

He fought the tingling of emotion she always seemed to draw out of him. "Don't."

"Rosalyn."

"It's none of your affair."

"Did your father disappoint you, as well?"

Colt balked, then steadied his thigh against the rail. "What does my father have to do with anything?"

"Did he disappoint you because he went in search of Almighty Gold?"

"This conversation is getting too personal."

"Those are your words, Colt, not mine. Almighty Gold."

Colt shifted his legs, ready to leave. He drew back his shoulders and turned.

She touched his forearm and stopped him. "And I suppose you're adding me to that precious list."

He clung to his silence, unwilling to yield.

Her brown eyes sparkled with the warm hue of the setting sun. "It's hard to imagine how I could disappoint someone I've barely had a conversation with in eight years' time. Do you know how often I've tried to engage you?"

"What do you mean?"

"Do you remember that summer when I was about to leave for college, and I came with my father to watch you and your men in the sailing regatta?"

He refused to let her words touch him. "You were there with your sister, Beatrice, if I recall."

"I so desperately wanted you to take me sailing."

"You knew I couldn't do that. I explained. They were organized games, and later I was on duty guarding your father."

"But you had the time to take Mary Beth Spencer."

He said nothing. But he took her elbow and led her along the outer deck. He'd deliver her to her cabin door, and this conversation would end.

They nodded to passing couples, to an elderly man who stood watching the ocean rise and fall. When he'd chosen this ship, Colt had ensured it was solid and relatively uncrowded compared to most. At times like these, it was pleasant to stroll the wooden decks and enjoy the view of the water. Quarters were tight and cramped, but the common spaces were ample.

"And do you remember that first Christmas dinner," said Elizabeth, unwilling to let the topic drop, "when we were seated around the dining table, you between my father and I? I asked you what it was like to grow up in such a large family. Raising hogs and corn…but you barely spoke two words."

"Talking about my childhood is never my favorite topic."

There, he'd delivered her at her door. Now he could leave. It was only three steps to the next cabin, which he shared with the five other men.

"Then how about that summer at the Charity Dance?" she implored. "All the young ladies could convince you to take them on a spin around the dance floor, but never me."

He stabilized himself against the churning water. A splash hit his cheek. The first strands of moonlight reached them, weaving shadows from the deck above to the brunette beauty who stood before him, demanding answers he didn't wish to give.

Her scent would always be unforgettable. A crush of blushing powder, new-fallen rain.

And of course, that hint of shoe polish. At least the swelling of her lids had subsided, and gone was the paste.

She cleared her throat, peering up at her cabin door as if pretending they weren't standing so intimately next to her private quarters. As if pretending she didn't feel the current of danger passing between them.

"Don't you see?" she asked softly. "Maybe it was you who disappointed Rosalyn. Maybe it was you who disappointed me."

Elizabeth detected a change in him. It was a subtle shift in the manner Colt looked at her, a slight puckering at the corner of his eyes that indicated a softening.

The breeze rolled in off the ocean, dampening her brow. With him standing so close, she was aware of her own vitality, of her body beneath her clothing. Her skin tingled in the rush of wind, her breasts heavy in her corset.

"The reason we took Mary Beth," Colt murmured, "was because she was saying goodbye to one of my men. I didn't condone their relationship, for she was promised to someone else by her parents. Nevertheless, it happened. Sailing around the harbor for an hour was the only time they could say goodbye without being seen by her folks."

Elizabeth's breath came in a rush. "I didn't know that. I didn't know she was involved with anyone but Oliver."

When Colt turned his head toward the glittering water, the clear lines of his profile turned orange against the moon. "The reason I didn't say much about my family at that Christmas dinner was because my mother had passed away three weeks earlier. I couldn't get through a dinner conversation with you…without the sadness…and still remain alert in my duties protecting your father."

A lump rose to her throat.

"I didn't know about your mother," she said softly. "I'm so sorry." And sorrier still, for Colt, who apparently excelled at hiding his emotions. How could he have masked the depth of his pain while seated next to her at a dinner party?

"And as for the Charity Dance, Gerard was standing by your side from the moment the band struck up till the moment they ceased. He glared at any man who so much as approached you."

"I didn't think you noticed."

"I notice everything. It's my—"

"Duty," she finished for him.

"Is there something wrong with that? Sometimes, the way you say the word makes it seem unpalatable."

"Following one's duty is very admirable. Honorable,

worthy of the highest regard." And she did respect him greatly for it. "But sometimes…duty is a cross to bear for all involved. Look at poor Mary Beth, betrothed to one man and loving another. Yet, she's obligated by duty to marry the man her family decided upon."

"And I suppose that's the lecture you gave Rosalyn when she left me."

"No…I…*no*…" Humiliation swept over Elizabeth.

This man was human, after all. So very human.

And she was a fool.

She turned and placed her key in the lock, opening the door before she said anything more.

His hand fell upon hers. He'd entered behind her. A sliver of moonlight cascaded through the door.

It was so dark she could barely see him when he yanked her close. But she could feel his lips brush her cheek and then, more firmly, without the slightest hesitation, her mouth.

Heaven, he kissed her. Absolute heaven.

Encircled in his arms, she couldn't think of anything but how warm his lips were. How his chest pressed against her soft bosom, and how much she longed for him to touch her everywhere.

But how on earth could she let this continue?

And then it came. Shouting from somewhere on deck, interrupting their quiet moment. Or perhaps saving her from this risky situation and everything wrong between them.

Chapter Six

"My daughter. Someone, please!"

"What's wrong with her?" Elizabeth shouted to be heard above the group of men already gathered on the deck by the time she and Colt reached them. She tried to jostle her way through the tight bodies. No success.

She bounced on tiptoes to see, but it was too dark with only moonlight illuminating the scene.

At the center of the spectacle was an elderly couple dressed in country clothing—the one Elizabeth had seen boarding the ship earlier with their weakened daughter. The young lady, roughly the age of sixteen, seemed to have fainted and was lying supine on a bench.

"She's been drinking," suggested one man.

"Maybe she hasn't eaten," shouted another.

Colt pressed in beside Elizabeth. "Liza, there are others going to her aid."

Elizabeth grimaced. "But are they helping?"

This ship was as poorly staffed as the others heading to Alaska. No doctors on board.

Frantically, Elizabeth scanned the faces for Dr. Wellsley. He could help. But he wasn't in sight. Perhaps he was already kneeling over the young lady. Elizabeth strained to look, but there was no one resembling the London doctor. Only the girl's mother and two young deckhands, at a loss at what to do.

"Please," begged her father. "Someone."

Elizabeth silently pleaded with Colt.

"There are others helping," he insisted, but his posture softened. He seemed to have a change of heart, for he pivoted, about to run. "I'll find Wellsley."

The young lady's moans pierced the air. Elizabeth and Colt rushed to move at the same time. She shoved forward through the crowd, unable to push through, at the same moment Colt grabbed her by the waist and lifted her.

"Give way," Colt shouted. "Another woman is here to help. Give way!"

It was a relief to have his arms wrapped around her. The men parted enough for Elizabeth to be delivered at the feet of the ill young woman. Slumped over, with dark hair knotted in a tight bun, she wore a plain calico skirt and blouse.

"Hello," Elizabeth said quietly, not wishing to frighten her or her heavyset mother, who was just as pale as her daughter and on her knees trying to help.

The father, long white hair tied into a ponytail, his body as thin as a stick, hovered over them both.

"I'm Liza."

The young woman groaned. "…Milly."

Elizabeth turned to the parents. "Has she been drinking?"

"Only a sip of water this morning," said the mother.

"Nothing more?"

They shook their heads.

"Has she eaten anything?"

"Not since yesterday. She has no appetite."

Elizabeth pressed her hand to the young woman's forehead. Milly was fevered, shaking and perspiring.

Elizabeth palpated her abdomen. Thankfully, her corset wasn't too tight. When Elizabeth pressed in the abdominal region, Milly flinched and gritted her teeth.

Dr. Wellsley pushed through the crowd. Colt had apparently found him.

With a swoon, the doctor handed Elizabeth his topcoat and nudged her out of his way.

"Not to worry. I'm here now. Dr. Donovan Wellsley," he introduced himself. The parents nearly cried with relief.

Elizabeth sat back on her heels, bowed her head and stared at the fabric of his topcoat. She dearly wanted to help.

He did a cursory examination, much quicker than Elizabeth's. "Vermiform appendix, I believe."

"Pardon?" asked Elizabeth.

"It's a segment of the lower bowel. It's inflamed." He turned toward the anxious parents. "I'm afraid she'll need surgery. I could do it but I recommend we turn back the ship—"

"But how do you figure this?" Elizabeth interrupted.

Dr. Wellsley flicked his gaze over her, as if he'd never been questioned. "She has a fever. Profuse sweating. Her abdomen is rigid. When I palpate, she jumps toward the sky. Surgery is the newest technique in London—"

"Yes, but isn't it fortunate that her tenderness is on the left side and not the right?"

He frowned.

"I mean…I saw how carefully you did the examination, and I'm impressed by your thoroughness…"

He repeated the palpations and true enough, Milly quivered and groaned when he pressed on the left side, but not so much the right.

"Yes, of course, I hadn't completely finished with her."

"With *Milly,*" Elizabeth said, noting how white and withdrawn she'd become at their discussion. Elizabeth leaned forward and placed a comforting hand on Milly's shoulder. The touch soothed the trembling.

"Appendicitis was one possibility. That's all I meant. But the other possibility, the more likely, is a partial bowel obstruction."

The parents and Milly stared at Dr. Wellsley.

"This is much better news," Elizabeth explained. Milly relaxed, and her mother, welcoming the news, pressed her forehead against her husband's knee. The husband stroked his wife's neck.

Elizabeth whispered a personal question in Milly's ear.

"Not for a couple of days," Milly responded.

"And your folks say you're not eating or drinking well. That would explain it."

"Tea. Mild dandelion tea is what I recommend," said Dr. Wellsley. "I have some in my cabin. You'll need to drink more water and eat plenty of fruit."

"We have some apricots," said Elizabeth. She turned to the fair-haired Dr. Wellsley. "Thank goodness you came along."

Dr. Wellsley beamed with satisfaction. "Yes, well, it's

good to be of use. I'll need to get my medical bag and stethoscope from my cabin, to confirm all this." He handed his key to a deckhand, who immediately tore off.

"I'll get the apricots," said Colt, leaving Elizabeth's side.

He returned several minutes later as they were finishing, the diagnosis confirmed. Milly was sipping on a wineskin filled with water.

"Thank you, Dr. Wellsley," said her father. He'd introduced himself as Mr. Theodore Thornbottom.

"And, thank you, Elizabeth," said Mrs. Abigail Thornbottom.

Elizabeth smiled and patted the topcoat she was still holding. It's Dr. Langley, she thought. I'm Dr. Langley. But this woman would likely never know. And it didn't matter, for her gratitude was unexpected, and the wonderful prognosis for her daughter was all that counted.

The woman whispered, "Do you think we should go on with our journey? Mr. Thornbottom and Milly are determined to see the Klondike."

"It might be wise to disembark at Skagway and lag behind for a few days. You could continue with your journey when you're sure her strength is restored."

"I'll try to convince them."

"Good luck," Elizabeth whispered.

Two of the Mounties arrived on deck, along with the faithful dog. Apparently, they'd been down below, playing cards. "What's going on here?"

Colt explained, then she felt his sturdy hand again, gripping her upper arm, guiding her out of the situation. Colt yanked Dr. Wellsley's topcoat from her hands, rather rudely, and tossed it to the British doctor.

"Nice to have met you," Colt said to the Thornbottoms.

Elizabeth only had time to nod goodbye before being whisked back to her cabin.

Again they were at her door, with the moon casting shadows over the fine cut of his shoulders, the ship rolling beneath their feet.

"Thank you," she said. "For allowing me to get involved. For helping me to get to Milly."

"I couldn't let a young lady…"

"You carried me and set me right at the foot of danger."

"I thought with you being a woman…a female doctor…this sort of thing would be up your alley."

Elizabeth expelled a weary breath. "Right. Woman to woman."

She recalled the words she'd heard Colt say to his men. *Personally, I wonder why she doesn't prefer to stay at home as wife and mother, as nature intended.*

Colt slid the key from her fingers and unlocked her door. He walked right into her room and peered behind the door, behind the bed and underneath it. He was a bodyguard and she supposed he worked instinctively, but she didn't need protecting.

Except, perhaps, from him.

Colt came around to stand beside her at the door. This time, he left it firmly open to the deck and its strolling passengers, and deposited the key back into her hand. He seemed to be very careful not to touch her.

"You talked your way through that close call," he said. "Wellsley has a big enough head to fall for every line you fed him."

"It's not his fault. It's the way we and our class, our society, look up to male doctors."

"But some look up to you."

"Other women, mostly."

Colt ran his hand along the door's edge and she watched in fascination at the way his expression changed. Gone was the rough and dutiful officer. He mellowed into a listening, caring man who was perhaps embarrassed at how businesswomen were sometimes treated.

"What made you stand your ground that it wasn't surgery Milly needed?"

"Years of experience, I suppose. In the past, my lack of strength had dire consequences."

"You? A lack of strength? That's hard to imagine."

"Oh, it's terribly true. When I was in my final year, the Dean's wife...not the Dean of our College, but the University where Gerard studied—"

"The one where they don't allow women? Men only?"

Her lips pulled upward in warm surprise. "You do listen."

Humor tugged at his dark cheek.

"The Dean's wife came down with pneumonia. She lived across the street from the boarding house where I stayed. We often met at the market. I kept telling everyone, the Dean especially, that it was more than winter influenza. That they should pay attention. Apply poultices to her chest. Have her rest rather than attend to six children."

"Was the Dean grateful?"

"He discounted what I offered. He was getting better advice, he said, from men. Even she wouldn't heed my advice. Didn't wish to complain in front of her husband, she told me. Later when I insisted Gerard step in, they still let it go for another week. Finally, she collapsed from exhaustion. It took the poor woman six months to pull through."

Elizabeth bent to lift her carpetbag from the floor. Her skirts swept the planks. Colt beat her to the bag and placed it on her mattress.

The weight fell easily in his hands. "But there was nothing more you could do. You warned her. You warned her husband. You told Gerard. And she *did* pull through."

"My grandmother wasn't so lucky. She passed on, more than ten years ago, when I was still in grade school."

"What happened?"

"One morning when I came to milk her cow, she was sloppy, not her usual self. She knocked over the sugar bowl and forgot she had a jam roll baking in the oven."

He watched her remove a hand mirror from her bag. It was odd unpacking in front of Colt, yet the intimacy seemed almost natural.

"What was wrong?"

"Now I know she had a mild stroke. But back then no one realized. I tried to tell my grandfather something was wrong, I tried…he wouldn't listen."

Colt leaned against the wall. He filled the room. "But there was nothing you could do."

"If I'd tried harder, we might have gotten medicine to help strengthen her blood. To prevent what was coming."

Elizabeth removed a towel. It slipped toward the floor but he caught it in time.

"What was coming?" he coaxed.

"A devastating stroke. Or maybe it was a massive failure of her heart. We can't be sure. One day after school…I found her in the garden. She'd crawled for help but… that's where she died."

Colt moaned. "So your grandfather saw this, must have seen how keen you were to follow medicine—"

"No. My grandfather disapproves of what I've become."

She began unpacking again, but Colt placed a gentle hand on hers and stilled her.

"The grandfather you're going to see in the Klondike?"

She nodded into caring eyes.

"Why?"

"Sickness and death. Some people wish to stay away from things that terrify them. They want to shield those they love from it, too."

He released her hands and watched her wrap her fingers together. "I told him only once I thought my grandmother wasn't feeling well. Only once. Yet, I'd witnessed little details for two weeks. I was petrified to tell him, and he petrified to hear it. We failed her."

"You were only a child."

"I'm not now. I will never again remain silent, nor will I let myself *be* silenced by someone who is too afraid to hear the truth."

Colt was an inch away. The whisper of his breath hummed through the room, rolling along her temple. The heat of his body radiated between them, and a rush of blood pounded through her flesh.

His breathing grew shallow, he lowered his face. Moonlight from the porthole highlighted his firm dark cheek, the straight slash of eyebrows, the curve of his lips. "Listen, about what happened earlier here, with the kiss…I shouldn't have…"

"It was my fault for allowing…"

"I won't cross the line again, I assure you."

"You needn't assure me, for I assure you it will *never*…"

He lowered his lids. Then he slammed the door shut and pulled her in his arms again.

Dammit, he should leave. He shouldn't do this. But Colt reached up to touch her cheek's downy surface. His fingers grazed her luscious skin.

Such a mystery, this one.

Elegant. Shy. Yet a deep, moving sense of obligation to her grandmother.

He trailed his thumb along her jawline, taking pleasure in the softness of her skin and the sparkle of disbelief in her gaze that danced in the moon's glow. His stomach tightened with his own apprehensions, knowing this was wrong, and yet basking in the guilty pleasure of his sexual thoughts.

To see more of her skin, *all* of her skin, beneath his own naked body, rocking in a splendid coupling; the image caused his heart to race. But wasn't she his nemesis?

Not at this moment. At this moment she was fashioned of a clay that he could mold with heated fingers.

His heart hammered against his ribs as he tried to pry away from her in one last, futile attempt. Instead, he cupped her ear, breathed her in, lowered his head and eagerly met her lips.

She tasted of all things womanly.

At first resisting softly, she then allowed the kiss.

Unable to bear the gentleness of their touch, he crushed her mouth with his own.

He pulled her close, embraced her and thrilled in the sweet sensation. Her lips were warm and inviting. When she responded with an urgent moan, his sanity fled.

She roped her arms around his shoulder, brushing her fingers against the soft hairs at the back of his neck, causing his skin to rise with goose bumps in a wild fever. He dipped his tongue against hers and she imitated the touch, melting him like maple candy on a warm summer evening. He had her. He had the beautiful Dr. Elizabeth Langley in his powerful grasp, could feel her breasts brushing against his chest, could feel the heat of her tongue and the wanton abandon in the way her soft round body clung to his.

She was wickedly delicious and it surprised him.

He cinched her waist with a firm grip. She allowed him. He slid his greedy hand upward, feeling the tightness of the whalebone in her corset. She allowed him. With an urgent touch, he held back from doing what he really wanted—to firmly grasp one beautifully shaped breast and draw it to his mouth—instead, he lightly skimmed the surface of the flesh above the soft cotton fabric as the curvature rose above her corset, teasing her, and himself, in the process.

She allowed him.

It drove him crazy.

The splendor of the kiss was like none he'd experienced, a willing bond between two people starved for mutual touch. How could this be? How could it be that he thirsted for this woman?

He nibbled on her cheek, her temples, her earlobe. Everywhere his mouth could reach. She made a guttural sound at the back of her throat and willingly arched her neck as his lips sped there, too. He couldn't get enough. The slow and pounding yearning of his body, making him hard, drove him to unfasten one of her buttons and then another and another.

"Elizabeth…" He groaned, viewing the charms of a woman unleashed from the constraints of fabric. The top curve of her bosom heaved with golden specks of dust cascading down the moonlight on her skin, as if sprinkled with the gold dust of the Yukon. "You're more beautiful than I ever imagined."

Her breath was warm on his neck as she moaned in reply and trailed her fingers along his throat.

He let his desires lead him, unable to stop. With a slow and careful step, he led her deep inside her cabin until she was pressed up against the wall, shimmering in moonlight and rocking in unison with the ship.

Working with lightning speed, as if he were a virgin and this might be his first and last time, he undid her blouse, slid it off her shoulders to expose her corset, and targeted her naked flesh. He slid his mouth to the sweet juncture of her upper arm and the side of her breast, the part that bulged softly. Then he whisked his tongue along the top of her golden breasts, first one and then the other. She cupped his head as though guiding him, this approval making his blood rush to this thighs, hardening his erection and driving him to a frenzy.

He was mesmerized by the contrast of her Sunday-school-blouse, set against an alluring body that was paradise-alley illicit. He tugged lightly on her lacy corset, and her breasts, gorgeous breasts that were certainly meant to be painted in a portrait, popped out.

His gaze lingered on the rich, round areolae, the perky nipples pointing upward and the creamy round flesh. Shadows of moonlight illuminated the curves in a poignant landscape that was intended for Rubens's brush.

"You take my breath away," he murmured.

He couldn't read her expression—she seemed trapped between her own heated desires and the imprudence of what they were doing, what they should never be doing aboard this ship, on a journey stemming from his line of work.

Unable to deny himself, he kissed the tip of one breast and she responded. "Hmm."

He kissed the other and she wove her fingers in his hair. When he suckled, flicking his moist tongue over and over her areola, drawing circles around her nipple, she sighed with abandon. "Feels so…"

Voices outside on the deck carried through her door. They seemed to startle her, as if she finally became aware of who she was with and what they were doing. She pulled away from his eager mouth.

"You needn't say it," he whispered. He cupped her delectable throat, running his fingers along her hot flesh, searing the memory of her naked body into his mind for a future lonely time he knew was sure to come.

She said it anyway. "I've…I've taken leave of my senses."

He had no wise response.

His arms slackened and she escaped his embrace. She slid her corset up along those gorgeous ribs and the creamy mounds of flesh, the areolae that beckoned to him and the nipples that rose like beautiful stars toward the heavens. Her cleavage turned and twisted, hypnotizing him into a trance from which he didn't wish to awaken.

Deftly, she buttoned her blouse, no longer able or willing to meet his eyes. As if shamed.

It was shameful. Shameful of him to treat her as a wanton woman available for him and his touch.

"It's my fault," he said. "I shouldn't have let this happen. I'm the guard who's supposed to be watching over you." He took a step back and ran his hand through his hair.

"Well, this can't happen again. This isn't what I want."

He heard her loud and clear. *He* wasn't what she wanted. *He* could never replace the touch of her former lover. Judging by the way she'd responded to his caress, he was certain she'd had a lover before.

God curse the man.

And God curse Colt for the resulting streak of jealousy raging through him.

Elizabeth turned away toward the bed and her carpet-bag, as if dismissing him. *All done now. You may leave.*

Colt felt like a servant.

Dammit, he was a servant. Just as she'd said. He should know better. He was the one always harping on expectation and honor and all it entailed.

"I apologize. Good night." He let himself out the door.

Waiting for him on the other side was his faithful new friend, Saint. The dog tilted his head and whimpered.

"How long have you been sitting here?"

"Awhile," Buxton replied, coming out of nowhere on the deck, approaching the cabin next to Elizabeth's. Will was with him.

The prickly heat of guilt raced up the back of Colt's neck. What had they witnessed?

Buxton unlocked their cabin door and he and Will stepped inside.

"All clear, Liza," Colt said loudly through her closed door, hoping to mask the impropriety. "No more trouble on deck. Good night."

But as he stumbled to the railing to catch his breath, he looked down at hands streaked with shoe polish, his shirt, as well. With aching breath, he pointed his face to the salty wind and wondered how much his men had observed, how badly he'd compromised Elizabeth, and what on God's green earth had possessed him to kiss her.

What would he say to the beautiful doctor tomorrow?

Chapter Seven

Elizabeth could hear his voice through the wall.

The moon, as rich as butter cream, poured through the porthole and over her bare dangling leg, highlighting the smooth cliffs and valleys of her knee and calf. Her nightgown, unbuttoned from top to bottom due to the soaring heat inside the tight four walls, gaped open to reveal her nakedness.

Colt had kissed her breast and she had inhaled the earthy scent of his skin. How could things ever be the same between them?

Back and forth, the motion of the ship lulled her into a drowsy state, yet she couldn't fall asleep. Her restlessness, ever since Colt had left her cabin hours earlier, wouldn't abate.

His voice drifted over her. She couldn't make out the words, but he was talking to his men. Sometimes his tenor was smooth and coaxing, as he'd been with her, other times his sentences ended in a round of laughter from the Mounties.

She wondered how Colt could carry on a conversation as if nothing had happened. As if he hadn't kissed her, as if he hadn't unwrapped her bosom and placed his lips upon her.

Groaning with the need of his touch, she rolled over to her side. Her breasts rolled with her movements and she looked down to assess what he'd so openly claimed.

Nakedness was natural. Making love was natural and nothing to be ashamed of between two wedded people. Or perhaps two people intending to wed—that was how she'd slipped up before, with Gerard. But any hint of seduction between her and a man who thought her uncle capable of murder…

Colt thought her interest in medicine was to be commended, but she'd heard him say that she should settle down with a husband and children. How could she give up the very thing that was a part of her soul?

She hadn't done it for Gerard. She'd never do it for Colt.

Would Colt want that, though? After their discussion this evening about her grandmother, was he thinking differently? Did he appreciate Elizabeth more in her role as a physician?

It didn't matter. She was going to the Klondike. Colt might be commanding this journey, but he would not command her in any other way.

The sooner she let him know their interlude had been a mistake, the sooner they'd return to the way things were, to their normal state of being. But remembering the way he'd looked at her in the moonlight tonight, his face silhouetted in shadow, his full lips parted with anticipation, made her stomach throb.

She cupped a hand beneath her warm, heavy breast, rubbed gently and then ran her hand beneath the other. He'd touched her here, and here, and here, and made her quiver.

She flicked her thumb over her soft nipple, reveling in the sensation. Closing her lids, she thought of his handsome face captured in the moon's glow. Wondered what he'd think if he knew what she was doing now. Remembered how his hot mouth swirled against her nipples, and how his riveting touch had caused her to melt between her thighs. She slid her hand along her belly and lower still, till she found the exquisitely sensitive spot Colt had been searching for. She moaned softly and imagined how his fingers might feel here, and what expression he would wear upon his face.

Two days passed on the heaving ocean. They barely spoke.

Colt sensed Elizabeth's disapproval of him by the way she avoided him on deck, by the cool set of her lips whenever she and the brothers met for a meal. Finally, on the third day after their unfortunate kiss, the waves subsided till the Pacific took on a glossy blue sheen, as rich and smooth as the coat of a seal, and Elizabeth was once again tolerating him.

"You know, you two certainly look like brother and sister. I could spot that from ten yards away."

Colt smiled at the humorous comment made by Mrs. Thornbottom. Seated on the crowded bench beside Elizabeth for breakfast, he was enjoying a spread of marmalade and eggs. It was surprising what tricks the mind could play when a person really believed he and Elizabeth were related. In this case, Mrs. Thornbottom saw a physical similarity where there wasn't one.

Elizabeth nearly choked and took to lathering her slice of bread with more butter. Milly and her father stared at Elizabeth and Colt as one might do at an odd painting. The Mounties seated on Elizabeth's other side were too busy gulping coffee and pointing at the ocean to pay attention.

Colt yanked on the brim of his cowboy hat at the same time Elizabeth did hers.

"I mean," said Mrs. Thornbottom, obviously having recovered quite nicely from her daughter's illness two evenings prior, "you've got the same nose."

"Do we now?" asked Colt, amused.

"Yes, indeed. Look, look Milly, don't they have the same forehead and the same look of…what is it in their eyes? The same look of…combat. That's it! Combat!" The woman slapped her own round cheek, causing it to shudder, and laughed.

Colt glanced at Elizabeth. Beneath the painted brunette hair, she puckered her mouth. Her blackfly bites had turned into teeny scabs. She squirmed beside him as if someone had lifted a rock off a worm and she, the worm, was squiggling to escape. He wished he could take back those kisses. He wished he didn't have the image of her bouncing naked breasts burned into his mind.

"Folks say that a lot," said Colt, playing along. "That we look alike."

He poured himself another cup of coffee from the tin pot as Elizabeth chuckled weakly.

Sunlight mirrored off the ocean as their ship chugged along. The ocean blues and aquamarines swirled in the depths below. To their right along the coastline, mountain cliffs rose from the water, topped with ice and snow. Mother Nature at her most magnificent. *Other than the mesmerizing body of a woman. Mother Nature certainly knew how to sculpt.*

He bit into a slice of rye. "Hmm, very good."

Mr. Thornbottom engaged the other Mounties in a quiet conversation about his business as a rope and broom salesman in Montana while his wife and daughter stared at Elizabeth and Colt.

"Yes," said Elizabeth, toying with her napkin. "Some folks say we have the same…same chin. Then they comment how Colt is so much more flamboyant. He has always sought attention, even as a young boy."

Milly giggled and Mrs. Thornbottom pressed her large bosom to the table in an eager attempt to hear more.

"Why I recall on more than one occasion, Colt acting up in church. He always sang the hymns much too loud, just to get attention."

"No!" squealed Mrs. Thornbottom.

A muscle twitched at his lips. Where was Elizabeth taking this? Was she trying to show him how well she could lie?

"Oh, yes," said Elizabeth, smiling and gaining momentum. "And he once put a mouse in the Reverend's wife's pew."

"Uhh!" Mrs. Thornbottom nearly popped a blood vessel.

"Don't you worry," said Elizabeth. "He got a switch on his behind for that one."

So this was how she wanted to play the game, was it? Could be a fine one, at that.

Colt leaned toward the plump woman. "Don't think

she was an angel." He turned to Elizabeth. "Why don't you confess to some of your crimes?"

Elizabeth gave him an uninterested look and bit into her jam sandwich. The honey dribbled onto her fingers and she licked one. And licked it again. He swallowed hard, wondering how that tongue of hers would feel pressed against his—"

"Do tell," said the old woman. "I can't imagine Elizabeth doing anything as rascally as you."

"Would you believe she stole the Reverend's wife's handkerchief?"

Elizabeth gasped. "I did not!"

The corner of his lips turned upward. "Remember how you admired the blue lace trim, and how you said her monogrammed initials were the same as yours? LB." Slowly he sipped his coffee.

Mrs. Thornbottom's jaw hung so loose it nearly hit the chunk of cheese she held between her fingers. "Blasphemy."

"It's not true," said Elizabeth. "Don't you remember, dear brother, the culprit turned out to be that…that girl you used to court…the one who never stopped talking about herself…Lydia Bartholemew?"

"Oh, yes, Lydia." Colt smiled at Elizabeth's ability to make up a name so quickly. "She was the most accommodating girl, as I recall. Loved it when I kissed her."

Elizabeth flushed deep, apple-red. Was she, too, thinking about *their* kiss?

"I wouldn't sit there so self-righteous if I were you," Elizabeth said. "Shall we tell Mrs. Thornbottom about the time you were arrested for drunken and mischievous behavior?" Elizabeth chuckled as if she were about to burst. "They found him on the neighbor's roof, singing those church hymns. Stark naked."

The women tittered. Mrs. Thornbottom fanned her cheeks with her hand. "Gracious, he does love to sing those blessed songs."

Colt rallied. "Perhaps you should tell them about the time you got into Mother's perfumes."

Elizabeth sniffed. "A little perfume never hurt anyone."

"But *you* wound up naked in the cornfield."

"I was only six." Elizabeth sipped her coffee. "He's very mean. He doesn't allow me to forget things like that, and I was only a child. That was the year our mother died. I wanted to remember her by trying some of her perfumes."

Mrs. Thornbottom clucked her tongue and scolded Colt. "She was *only a child.*"

Blazes. Where did Elizabeth learn how to fib like this?

"He's a very bad dancer," said Elizabeth. "Once, my brothers and I caught him practicing for his twelfth-grade graduation."

"Did he go with Lydia?" asked Mrs. Thornbottom.

"The one and only."

"*Lydia* quite enjoyed my dancing," Colt interrupted. "She was quite willing to stay up all hours to help me improve my…twirl."

All three women gasped.

Elizabeth shuffled in her seat, her skirts billowing over his thigh. Mrs. Thornbottom looked askance.

"Why don't you tell us about the night of your own graduation?" Colt prompted. "This time you were sixteen."

"It was nothing. A figment of your imagination."

Colt lowered his shoulders and dropped his voice to a whisper. "She decided to go without a corset."

"Oh, my. Oh, my." Mrs. Thornbottom cupped her mouth. "What on earth possessed you?"

Elizabeth's mouth gaped open. Speechless.

"Oh, she still does it on occasion, when she has her sights set on a man. That's why my brothers and I have to keep such close guard over her."

The old woman's eyes dropped to Elizabeth's bosom, where they remained for several seconds. Colt took the opportunity to scrutinize the area himself.

It was such a lovely area. The buttons of her thin blouse dipped against her chest and then over the delicious mound of flesh. It conjured a picture in his mind, the beauty of her faintly colored areolae and the warmth of her nipples.

Elizabeth swung toward him, her cheeks splotched with color. "I do *not* go without…without my…"

"I certainly hope you've cured yourself of that habit. Your brothers and I can only pray." He leaned back and took a sip from his cup.

"Listen to your brothers," implored Mrs. Thornbottom. "They mean you well. You wouldn't want to wind up—" she dropped her voice till it was nearly inaudible "—in some back alley. I can understand how losing your mother at such an early age impinged on your upbringing, but good heavens—"

"Good morning," Dr. Wellsley interrupted. He stood above them with clean plate in hand.

Rather pale and weak for a man, thought Colt.

"And how is everyone feeling today?" Wellsley smiled and nodded first at Elizabeth, then pointedly at Milly.

"Much better," Milly squeaked.

"Everything is working normally this morning," her mother sputtered. "If you understand my meaning. Please, please join us."

Elizabeth's eyes opened to the size of eggs as she downed a mouthful of coffee.

Colt didn't think Wellsley had overhead much, but couldn't be sure.

Elizabeth, however, kept her eyes on her sandwich. Then calming down, she shoved Colt in the ribs to make room on the bench for her beloved hero.

Colt refused to budge. Let the squirmy fellow find his own bench.

"*Excuse* me," muttered Elizabeth, again elbowing Colt. "Could you please make room?"

"I'm already sitting on the edge. There's no place to go."

"Well, bundle up your shoulders and slant them another way."

He refused. So she pressed up against him good and solid. In other circumstances, he might have enjoyed it. When Wellsley squeezed in beside her, Colt assumed the other man had a good feel of her, too. His blood began to cook.

"It's good to see you, Donovan," cooed Elizabeth.

"And the same for you. How did you sleep?"

"Exceptionally well, thank you. I think our stroll last night cast me into a very deep slumber."

Colt fidgeted. His eyes still stung from lack of it. "It's time we go recite our morning prayers." He rose, tossing his napkin to the table. "Are you coming, Liza?"

"But we've only begun—"

"Liza," Colt repeated. He glanced at Mrs. Thornbottom as if to say, *See what I mean?*

"Go with your brother, Liza, go. I feel an urge to act as your mother would in this situation. You need to say your prayers."

"What's this?" asked Wellsley. "I thought we might have a conversation."

"Liza," said Colt, "please don't make me repeat any stories to Dr. Wellsley."

"What stories?" The doctor stuffed his mouth with a prune.

At that moment, Mrs. Thornbottom screamed.

Colt shuddered. Elizabeth froze.

They turned toward the ocean, where the buxom woman was staring and pointing with her handkerchief.

"A sea serpent!"

"Good grief," said Colt. "It's a whale, Mrs. Thornbottom. A whale."

A collective gasp went through the group. Eight shiny black mammals were swimming fifty yards from the ship. Their moans, a low hum through their blow holes, skimmed along the water and dropped like stones on the deck, echoing around the men and women.

"What are they doing?" asked Elizabeth.

Colt watched as the whales dived up and down, their white chins glistening in the sun. The smaller calves followed, imitating their parents and grandparents. "I believe they're probably trying to trap a school of salmon against that cliff."

"They eat salmon?" asked Mrs. Thornbottom.

"Well, certainly not us."

A large black dorsal fin flopped in the water close to

them. He was one of the braver ones, perhaps wondering about this wooden beast that was blowing smoke and chugging in their ocean.

Elizabeth's expression was one of awe, and Colt shared her sense of marvel. Their souls held together for a few brief seconds, connected by the joy of being alive, of being a part of this wild adventure.

Then as quickly as they came, the whales disappeared around the bend, beyond the cliffs. And he and Elizabeth glanced away from each other.

"What stories, then?" asked Wellsley when the group nestled back into place. "What stories of Elizabeth?"

"Well, it's about her grad—" Colt began.

"Never mind." Elizabeth scooted out of her seat. "Perhaps we can take a stroll along the deck later this morning, Donovan."

She didn't bother looking at Mrs. Thornbottom's curious stare, or Colt's suspicious regard.

But Colt knew one thing as Elizabeth huffed away from the table with him. He had an ally in Mrs. Thornbottom in protecting his baby sister.

"Thank heaven for old busybodies," he said to Elizabeth, once out of earshot. The deck leading to their cabins was almost empty. No doubt, most folks were on the stern, still talking about the whales.

"I will *never* forgive you," she said. "That nice old woman thinks I have a problem keeping my clothes on."

Colt quirked an eyebrow. Well, didn't she?

"How dare you insinuate it was me who—who shed them and not you who—who ripped them…"

A lazy smile worked its way over his mouth.

Elizabeth gasped. "Never mind. But now that I've got you alone, I'd like to make one thing painfully clear."

"Painfully would be your choice of word."

The mood turned serious. He didn't like serious. Dammit, he just wanted relief from this whole headache of having her as a make-believe sister. Serious and truthful was harder to take. And what was the truth about him, when it came to women? That he couldn't forgive her for the things she must have said to Rosalyn? Or that he couldn't forgive himself for not being man enough to hold on to Rosalyn?

"I'd like you to know how very much I regretted the other evening."

"You mean the shoe polish?"

"No, not that evening. Two evenings ago."

"You mean last night when you ate that spinach—"

"Stop it. Be serious. You know which evening I regret."

"At the time, it didn't seem to me like you regretted anything."

She closed her lids and uttered something he couldn't make out.

Her eyelashes flashed up at him. "Everything that comes out of your mouth is somehow…dipped in a lie."

"You did pretty good yourself back there."

"What I want to say is…my behavior wasn't the type of behavior I'm proud of."

"I wasn't proud of my own."

"Well, I need to repeat that it will never happen again. You took me by surprise and…and I'm not good with surprises."

With a fashionable twirl, Elizabeth unlocked her door, stomped inside and shut it. The interior latch clicked in his ear.

He called through her door. "You're to begin with the Lord's Prayer."

When she didn't respond to his brand of humor, he sighed, unlocked his cabin and slid into emptiness.

"You took me by surprise, too." The words echoed softly against the walls.

Chapter Eight

"It's time you came clean with us, Colt. What's going on between you and Elizabeth?"

Tall and shirtless, Colt was shaving at the washstand in his cabin. At Buxton's unexpected question, Colt paused with razor in midair. An early-morning breeze from the porthole swept over his bare chest. The other five Mounties were folding clothes and packing duffel bags, preparing to leave ship. By noon, they'd be in Skagway, Alaska.

Colt scraped the razorblade against his cheek. White stripes of shaving cream contrasted with his brown skin. "Nothing's going on."

"You came in one night covered in shoe polish," said Buxton.

"I was helping her with…her luggage."

Buxton scowled, the ridge of the scar beneath his eye deepening. "You were doing a hell of a lot more than that."

"You can't let her control things," said Tommy.

Colt regarded the men reflected in the mirror. Tommy's

hardened expression conveyed his rancor. What was he so pissed about? In all the years Colt had known him—hell, since they were fifteen—had Colt ever let him down? And Buxton…he'd had it in for Elizabeth since the moment he'd met her. By the way Will was flinging clothes into his bags, Colt knew he was extremely bothered, too. Anderson was pretending he was more interested in patting the dog than listening, but even his easygoing nature was strained. Eddie, lying on his bunk with hands behind his head, was the only one not displaying outright anger.

"It wouldn't hurt for you men to ease up on her."

Tommy tugged his boots on. "We've got a lot riding on this mission. If you need to pull out—"

"I *don't* need to pull out."

The other men eyed each other.

"It took a couple of days for Elizabeth and me to get acquainted. For me to let her know who's boss."

"You've got to let her know she takes orders from you," said Buxton, speaking as though he was the oldest brother here. Which, actually, he was, but Colt ignored his pushy tendencies.

"Don't worry, she knows. That's why she's fighting it so hard."

Finally, Anderson, with his trademark good humor, nudged Will. "All women dislike taking orders from men."

The tension eased. Will grinned. Buxton relaxed. Tommy sighed. Anderson whistled at the dog. Eddie rose from his bunk.

Colt toweled his skin and peered into the mirror with disdain. His relationship with Elizabeth was hardly that of a police officer investigating the possible murder of an innocent man by *her* uncle. Colt slapped the towel over his shoulder. He wouldn't enter her cabin again. He'd protect her from the idiotic Wellsley, but Colt himself would not set foot in her room again.

He broached another topic. "Have any of you heard more about the gang we're looking for?"

"Some folks are warning me to watch our supplies between Whitehorse and Dawson," said Buxton. "It's where the worst thefts are occurring. But we already knew that."

They wouldn't be there for another two to three weeks, thought Colt.

"It might not be the same gang that's doing all the robbing," said Tommy. "That's something new. I've heard different descriptions of the leader. Some say to watch out for a dentist with a beard, others say it's a clean-shaven schoolteacher."

Will shoved a towel into his bag. "And if it's the same guy, he uses a different name with each robbery."

"Always poses as an educated man," Colt pointed out. "I've heard he orders his men not to use violence."

Ed looked over from his bunk. "I've heard that, too. Seems like an odd rule for a man who robs folks blind. I wonder if he knows he's left some travelers so desolate they've died of starvation anyway after he and his men leave."

Colt clenched his fist on the stick of the razor. "When we catch the son of a bitch, I'll get the answer out of him."

Pierce Rawlins bit into his chewing tobacco, swirled it in his mouth to savor its kick and spit it to the ground. The eyes of a dozen men riveted on his face. From behind their hiding spots, they waited for his signal. His chest expanded with pride. His heart thumped with anticipation of the new prize about to fill his coffers.

Smoke from the nearby campfire bit his nostrils. The call of eagles on the mountains made his senses soar. He'd been raised on land as flat as a pan, and to him, the mountains rose like strange creatures from the earth.

"Now," he ordered.

With rifles and revolvers drawn, a dozen men jumped out from behind bushes. They wore bandannas. They leaped from boulders. They sprang from canoes on the Yukon River and surrounded their prey.

At the campfire, the trapper and his wife stumbled to their feet in shock.

Rawlins adjusted his clerical collar. Exhilarated, he stepped out from the aspens. His boots pounded into the earth.

"Reverend," the trapper's wife cried. "Have they hurt you?"

Rawlins grinned and rubbed his bristled jaw. Unexpectedly, he slid his rifle up to greet her. "Not at all."

The trapper, a burly fellow in his thirties, stepped in front of his wife with a six-shooter in his fist. "What the hell is going on here?"

"Drop your weapon and you won't get hurt."

The trapper recoiled. "How can you do this, Smith? You're a man of the cloth."

They still believed it. And that his name was Smith.

"Even men of the cloth grow hungry."

"We fed you dinner. We invited you to join us."

"You should have known better than to flaunt your pelts." Fox and beaver and caribou overflowed on the couple's raft. Why were people so stupid? They made his job too easy. There was more honor, more victory in outsmarting someone his equal.

The trapper slid his gun to the ground. "Don't do this."

"It's already done." With a nod to his men, Rawlins watched them strip the boat of pelts. They'd fetch him a mighty fine dollar. What's more, he was thrilled to partake in the wild adventures of the far-north trappers that he'd read about in journals and newspapers.

The trapper's hands trembled. "You can have the pelts. Just leave us be."

His wife sobbed and sank into her husband from behind. They both fell to the ground on their knees.

Rawlins winced. He'd never hurt them. Blood and gore made him vomit. The calm way he handled things was how he'd earned his nickname this last year on the trail. The Reverend. The name held a certain charm. He wasn't truly a man of the cloth, but he enjoyed the disguise. He'd worn a clerical collar on the heist with these people for the first time.

Fascinating, really, how the fear of violence was more powerful than violence itself. Rawlins gloated.

Shit. There was that man down in Dawson, though. Last year. Shot and killed. Queasiness gripped him. The incident couldn't be helped.

Rawlins swallowed at their misery. "Get off your knees," he roared. "There's no need for that. Now, stay put for four hours. If you so much as flinch, we'll be back, and so will our bullets."

"Colt? Would you mind stepping into my room?"

Colt groaned. He was coming out of his own cabin onto the deck when Elizabeth called from her opened door.

"Please? If you could just take this bag, I could manage the other."

The ship had anchored, and disembarking passengers swarmed the deck. The Skagway harbor was nestled in a gorge between half a dozen mountain peaks. Fir trees ran halfway up the slopes, then nothing grew beyond the timberline. There, gray boulders and rocky crags met with snow and ice. The blue ocean sparkled beneath them, waters so deep they allowed ships of many sizes. Above them, the sky was streaked with white cotton candy. When Colt inhaled, the air smelled and tasted so pure and clear that it rushed down his lungs like a waterfall.

On the dock, his men were tending to the animals, to the crates of apricots and sausages. Colt had already organized his team and instructed them all, including Elizabeth, to meet by the horses. He'd come back for his duffel bags, while Anderson had volunteered to help Elizabeth.

The dog circled beside Colt, restless to get on solid ground. Saint looked better already from the five days on board. Softhearted passengers had taken to feeding the poor mutt every scrap they could spare.

"I thought Anderson was helping you," Colt hollered.

"I wasn't ready, so I told him to go ahead and get Amelia for me. Would you please just come here?"

Inside her room? "You know, when you break a little vow, it gets easier to break a bigger vow, and before you know it, you're breaking every damn rule you've ever set for yourself."

"What in tarnation are you talking about?"

"Never mind." He set his two bags inside her open door, then, looking down the deck, he caught sight of a suspicious character, playing card tricks for money. "You!"

The young lad shot Colt a nasty look, then scrambled to collect his crate and cards.

"I told you to stop that!"

But he was already gone, lost in the crowd. It served some folks right to lose everything they owned, if they thought they could double their money in a fast game of twenty-one.

Folks should pay close attention to their wallets. Scoundrels were no longer trapped at sea, easily caught. For five days they'd been prowling the ship, targeting their marks, and now they were making their moves. Ports were the worst place for these sordid characters.

"Could you please help me with this?"

With an impatient sigh, Colt appraised her standing at her bedside, pounding on a bag, trying to force her clothing to fit inside. With every movement, her bosom and hips swayed.

"I can't seem to close the buckle." She kneed her bag and yanked on the clip. Exasperated, she wiped her damp forehead with her sleeve and stared at him.

"Colt?"

"It fit before. What's the problem?"

"I washed my laundry and nothing fits like it did."

With a groan, he stepped into the hot room and came around to her side. He tore the clothing out of her bag.

"That's no help!" She snatched the first thing to pop out. Her thin nightgown.

"Roll them instead of fold. You can jam more in."

While she tried to conceal her nightgown, his eyes strayed to the buttons down the front and the pretty lace trim. She grabbed her corset, a rose-colored one, before his gaze could fully catch it. But it was getting harder to breathe, watching her put the lacy thing away. The corset he'd slid off her the other evening had been a white one.

"Not everything can be rolled."

"Do your best." He grabbed one of her skirts, a thin brown muslin, folded it in three and then rolled.

His touch on her intimate things was wrong. He became aware of the faint sound of bedsprings creaking as he kneed the mattress. He noticed the sound of her breathing, the shuffle of her soles on the floorboards. Sticky heat from the noon sun drizzled down the back of his neck and dampened the spot between his shoulder blades.

She looked out at the crowd on deck. "Maybe we should wait here till it clears."

"No."

The soft down on her cheeks shimmered with perspiration. Outside, there was snow on the tips of the mountains, but the daytime temperature was stifling at sea level. With a handkerchief, she rubbed the back of her neck. She sopped up the moisture beneath wisps of hair that had escaped from her braid. A pulse at her throat hammered against her flesh. Her lips trembled slightly when she met his heated gaze.

"Oh, oh…" She sprang away from the bed and him. "We should really leave and…and join the lineup as quickly as we can."

"After you," he said. He did up the last of the buckles, hoisted her extra bag with his own and trudged toward the door. He wasn't staying one damn minute longer.

"I can't get out," she said. "The crowd's too thick."

A young man, roughly eighteen, swung past and peered at Elizabeth, his face mottled with red spots.

"Russell, how are you feeling?" she asked.

"Fine, thank you ma'am. Gettin' rid of my wool clothes did the trick."

"Your rash has faded an awful lot. Glad to see it. From now on, cotton and linen only."

"Yes, ma'am."

He disappeared and Elizabeth whispered to Colt inside the doorway. "Thank heaven it wasn't measles. A bout of that could have wiped out half the passengers."

"Liza," said Colt, exasperated. "Why are you going around helping everyone? And he's a man, for God's sake—"

"He's a boy. And I never touched him. I didn't need to—"

"Didn't we agree—"

"Shh." She cut him off, motioning to the listening ears.

Colt clenched his jaw. "We'll continue this conversation when we're alone."

He pushed his way into the group of strangers, flexing his muscles and heaving his broad shoulders. Someone took pity—Mr. Thornbottom and his family—and cleared a spot in the crowd.

"Come along, dear," said Mrs. Thornbottom, trying to squeeze her large frame into a tight opening beside the rail.

"Thank you." Elizabeth smiled, lifted her bag and wove her way into the summer sunshine, Colt beside her.

With a rush of exhilaration, Colt studied the scene sprawled out below the railing. The dock itself ran for half a mile up the Lynn Canal. Thousands of people were unloading crates of canned food, sacks of flour, tins of coffee, pots and pans, axes and shovels. As far as the eye could see, people covered the banks. Hundreds of white canvas tents flapped in the wind. Dozens of log buildings lined the muddy main street with its gambling halls, saloons and false-front shops.

People were selling and buying whatever the imagination could think of, whatever folks had had the foresight and stamina to carry here. Signs read: Bunks for the Night, English Tea, Klondike Gear and Outfits, Fine Hats, and Colt's personal favorite, Used Gold Pans Half Price.

Many of these makeshift stores had an additional sign in common: Open Twenty-Four Hours.

"Twenty-four?" Elizabeth said beside him.

"It's already June. We're nearing summer and we're so far north, the sun never sets."

"Ah." She paused to absorb it all. "It's so loud."

He noticed the buzz of voices then, too. The pitch of excitement from those on their way out, or, from the ones who'd tried but couldn't make it—the delirium of hope and failure. They came from everywhere. Norwegians, Scots, Italians, Russians, Americans from every state and territory, and Canadians who'd never seen much more than the front of a desk their whole adult lives.

"Take a good look," he said softly, torn between awe and disgust. "This is gold fever."

When she leaned over the rail, Colt's thigh brushed hers. She reacted as if a stray spark of fire hit her, jolting sideways to avoid more of him.

It was impossible to get away from her. The fleshy part of her upper arm brushed his, conjuring in him the image of Elizabeth in her corset, of him pulling down the whale-boned fabric to reveal enticing breasts.

Trying to erase the lovely thought from his mind, he straightened, ran his hand along his rough jaw and looked for his men. He spotted them by the horses and supplies. What Colt was more interested in, why he'd timed it so he could lag behind, was who else had their eyes on the crates.

There were several interested parties in the crowd.

Two men dressed in rags, smoking cigarettes and mumbling to each other as they walked down the gangway, eyed the apricots. Another three men, several feet behind them, said nothing, but Colt noticed their feverish look of greed. Another sole gentleman chewed on a cigar while observing the Mounties. The gent was also studying two well-groomed men on the dock who were dressed in expensive suits and carrying fancy pocket watches.

Colt and Elizabeth shuffled their way through the folks on deck. They said goodbye to the Thornbottoms and wished them luck. When Colt followed Elizabeth down the gangway, he noticed the envious looks of male passengers.

"Where are the women?" she asked as they approached their brothers on the shoreline. "There are no women."

"There's a few," Colt replied.

"One in a hundred."

A gull swooped down and captured a piece of bread someone had dropped in the water.

"Would you care to buy your wife some oysters?" A burly man in plaid trousers, stiff with dirt, nudged Colt.

"Sister, not wife," said Elizabeth.

Colt frowned at her. Better for her own safety that this man consider them married.

The man grinned, revealing a sturdy set of teeth. "Ah, sister."

"No, thanks," Colt told him.

"Where'd you get the oysters?" asked Elizabeth, breathless.

"Seattle. Iced all the way here."

"Must be pricey," said Colt.

"Worth every penny. For your sister."

Colt shook his head and elbowed his way and Elizabeth's past the other Mounties. He gripped the reins of one black mare and Elizabeth took hold of Amelia's, just as someone hollered behind them.

"Make way!" Two old men, laden with sacks marked with the stamp of Canadian postal services, pushed through. Two younger men followed, on either end of a leather trunk. Sacks of more mail and parcels shifted on top of the trunk.

Colt was intrigued by the items some folks were shipping. "Wow," he said. "Is that a book? Look at the size of it."

One of the older mailmen chuckled. "Two full volumes of the English Dictionary. Some bloke—a reporter—ordered it for Dawson."

"And two hatboxes?" asked Elizabeth.

"They're costing a fortune to deliver. Ordered by two ladies who struck gold."

Folks around them whistled. There was also a banjo in a leather case, and a crystal bowl marked England peeking through the slats of a wooden crate.

Most of the mail to the Klondike was delivered by the

Mounties, but Colt didn't recognize these men. They had to be locals from the Yukon who traveled specifically back and forth from Skagway to Dawson.

"It's the first mail run since the ice breakup," said one of the younger Mounties. "So we've got a lot."

For some reason, Elizabeth gasped. "Colt, this way. Come. Come, let's go this way."

"Just a minute." His eyes widened in disbelief at the trunk. "Tell me you didn't." His mouth dropped open as he glared from the red trunk to her, then back again to the red leather. She had asked the Mountie they'd left behind at Whippoorwill Station to ship the trunk, and he'd done well. "Tell me you didn't disregard everything I said."

"I addressed it to my granddad," she whispered. "And no one will ever know otherwise."

He pulled her to the other side of the mares. "It's full of the things I told you not to bring."

"I didn't think it would be traveling alongside us. I thought it would go on another ship."

"That's the problem," he whispered. "You didn't think. Now you'll be attached to that thing and whimper every time it hits a bump. You'll be a dead giveaway."

"I'll ignore it. I'll pretend it doesn't exist."

"That's about as impossible as convincing you not to look the other way when someone needs help."

"Me? What about you? It's harder for you to pretend-" she lowered her voice so he could barely hear her "—you're not an officer of the law."

He gritted his teeth. "What do you mean?"

"Stopping a crooked game of cards. Nabbing a pickpocket. Breaking up arguments between complete strangers."

"I go about my business without attracting attention."

"Mr. Thornbottom witnessed you a couple of times, I saw him watching you. And now he's watching us as if the Lord himself blessed him with the eyes of an eagle."

Colt led his mare a few paces ahead, then looked back. Sure enough, gray-haired Thornbottom, thin and deliberate, tapping his belt buckle, was watching them.

"I want you to stop talking for a while. We're heading to the top of that slope. We'll set up our tents for a couple of days to get our bearings, and go from there."

But it was too late to slip into the crowd. They only got partway up the slope into a small clearing, when behind him, Elizabeth screamed.

Colt jumped and turned around to look. The rough man in the plaid trousers who'd tried to sell them oysters was pawing at her. He twisted her arm from behind, gripped her by the waist and kissed her throat. He waved a shovel in one hand as if it was a weapon.

"Land's sake, I haven't had a respectable woman in over two years."

Incensed, Colt was the first Mountie to respond. "Maybe that's because you've got no manners, you piece of dirt."

The man lunged with his shovel and pierced Colt's thigh. The metal ripped through denim and dug into solid flesh. He yelped. Pain downed him to his knees. Blood oozed from his leg, then his livid anger blurred the pain.

Elizabeth shrieked. Her tormentor pulled her closer. Colt's head pounded with fury.

The Mounties, yards behind, dropped their reins and came running.

Colt ignored their warnings. He stumbled to rise.

"Colt, no!"

"Leave him be, brother!"

"We'll get Liza!"

"Let's not start a war!"

Colt rose from the ground, wobbly on his feet, light-headed and dizzy. "I'm not starting one. I'm finishing one."

The man sneered and charged with his shovel. This time Colt ducked out of the way and swung at the predator, ready to make him pay.

Chapter Nine

Elizabeth heard the crunch of Colt's fist. It rammed the teeth of the dirty man who held her. Thankfully, his grip on her slackened and he collapsed to the dirt. The Saint Bernard shot out from behind her legs and growled.

Colt collapsed on her other side. His eyes closed.

Elizabeth dropped to her knees. "Colt!" She shook him frantically by the shoulder. Colt!"

Slowly, he opened his lids. "Stop yelling. I can hear you."

Saint circled his master, whimpering and nudging him to rise. Colt tried, gave a slow heave, then crumpled again.

She assessed him quickly. The pulse in his neck was strong. Breathing too fast. Leg bloody and oozing. The blood glued his pants to his skin, so she couldn't assess the wound. She ran her hands down his leg. No broken femur, thank God.

"Keep talking to me," she said. "Keep talking."

"What should I say?"

"Anything. Just talk."

"The clouds are rolling…."

"Yeah, the clouds. The clouds." Trying not to panic, Elizabeth tugged the kerchief from her neck, placed it smack on top of the wound and pressed hard to stop the bleeding. Peering up to the stunned crowd for help, she glanced to the Mounties. Two of them held her attacker, who was wrestling to get up, and two tended to the frightened animals.

Buxton scrambled to her side, pale and stiff himself. "How bad is it?"

"I don't know. I can't get a good look at the injury till the bleeding stops."

Her attacker cursed the men holding him. The Mounties gave him a good shove and released him. The crowd parted and he ran down the hill.

Her mouth fell open. "You're letting him go? Aren't you going to report him to the law?"

Buxton looked at her in a funny way. She didn't much care because Colt was drifting off again.

Panicked, she nudged him. "Colt. Colt."

"Yeah."

"I need to take your pants off."

"Yeah," he murmured. "I mean *no*."

"I need to see the wound." Her pulse raced along with his. "It's got to be cleansed. Bandaged."

"Let Buxton do it."

"I can do it better," she urged.

"No. Buxton and Anderson."

The men gaped at her as if expecting her to stand up and leave. This was no time for politeness. Blazes, as soon as she released her hand from his thigh, the blood oozed again. She glanced at the hunting knife attached to Buxton's belt, and moving quickly, heart pounding, she reached over and yanked it out.

With a swift hand, she made her threat. "Either you pull his pants down for me, right here, right now, or I will cut them off." Her voice escalated. "Do you hear me?"

"Dammit, woman. He'll need his pants for later." Buxton unbuttoned them and gave the denim a hard yank.

Colt groaned, but didn't fight. The pants slid down and her eyes went straight to the wound.

"Anderson," Elizabeth ordered, "get rid of the crowd. Set up a tent around me to block their view."

"What are you doing?" Colt murmured.

She raced to clamp the bleeding, using both hands. "I'm helping you."

"I don't need…don't need…"

"You *do* need."

He tried to add something. She lowered her ear to his lips.

"I promised your father," he said. "I wouldn't let you touch a man…no male patients…no man."

"You're not a man. You're my brother."

Colt tried to grin, then winced. "Everyone…can see."

"I'm helping my brother," she whispered. "No one will think there's anything odd about that."

"But…*I will know*…and you're not…not to lay your hands on a man."

"It'll be our secret. Don't tell my father."

"So many…many secrets."

Colt lost consciousness.

Her fingers flew over him. She called for her two carpetbags and they appeared within seconds. The Mounties worked fast, clearing the crowd and blocking her and Colt from view by using the animals. By the time she cleansed the wound, they erected a tent behind her, then one on either side.

Anderson and Buxton stayed by her side, assisting.

She sutured Colt's wound in less than twenty minutes—it was deeper than it was wide—and wrapped his leg with strips of cotton.

He was stirring by the time she finished. Now with complete privacy, shielded by the tents, she knew his skivvies needed to come off, too. One leg of the underwear was drenched with blood. She wasn't about to pull the soiled things over her clean bandage, so took out her scissors and cut.

Anderson and Buxton groaned aloud.

"He's gonna kill us," said Anderson, "for letting you do that."

"Then I imagine he'll never forgive you for what I'm about to do next." She glanced at the pan of bloody water beside her heel. "Run to the river and fetch some clean water. Please, before he comes to. Unless of course, one of you gentlemen would care to wash him?"

Colt groaned in his sleep. *Someone*…a woman… was kissing his cheek. Her lips were soft and warm and moist….

His thigh throbbed with pain. He'd been hurt…didn't recall how…but the kisses eased his pain…made it worthwhile.

Her touch was cool and soft on his foot, pressing along the arch. She ran her hand along his calf and pressed behind his knee. And then, sheer heaven…her cool, expert fingers lingered along his hairy thigh and settled in the bare crevice where his leg met his hip.

"Pulses normal," she whispered.

Pulses? What did she mean?

"Hmm," he responded to another round of her kisses.

He turned his cheek in that direction, willing his lids to open so he might see her face…but her hands touched his feet again. Two women? Were two women with him? Praise the heavenly stars.

Another moist nibbling on his throat, and he was gone….

What was that sound? Chuckling? Giggling? Were the two women giggling at what they were about to do to him? That he might lie here forever, basking in their warm and delicate caress…laughter was fine…they could laugh all they wanted. He, too, found himself grinning.

With monstrous strength, he forced himself to open his lids to the heavenly wench kissing his face.

A burst of sunlight. More laughter. He squinted. Where was she?

A Saint Bernard licked his mouth.

"Eww!" He jolted up on the grass, inside a tent. Still wearing his shirt, he was covered from the waist down by a sheet.

"Shoo!" said Elizabeth to the dog. "I told you, shoo! Could you men please stop this animal?"

"But we were enjoying their reunion," said Anderson.

"Get outta here." Colt shoved the dog. "I don't need your lips." What a bloody disappointment. Not two beautiful naked women. One smelly dog and a no-nonsense doctor. And Buxton and Anderson laughing.

Elizabeth pushed her sleeves up to her elbows. She

knelt on the ground next to him, her long brown skirt ballooning at her knees.

Buxton and Anderson chuckled again.

"Do you have to stare at me like a couple of gossipy old women?"

"I think you were dreamin' of better things." Anderson rose from the log he was sitting on.

"Who's tent are we in?" asked Colt.

"Our own."

"How long have I been out?"

"About two hours," said Elizabeth. "How do you feel?"

"Groggy. What happened to…oh, yeah…you okay?" he asked, recalling she'd been attacked.

When she nodded, dark wisps of hair slid around her face. She looked at him with gentle concern.

He tore off his sheet but when he saw his nakedness, yanked it back. There was nothing on his legs but a thick white bandage.

"What the hell…?"

"Gotta go." Buxton rushed out.

"See ya." Anderson was right behind him with the dog.

"I've got to wash your pants," Elizabeth chattered on. "And my skirt. They're covered in blood." She sprang to the door flap. "I'll ask Tommy to sit with you. It's best not to move. I gave you a shot of morphine, but I don't have much more in my bag and it'll wear off soon. Maybe I should try to find my red trunk—"

"No. Just a minute. Hold it right there."

She froze but didn't look at him.

"I just woke up, completely dressed on top, but completely naked from the waist down. How did I get this way?"

She toyed with her fingers. "Your leg was bleeding. We needed to see it."

He relaxed. "Ah, and Buxton…"

She shook her head. Her braided hair jostled along her spine.

"Anderson…"

She puckered her lips.

"Tell me it wasn't you."

"It wasn't me."

His gut twisted. "You're lying."

"You're right."

"Oh, hell." He sank onto the blanket that cushioned him on the grass.

She turned her cheek his way. "Don't worry, I won't tell my father."

"Oh, hell."

"There's nothing wrong with a doctor looking at a man's…at a man's…at washing the blood from…"

"Oh, hell."

Elizabeth didn't want to listen to their conversation. She shifted with discomfort at her own eavesdropping. She was trapped doing the laundry in a shielded spot between the three tents. Consequently, she heard every word spoken between Colt and Tommy inside the tent.

The other Mounties had left to finish what they'd intended before Colt had leaped to her defense—hauling their tons of supplies uphill to their makeshift camp. Considering her earlier attack, she didn't feel safe leaving the tents on her own. So, she continued to wash Colt's pants and her skirt. She'd planned to mend his pants when they dried.

Sunshine poured down on her. She swatted flies.

"It wasn't as bad as the time you got knifed for snatching his wallet," said Tommy.

Whose wallet? thought Elizabeth.

"I was only sixteen," said Colt. "Didn't know any better."

"Bloody Angus himself. Biggest prizefighter Ireland had."

"He should've let me go. He didn't need to knife me."

"Pickpocket like you? Nah."

Colt a pickpocket?

"You should talk. What about the shotgun you got sprayed with when you stole that cow?"

"At least he said I had balls."

"How'd we wind up here, Tommy? Mounties. Sometimes I can't believe it."

"Never got caught. That's how. These days, I always try to give a young man a break. I remember how it was with us."

"What are you trying to say? That I never do?"

There was a long pause.

Colt's voice turned into a soft grumble and she couldn't hear the rest, but his tone suggested he was hurt by Tommy's insinuation.

Elizabeth sagged beneath the weight of what she'd overhead.

Colt had a criminal past. He was never caught, but at one time during his juvenile years, he was a thief.

Is that why he was so rigid? So harsh with others?

With her and her uncle? Suspecting the worst…looking for it…even hoping to find it.

What a hypocrite.

"Those were lean years, Tommy."

A fly buzzed around her ear. She reached high and clapped at it instinctively. The conversation inside the tent stopped.

Why?

She stood perfectly still. Then saw the shadow of her boot against the tent. When she'd swatted the fly, the men inside had likely seen her shadow.

Sickened by what she'd overheard, Elizabeth dropped the wet garments into the pan of water and stepped around the tent to locate the other Mounties.

Colt, so high and mighty, had fallen to the basest level. Sergeant Colton Hunter, a man who roared about duty and honor, was no better than anyone else. In fact, he was worse.

Pretending to have such lofty ideals, such high regard for the law and proper procedure. She scuffed the ground and fought an inexplicable wave of tears.

How much had Elizabeth overheard?

Colt turned over on his side, moaning at the throbbing pain. Elizabeth was right about the morphine. It was wearing thin, and only two hours had passed since he'd awoken.

"Hey, fella," he muttered to Saint lying on the grass beside him. "I need to get up and out of here."

"I'll help you get your things." Elizabeth burst into the tent but avoided his stare.

Humiliation seeped into Colt. It was better she didn't look at him, for how could he explain away what she might have overheard?

Every word of it was true.

She rubbed her hands together and peered at the pile of duffel bags. "What bag do you need?"

He noticed that the blackfly bites, at one time riddling her eyelids and temples, had cleared.

"The one on the right."

She slid it over to him. Her skirts ruffled at her ankles. "Thanks for stitching me up."

Her cheeks rose in a polite nod. "My pleasure."

"Pleasure? You've got a strange way of wording things."

Her eyes flickered. "I need to thank you, too, for rushing to my defense."

"My pleasure."

No smile from Elizabeth.

"Why didn't your men take that man who attacked us and bring him to the sheriff? Why'd they let him go?"

"Because the sheriff here is bought and paid for by the same criminal who runs the rest of the area. Fellow by the name of Smith. We're on American soil, so we don't have any jurisdiction to stop him."

"Oh." Aghast, she finally turned his way. The golden brown eyes sparkled with alarm.

"American law hasn't caught up to the Alaskan frontier." He pressed a large hand to the sheet that covered his nakedness. "Too many folks have arrived in the past year. Tens of thousands, with not enough lawmen to balance the numbers. Jefferson "Soapy" Smith is running things here. At first, we suspected Smith or the sheriff might be the leader of the gang we're looking for, but we've ruled that out. The man we want works on his own in the Yukon. He never crosses the border."

"On our side we've got our Mounties, don't we?"

"Yes, we do. Our government set up the Mounties at the border to protect what's ours. Klondike gold," he said. "But once in the Klondike, there's a great shortage of Mounted Police. They can't patrol everywhere."

"So, here in Skagway—" she nodded toward the tent flap "—even if you turned that culprit in, he wouldn't be jailed."

"He makes enough money selling oysters to bribe his way out of anything."

"And why bring attention to ourselves, right?"

"There's that, too."

"Criminals," she said softly. She tilted her chin in defiance, and yet her lips trembled slightly. Her nostrils flared as her searching gaze ripped straight through him. She conjured shame in Colt deeper than he'd ever felt.

Chapter Ten

"I came to give you another dose of morphine."

"Save your supplies for a real crisis."

"But you've had twelve stitches—"

"I'll be fine."

"At least let me give you a shot before bedtime. So you can sleep."

"We'll see."

From his bedroll inside the tent, Colt watched Elizabeth weave her fingers into her skirt pocket.

"What…what are the sleeping arrangements?" For a doctor, she was firm with her orders, he thought, but for a woman, she was soft and unsure of her place.

He sighed. "I don't think you should sleep alone, considering the dangers. There are a lot of men out there just like the fool with the shovel."

"I agree with you on this one. And…I was wondering if you have a spare gun I might keep with me."

He gripped the sheet in surprise.

"I mean, I asked the other men and they're under a misguided impression I need your permission first."

"You can have a gun. I'll show you how to use it."

"Thank you. And I think—I—I think as far as sleeping, I should stay by your side in case you need me."

Could he sleep with her nearby? "All right. You, me and another man in this tent. The others can divide the remaining two."

"Fine."

"Fine."

"Fine."

But they both knew it wasn't.

Continuous daylight could be very annoying.

It seeped into the white canvas tent and cast everything a brilliant alabaster. For the first few hours, Elizabeth found it charming. The sun was so strong and sharp at ten o'clock in the evening that one could get a sunburn. She was still tossing at the brightness at twelve, one and two. But by three in the morning when the sky was somewhat dimmer, twinkling in a strange twilight blue, she was punching the sheepskin jacket that doubled as her pillow. She accidentally brushed the cold pistol Colt had given her, resting beneath the sheepskin.

Tommy stirred at her feet. "You sleeping with that thing?"

"I—I cleared it with Colt."

"Did he show you how to use it?"

"Mmm-hmm."

"Something wrong?" Colt muttered from his bedroll, six feet away from her. "Can't sleep?"

She shifted her head on the jacket. "I would dearly love to fall asleep, but my body refuses."

"You'll get used to it…" And off he went, snoring again in his morphine-induced state.

He snored almost as loud as Tommy, who started again within minutes. The three of them lay head to feet, stuffed together like strips of bacon.

She hadn't anticipated that she'd have to look at Colt while he was sleeping. For pity's sake, she thought once they went to bed it would get dim and dark—how, she hadn't fathomed—and she'd forget about him. But here he was straight in front of her, eyelids closed, nose in the air, cheeks darkened with unshaved stubble, hair tousled above his ear.

She studied his hands. The sinews of the flesh, the ropy veins, the golden hairs, the strength she saw there. He was different than any man she'd ever known. Different and disappointing.

For one blissful moment, before she finally fell into a deep slumber, she thought of Gerard and how much she missed his gentle touch. How much she missed being loved by a man, being physically moved and touched and desired…. And then her dreams were overrun by the intimate moments she'd spent with Colt and how he'd kissed her breast.

A sense of danger pervaded everything they did.

Colt was aware of it the next morning when they took a walk down the wild frontier street in Skagway. Elizabeth strode beside him. Strangers watched from the other side of the boardwalk, and eyes peered out of second-story windows. The chill of the morning air—almost frigid overnight—kept them alert. Colt had ordered two men to stay with their supplies at all times, rifles drawn. Buxton and Ed were there now, but Tommy, Anderson and Will were strolling right behind them, looking to buy last-minute equipment for their journey into untamed wilderness. Saint, good dog that he was, galloped beside Colt.

Colt limped slightly. The pain in his thigh had eased to an ache, so he would stay away from the morphine, no matter how much Elizabeth insisted. He didn't like its groggy effects. Luckily, his injury wouldn't hold them back. Hell, he'd suffered gunshot wounds worse than this.

As for Elizabeth's safety…she was learning to stay close to her brothers. Anderson had kept her company this morning when she'd gone for fresh water, and had also helped her clean the breakfast dishes.

It was just as well, thought Colt, gritting his teeth at the image of Anderson and Elizabeth together, for the more time his men spent with her, the less he had to.

The team made an intimidating sight, dressed in long leather dusters, cowboy boots and hats, strolling together like a band of outlaws. Elizabeth wore what they wore. Anderson had supplied her with a pair of new denim jeans and a leather duster. Colt had given her his newest blue cotton shirt, and of course, her brown cowboy hat. She looked a little sinful, he thought, long brunette hair flowing down her back, pounding her boots into the boardwalk and wearing the same cool expression on her face as her brothers—one of disinterest and calm control.

Their guns were firmly planted in their holsters, visible to all. Elizabeth had bought a holster of her own this morning from a nearby tent, and slung her pistol on her right hip. Her attack from yesterday had caused a change in her.

She was no longer an innocent traveler. She'd come

close to being snatched and raped, and wouldn't put up with the possibility a second time. Hats off to her, thought Colt, still surprised at how quickly she'd adapted to the circumstances.

Sinful, Colt thought again, stealing a glance at her legs, encased in tight denim, his leather belt cinched around her slim waist. The corset beneath her shirt—*his shirt*—held her breasts firmly in place, and the loose fabric, rather than hide her figure, accentuated it.

"Right here." Colt stopped at a store marked Klondike Outfitters. They stepped inside the wooden building. A fire crackled from a cast-iron stove planted by the till.

"Morning." Colt nodded to the unshaven gent behind the counter.

"Mornin'. What can I help you with?"

"Working clothes. Denim pants. Shirts."

"They wear out fast in these parts. We had a shipment come in last Wednesday."

Colt glanced around the cramped shelves. "Where do you keep them?"

"They sold out in a day."

"Oh."

"Had another shipment in yesterday."

"Show me."

"Sold out in five hours."

"Can you help us or not?"

The gent scratched his ear. "'Fraid not. You'll hear the same story all the way down the street. Your best bet is to wait another six days when the next shipment comes in."

"Don't have that kind of time."

"Looking for anything else?"

"Nails."

"Sold out."

"Saws."

"Sold out."

"Do you have any bedding?" asked Elizabeth. "Pillows?"

The gent laughed. Colt and his men joined in.

"Sold out. They're the first things to go. Even though it's mostly men in these parts, we like some comforts, too."

"Bullets," said Colt.

"We're definitely sold out of those."

Colt didn't like the sound of that.

"All right, then. One more thing. We're looking for packers to help us carry our things up the Chilkoot Trail."

"Keep walkin' down the street. Take the second right. First building on your left."

"Much obliged." Colt tilted his hat and they left the store.

The team stopped at the corner of the boardwalk beneath a canvas awning. Buxton signaled, and they circled around him to listen.

"We can't take the horses up the Chilkoot. The climb's too steep. We'll be crossing gorges. We'll be balancing on logs. No large animals can do it."

"I'm not leaving them behind," said Colt.

"What's so important about bringing horses?" asked Elizabeth. "You could sell them here."

"Imagine," Colt answered, "how valuable they'd be to the Mounties in Dawson. Horses are few and far between. Right now, most men travel on foot or use the rivers."

Buxton raised his palm. "Four or five other trails lead around the mountains and converge at Lake Bennett. Besides Chilkoot, the other major one is White Pass. But it's been nicknamed the Deadhorse Trail."

"What?" asked Anderson, pushing back his hat in disgust.

"Too much mud," Buxton explained. "Too many boulders. Folks overpack their animals. Two to three thousand horses have died already."

The group moaned.

"There's got to be a way," said Colt. "Because I've heard some animals *have* made it through."

"We could hire guides," said Buxton, "the same Chilkat Indians we'll be using as packers. We could ask 'em to bring our horses along a gentler slope. They could meet us at Lake Bennett. They'll have a longer route than us, but their load will be lighter. So they'll travel faster. We could aim to meet at roughly the same time."

"Why don't *we* take that route?" asked Colt.

"Too rough for most men. The Indians know what they're doing. They charge a hefty price for it, too. Some of 'em are rich, without ever having dipped a single pan of gold."

"Are they trustworthy?" asked Tommy.

Buxton nodded. "They treat animals with a lot of care. They won't pack the horses. They'll let 'em go light."

"Arrange it," Colt commanded. "Include the mule."

They continued on their way, heavy boots pounding the boardwalk when Colt felt Elizabeth press his arm.

She whispered, "I saw some hair dye back at the store. Shoe polish is staining all my clothes. I have to wash laundry almost every night."

"You can't be seen buying it."

"I know. That's why I'm asking you."

"Give me a few hours and I'll see what I can do."

"All right. What about the rest of the stuff you asked for? We're in need of an awful lot of things."

"Not really."

"But nails and bullets…"

"No, no it's okay. We want them to think we're out of those things. I predict by noon, the whole town will know which trail we're headed for."

Elizabeth adjusted her cowboy hat. The chestnut color matched the tint of her thick braid; it accentuated her dark lashes and deep rich lips. "You want the crooks to follow us."

Frowning, Colt shifted his body in the long duster. He watched the other men reach the corner and turn right on the street that housed the guides.

"Liza, the best advice I can give you is to keep your hand close to that gun."

She eyed him critically, too deep for his comfort. "Aren't you making this more dangerous than it needs to be?"

His defenses went up. "You've got it wrong. I'm trying to make it safer."

"I don't feel safe."

Exasperated, he stepped closer, not caring how intimidating he must be in size, standing next to her. "I keep asking myself why your father let me take you on this trip. He knew it was dangerous. Why?"

Her mouth quivered and he was reminded again of that blazing night on the ship. Her willing response beneath his exploring fingers, the sight of her naked flesh, her tempting nipples, coaxing him for a kiss.

"The truth?"

He blinked. "Yeah."

"My father never agreed with my decision to end it with Gerard. He's hoping, once I see him in Dawson, that I'll change my mind and we'll marry."

Colt's heart thudded. He inhaled a sharp breath, as though someone had slugged him in the gut.

He needed a moment to grasp it. What upset him more? That her father hadn't trusted Colt enough to confide this? Or that it might not be over between Elizabeth and Gerard?

"What makes you so sure they won't rob us right here and now?"

Elizabeth buckled up her holster and watched Colt slip into his the following morning in the tent. Tall and muscled, he was a potent combination of courage and nerve. Like everyone else, they were camping out on the hills all over town.

"Because they're not stupid. The stuff we're hauling is worth fifty times more in Dawson City. Miners who've struck gold there have nothing to spend their wealth on."

"So you figure the thieves want us to carry the apricots and sausages to the Klondike, *then* they'll jump us?"

"Why should they haul it through the mountains when we could do it for them?" He removed his gun and checked his ammunition.

Outside, the team was nearly packed and ready to go. She heard the horses whimper. Amelia was ripping grass on the other side of the canvas. Elizabeth took out her mirror and looked at her newly dyed hair one last time. It was fine. Colt had managed to get the dye delivered last night, undetected. She'd washed all her stained clothing and bedding. Due to the daylight hours, it had dried overnight.

She tucked away her mirror, wondering how Cold acquired the hair dye. Had he used his pickpocketing skills? Despite what she thought of Colt personally, she believed in his abilities as a marksman and bodyguard.

Perhaps that faith was the reason she was so disappointed to learn of his past. Colt, like Gerard, was a man she didn't truly know in the private sense, in matters of the heart, and shouldn't completely trust. But she was here, and she would stick to Colt until delivered at her grandfather's door. Traveling with a band of Mounties was the safest way to get to the Klondike.

They didn't need to like one another to get where they were going. And she believed Colt was looking forward to the day of delivery as much as she.

Elizabeth finished packing, lifted her bags and headed toward the tent flap.

Two hours later, they'd delivered their pack animals to the guides and she and Colt were floating on a barge up the river toward the newly sprung town of Dyea. There, they'd disembark for the long climb up the mountains. Elizabeth smiled at the sight of the Thornbottoms on a huge raft. The family was dodging other boats while trying not to crash into the Mounties.

Elizabeth waved and hollered across the current. "It's good to see a familiar face!"

Mrs. Thornbottom flapped her hanky. "Looks like we'll be traveling together!"

"You've decided not to rest?"

"Milly seems fine, and Theodore is anxious to get there!"

Mr. Thornbottom, standing beside his wife on a raft

surrounded by their crates and sacks, nodded to Elizabeth. His long white hair blew in the breeze.

Elizabeth turned to view the scene ahead. Saint panted at her feet, seated between her and Colt.

Shaggy vegetation engulfed the river. Individually, the trees were skinny—poplar, pine, white spruce, paper birch and alpine firs—but together they formed a velvet richness. Cotton grass, five feet high, grew between the trunks. The wildflowers of fireweed, prickly rose, white mountain avens and bright pink poppies colored the landscape. Mosses and lichens clung to rocks.

Every stroke of the oars propelled them forward and brought a ravishing new scent. Ripening raspberries, fresh grass, icy mountain waterfalls.

Colt seemed equally mesmerized as he relaxed, oar pulled next to his broad chest, dark hair rippling at his temples, jaw slack with awe. The current pushed past them, spring thaw from the mountaintops, and Colt dug in again with his oar.

When they reached the tidal flats of Dyea, Elizabeth was surprised by the endless sandbank. It spanned the low water mark all the way to higher ground.

"Colt, it'll take forever to carry our things across the sandy flats."

"That's why our five packers are behind us. They'll help carry the load."

To her delight, Dr. Donovan Wellsley appeared. It seemed he'd hired two packers, as well, for they were loading his things by oxen and cart to carry them to the base camp.

"Well, what do we have here?" He held out his hand for Elizabeth as she disembarked.

She slipped her hand into his, disregarding Colt's look of annoyance. Knowing they were short of clothing, Elizabeth had reverted back to a long skirt and simple blouse. She'd save her pants for tomorrow when the rough uphill trail began.

While the professional packers went about their task, the travelers exchanged hellos and stories about Skagway, though Elizabeth refrained from telling them about her attacker.

They stopped for a brief lunch and continued chattering, the Mounties, the Thornbottoms and Dr. Wellsley. Elizabeth felt almost as safe as she had on the ship. It was late evening by the time they settled in camp. Hundreds of people had trampled a wide path into the dirt. Smoke from nearby campfires twirled in the air.

Elizabeth arranged mosquito netting Colt had given her over her cowboy hat, and descended to the banks of the Taiya River to fill canteens. Mrs. Thornbottom joined her with theirs. Anderson and Will had escorted Elizabeth here and were rinsing dirty dinner pots a dozen yards away. When Elizabeth dipped a canteen into the chilly water, an otter wove its way through nearby reeds. Two feet past him, a turtle floated by on a broad leaf, sunning itself.

Mrs. Thornbottom eyed Elizabeth's skirt. "My dear young woman. What on earth is that strapped around your hips?"

"A gun, Mrs. Thornbottom. A necessary force in this neck of the woods, I'm afraid."

"A gun." The older woman braced herself. "I let Theodore handle those things."

"Perhaps you shouldn't. Where's Milly? She should never be left alone."

"You're quite right. She's with her father."

"We'll walk you back to your camp. Please don't go out on your own again. It's not civilized here."

"It's lovely of you to think of my well-being."

They hushed for a bit, clinging to the banks, scooping water and filling their senses with heaven's gold. Crickets chirped and frogs croaked in the calm.

"It's difficult traveling with so few women around," said Elizabeth. "My brothers don't understand my need for constant hygiene. And why I like to wash my clothing so often."

Mrs. Thornbottom chuckled. "I met a lovely woman earlier this morning when we set out. Right over there, walking down the slope with her brother." Mrs. Thornbottom waved to them and they responded in kind. "I feel sorry for her. She's widowed. Lost her husband last year in the Yukon and had to move—"

Mrs. Thornbottom said no more because the woman was approaching earshot. On the hill beside her, Colt was also heading this way. Folks were dressed in either jackets or shawls for the evening chill. The bugs weren't out in full force yet, but Elizabeth was prepared.

"Good evening," Elizabeth called to the young widow. "We were just saying how comforting it is to see another woman."

The widow smiled from yards away. Roughly thirty, with black hair laced into a beavertail, she was on the thin side, almost bony, but moved with energy and appeal. "I know what you mean," she hollered. "It's very nice to meet you, too."

Her brother, slightly older but equally thin and dark, nodded hello.

"You're headed toward Dawson?" Elizabeth raised her voice above the gushing river.

"Yes, ma'am," said her brother.

Colt reached Elizabeth's side before the couple did. Without a word, he took four of Elizabeth's filled canteens and strapped them over his broad chest. She appreciated how he always noticed when she needed help. When he adjusted the netting over her cowboy hat, his touch on her bare neck sent a tingle across her skin.

Mrs. Thornbottom watched them with curiosity. "It's a sad story about the widow's husband," she whispered. "They tell me he was murdered."

"Murdered?" Colt said softly. His gaze shot to the brother and sister.

Elizabeth's stomach squeezed with sympathy. This territory truly was uncivilized.

Mrs. Thornbottom wiped her damp hands on her skirts as the widow reached them. "Allow me to do the introductions. Mr. Colton Blade and Miss Liza Blade, this is Mr. Frank Kolya."

They shook.

Mrs. Thornbottom turned to the timid widow. "And his sister, Mrs. Vira Mishenko."

A chill went through Elizabeth, straight down to her bones. Her startled gaze met with Colt's.

Vira Mishenko. Wife of Ivan?

And she was claiming murder.

Chapter Eleven

Elizabeth wanted to scream, *Your husband was murdered? Some say my uncle may have done it!*

But she kept silent. Fear clung to the back of her throat as Colt exchanged small pleasantries with the couple.

Together they all trudged up the bank toward their camp nestled in acres of shrub. Even though it was past nine in the evening, the sun, a golden orb, twinkled above the ragged cliffs. Hidden birds called out from the thickets—ravens, geese and magpies.

Elizabeth's heart pressed against her ribs. *I won't let this woman affect my reasoning.* No matter how sympathetic, how touching the story, Uncle Sebastian was incapable of murder.

Compared to her, Colt seemed to have no guilt in concealing his identity while he asked direct questions.

"Murdered, you say? How awful." He touched the brim of his Stetson. "Our condolences."

"Thank you."

"How did it come about, if you don't mind my asking?"

"It's not something I care to get into."

"Someone stole his gold," said Mrs. Thornbottom.

Elizabeth felt like vomiting.

"It's not simple," said Vira. "The situation was muddled with Ivan and…I'm returning to Dawson to make sure…"

Her brother spoke up. "Vira returned to San Francisco after Ivan died. When she told me the story, I insisted we come back to reclaim what's rightfully hers. And press charges on behalf of her husband."

"Good for you," said Mrs. Thornbottom. "Good for you."

"It's not going to be easy," said Frank. "The people we're up against are…"

"Are what?" asked Elizabeth. Powerful? Influential? *Was Gerard involved?*

"Perhaps we've said enough," said Frank. "We'll let the law handle it from here."

"I must say good night." Elizabeth excused herself and bolted toward their camp. "It's been a long day."

If she'd stunned them by her abrupt departure, she didn't care. She'd gotten out of the situation before throwing up.

Five minutes later, Colt joined her at the campfire. He eased onto a log beside her and watched the flames dance. Crossing his long legs at the ankles, he resettled his hat.

"How can you do that?" she asked after a few moments. "Lie so easily."

"You get used to it if you do it often enough."

"You surprise me. A normal person would have denied that lying came easily."

"I think you and I are above denying anything to each other. At least we speak the truth, no matter how painful."

She watched the firelight flick across his broad cheeks.

"What kind of a person were you when you were sixteen?"

"Angry."

"Why?"

He crossed his arms and stared into red-hot coals. "I wanted to get even with the world for the murder of my father."

She closed her eyes. "But somehow, you stopped yourself from a life of petty theft."

"My older brother pulled me out of it when I was eighteen. Me and Tommy both." He glanced over to Buxton, who was chopping firewood. "Luke returned from the West and gave me hell."

"What happened to the man who killed your father?"

"He got away. There were witnesses, but he circumvented the law."

"So you're making sure, working as a Mountie, that no criminal will get away again."

"I wish I could do all that." He rose, slid off his hat and nodded toward Vira's camp. "Maybe, though, I can help turn a widow's nightmare into justice."

The fear of his power seeped into her blood. For the sake of Ivan and Vira Mishenko, Elizabeth wanted justice to prevail, wanted to know the truth, but she was terrified of the implications.

"There's nothing much we can do to a dead man," said Colt. "We can't prosecute Sebastian Langley."

But there were others involved. What about her Aunt Rose, Uncle Sebastian's widow? What of their children and families? What of Elizabeth's father and his place in the government? What of *her?*

Elizabeth got up slowly. She wondered how she'd sleep another night staring at his face. Tonight, though, they'd be dozing around the fire, so she'd have more space. Tents were too time-consuming to pack and unpack each time.

"I'd like you to know," she said. "As far as the investigation goes, I'll cooperate in any way you want."

Her fresh decision caused Colt to tilt his head in surprise. His dark lashes flicked in the fire's glow. When he nodded at Elizabeth with newfound respect, she found it difficult to breathe.

In the cold twilight hours of the Yukon, Pierce Rawlins listened to the howl of a lone wolf. He sensed danger and excitement. Sucking back on his chewing tobacco, he nodded to his gang of twelve waiting behind boulders. They crept up the banks of the lake and pointed rifles and revolvers at four sleeping men.

"Get up!" Rawlins shouted.

"Holy Christ…" The eldest man, white-haired but muscular for his age, turned in his bedroll. He sprang for his gun.

Rawlins cocked his Enfield. "Don't touch that."

The other three men, in their late forties, sons of the first, slowly rose from the ground to sitting position. They lifted their arms in the air.

"That's right." Rawlins coaxed them as he would children. "You got it. Nice and easy."

The old guy scowled. "You said you were a school-teacher."

"I'm teaching you a lesson, aren't I?"

"Go to hell."

Rawlins chuckled. "I'd be mad as a bull, too, if someone was about to steal my treasure." He peered at the numerous crates of canned salmon, stacked on two flat-bottomed boats. With a nudge of his revolver, he commanded his men. "Untie the boats, boys."

"Christ," said the old guy, "we nearly broke our backs hauling those tins over the Chilkoot."

"Thank you kindly."

"You son of a bitch."

He lunged, but Rawlins jumped out of the way and pointed his Enfield at the man's head. "Hey," he called to his man Jefferson, "you better tie these ones up. Don't think they'll sit quietly when we're gone."

Jefferson took out his rope. The old man kicked him, so Jefferson stomped on his fingers.

The man screamed bloody hell.

"Hey," Rawlins snapped at Jefferson. "None of that!"

"The bastard kicked me!"

Rawlins snarled. "Approach him from the back. He's old enough to be your granddad. Show some respect!"

Dammit, Jefferson had a difficult temper to control. Heaving with sweat, Rawlins wiped his brow with the back of his sleeve. Jefferson was the one who'd pummeled that man to death last year. Of course, the man had been deservin'.

"We're calling her the healer." Mrs. Thornbottom plucked a dry leaf from the ground and added it to her basket.

Vira bent beneath a spruce tree and picked up a twig. Six feet beyond her, Elizabeth added twigs to her collection of kindling. Dr. Wellsley, looking rather disheveled because he hadn't shaved for a few days, was still working on his pile.

"Should be enough to start a fire." Elizabeth tried to avoid the topic Mrs. Thornbottom was so persistent in pursuing. Elizabeth's skill in medicine.

Her arms ached from the daily chores. Muscles in her calves screamed with the tension of the climb, and they weren't even at the Golden Stairs yet. She swatted at the hordes of gnats and was sorely tempted to scratch open the itchy welts and sores covering her hands. She longed for a bath. Maybe she should ask Colt to draw her one. Wouldn't that light his fuse?

Mrs. Thornbottom wouldn't drop the topic. "She mended her brother's leg as if she had a wand."

"Colt's leg wasn't broken," said Elizabeth. "Just cut."

"Never you mind. I saw you on the ship, too, with my Milly. Ain't that right, Dr. Wellsley?"

"Huh? Oh, yes. Yes, of course. Miss Blade would make a wonderful assistant. She seems to have the knack for bandaging and taking care of minor details."

Elizabeth pretended to smile, still annoyed that he'd insisted on taking out *her* stitches. She'd put them in Colt's leg. It should have been up to her to remove them.

"Tell me where you learned it," said Vira. It was the first personal question she'd asked Elizabeth in their five days of traveling.

"My…grandmother taught me a few things. She used to be a midwife." *Liar.*

"Ah," said Dr. Wellsley. "Women helping women."

He said it as though women didn't matter.

Vira sidled next to Elizabeth and picked up a piece of

bark. "My grandmother came from Russia. She used to sing me lullabies about turnips and honey."

Elizabeth didn't want to know. She didn't want to get any closer to Vira than she already was. It was as though Elizabeth had to choose sides—her uncle Sebastian, or Vira and Ivan Mishenko. Still, Elizabeth had a hard time ignoring her and felt compelled to respond.

"Do you remember any of the lullabies?"

"One. She used to sing it all the time. If I marry again and perhaps have a family…I'll sing it to my own child."

"Your grandmother would like that," said Elizabeth.

"She was a midwife, too," said Vira softly, surprising Elizabeth. "You have a good family. Your brothers take care of you."

Elizabeth's guilt flared. Of all the people she'd met on the trail, Vira was the most difficult one to lie to.

The young widow waved good-night and disappeared beyond a clump of thin firs, delivering kindling to her brother.

Elizabeth marched back to her camp. The Mounties were preparing dinner around the fire.

Colt lowered a bowl of canned salmon, mixed with hard biscuit, to his dog and watched him slurp.

"Everything all right?" he asked her.

Everything except that Elizabeth was stuck in the middle of a nerve-racking situation between a widow she was growing to like, and the possibility that Elizabeth's uncle had something to do with the widow's grief. Everything except that Dr. Donovan Wellsley was a bore. Everything except that she was sick and tired of pretending to be Colt's baby sister. And mostly, mostly, everything except the galvanizing way Colt was looking at her now. Why did he always make her aware of her body and what she was wearing—beneath her duster, tight jeans clung to her thighs, and the taut lace of her corset dipped against her breasts.

"As right as it can be," she replied.

Anderson stepped forward and took the basket of kindling from her. "Thanks. I can use this."

His fingers brushed hers at the handle. He didn't seem to notice, but Colt caught it. She tried to ignore them both, but her heart surged at the doubt trapped in Colt's dark eyes.

Why did he watch her like a hound with his men? Did he distrust her, or his men?

Or himself?

She patted Saint when he lurched toward her. He looked fitter and heavier by the day.

She retired early just to get away from Colt's gaze, but became trapped in the spinning daylight that turned briefly to twilight. Her fears about the future raced through her dreams. She tossed to one side, irritated when she caught Colt with his lids half-open watching her. She yanked her blanket over her shoulder, concealing her loose blouson, feeling the tightening of her nipples in the cool air as she faced the sunlit white canvas and listened to his breathing.

The next morning when they reached the first slope of the Chilkoot Mountain, Colt made no attempt to suppress the teasing nature of his questions. His Stetson shaded his handsome face. Elizabeth wondered how he managed to look so well rested, blood pumping beneath the dark, bristled cheeks.

"Ever climb a mountain?" he asked.

"You know the answer to that."

"How would I know?"

She removed her pack, following the lead of the five dark-skinned packers in front of her. With their long black hair tied into ponytails, the muscled men worked brutally hard.

"You're my father's bodyguard. You know almost everything about my family."

"Not everything."

"What don't you know?"

"If you've ever climbed a mountain."

She huffed at him. "No, I've never climbed a mountain."

"What else haven't you done?"

"Built a cabin."

"Well, we won't be building any cabins on this trip. But you can help build a raft when we get to the lakes."

"Why would I want to do that?"

"Because I bet you've never built a raft before."

"Must we do things simply because we've never done them before?"

"Of course." Colt strapped two canvas bags filled with flour onto Saint's back.

Elizabeth slid two sacks of coffee around her neck. "Okay, then, what haven't you done?"

"Performed surgery."

"Ha."

"Do you think Dr. Wellsley would let me try it on one of his patients?" he teased.

She squinted in the bright sun. "You're a man, aren't you? That seems to be his only requirement."

Colt grinned. It warmed her, every time. "It still bothers you."

She clicked her tongue. "What?"

"That I asked him to take out my stitches."

"I don't care who you asked what."

"Yes, you do. You'd be very annoyed, for instance, if I asked Mrs. Thornbottom to gather the kindling for tomorrow's fire."

"Kindling is *my* job."

"Exactly."

"How would you like it if I asked Anderson if I could sleep in his tent tonight?"

That stopped him cold. The rush of embarrassment rose up her cheeks.

"I meant that it seems to be *your* job to protect me. It didn't come out the way I intended."

"Go ahead, ask any fella you want."

The argument dampened their mood, but put their relationship back into perspective during the next week as they trudged up and over the coarse steps that were beaten into the side of the mountain by thousands who'd come before.

She cupped her eyes from the sunlight and glanced up. A stream of people, silhouetted strangers, marched stiffly up the slope. They looked like a chain of paper dolls attached at the hands that a child might cut out with scissors. Shadowy figures on a ragged cliff, set against a blazing sun.

They were so high in altitude they were above the timberline and walked among boulders and shrubs.

With a thirty-pound pack on her back, Elizabeth hoisted one filthy boot over the other on the Chilkoot Mountain—nicknamed the Golden Stairs because these steps led to gold.

Her shoulders ached. Blisters on her right foot stung. The bandage wrapped around her left ankle after she twisted it during yesterday's climb gouged her flesh. Her thigh muscles burned, as if ready to tear from stretching so hard.

Snow, two to six feet deep, cooled them at the summit.

"We're at the top of the world," Colt hollered. "If you reach up, you can touch the sky."

The view was exhilarating. The translucent sky was saturated with layers of shimmering blues. They stood at the level of other mountaintops, dozens of them as far as the eye could see. Gray cliffs, clumps of snow, miles of moss and grass. Mountain goats bleated from a distant rise.

Elizabeth filled her lungs with a deep rich breath. "I can't get enough of this fresh air."

"That's because it's ripe with life. And we're miles closer to heaven."

Finally, the team crossed onto Canadian soil. The border on top of the summit was marked by a solitary log cabin with the painted words, North-West Mounted Police. The Canadian mail carriers trudged by Elizabeth in warm wool jackets and gloves. Colt's team waited in line to pay duties and taxes on their supplies. In front of them stood six Norwegian sailors, two Scottish farmers and an Italian congregation of former government clerks. Elizabeth wondered if Colt or his men would know the other Mounties, but no one glanced their way.

It had taken them ten days to climb a mountain that at any other time might take two, simply because they had to make so many trips up and down. Most men could carry sixty-five pounds on one trip. The Mounties and packers carried a hundred.

"Many of these folks made twenty or thirty trips," said Colt. "Because most can't afford to hire help."

"Like the poor Thornbottoms."

"They'll be all right. Theodore will take his time and Mrs. Thornbottom can carry almost as much as a man."

"Have you seen Donovan?

"He fell behind. Likely two or three days."

Vira Mishenko and her brother kept up, though.

The following day, Elizabeth sighed at the sight of her first Yukon lake. It was pure turquoise in the sun, a magnificent color due to silt runoff from the icy mountains.

She was overjoyed to notice a group of eight women ahead in the heat of midday, long skirts brushing the ground, some wearing outrageous little hats with colorful feathers. Men both young and old swarmed to help them with their things.

When Elizabeth approached closer, however, smiling and calling hello, she noted the charcoal cosmetics lining their eyes and the artificial rouge on their cheeks. Saloon girls. Likely prostitutes, as well.

"Nice to meet you," Elizabeth said, nonetheless. Everyone in life had their sad story, their burden to carry, didn't they? For the most part, the women looked healthy.

"Mighty fine bunch of brothers," hollered the bosomy leader who called herself Belle Moon.

"Thank you." Elizabeth smiled beneath the weight of her pack. "They're all looking for wives," she said with good humor.

"Really?" The women turned to view the sturdy men.

Will and Ed grinned, tipping their hats. Anderson winked at Elizabeth, which Colt noticed with a frown of displeasure. Buxton peered openly at Belle, the scar beneath his eye twitching with mischief. Tommy went over and boldly helped one of the women step over a boulder.

Colt turned his back on the scene.

At that moment, the two young men carrying her red trunk heaved by. She ignored Colt's pointed stare, pulled out her fan and shielded her face not only from the sun and heat but from him.

"You're not much fun." She teased him, motioning to the women who were smiling his way.

"I can help in that regard." Belle surprised Elizabeth by appearing at their side.

"Can you now?" Colt placed his hands on his hips and took a good look at the painted woman.

A velvet choker wrapped her creamy throat. Her silky red blouse dipped below her cleavage and a plain black skirt stretched across ample hips. How on earth did the woman manage to look so…so good on this difficult trek? Clearly, she did little of the manual labor herself. Elizabeth admired her for her ability to woo the men into doing it.

When Belle touched Colt's arm affectionately, Elizabeth stiffened. He was so much taller than Belle, dark and intense, a striking figure of a man. No wonder Belle was interested.

"What does your brother usually look for in a gal?" Belle asked her.

Elizabeth sputtered, fan poised in midair. Colt thumbed his hat, crossed his arms and smiled as he waited for her answer. The lines deepened below his cheeks.

"Someone…someone he can talk to."

"I like talkin'," said Belle.

"A woman…who does his bidding with no quarrel."

Belle laughed. "I say yes to pretty much everything."

Colt raised his eyebrows at Elizabeth. She gasped at the implication.

"Then...you two...you two should get along just fine."

To be so blatantly open about sexual favors shocked Elizabeth. Colt glanced down at her buttoned blouse. She pressed a hand to her throat, clicked her fan closed, wheeled around and left.

"Too hot for you around here?" Colt shouted.

Glancing back, Elizabeth opened her mouth but couldn't think of a single thing to say. His gaze traveled down her backside, which Belle couldn't see, but which made things worse.

Elizabeth was still perturbed by the image of the two an hour later, when they met up with the most fascinating man yet.

He wore purple pants and a yellow sombrero and traveled with an entourage of two dozen men hauling bath tubs. Elizabeth was the first to spot a white porcelain tub as they approached the group in the woods. She spotted another and another. Claw-footed tubs, some with high backs. Some five feet long, others six and big enough for two. The men were also lugging dozens of wooden crates filled with wine, it appeared.

"Good Lord, am I dreaming?"

Colt took a long look at them. An obedient team of huskies accompanied the men. "I've heard of this fellow. Champagne Charlie. Caters to the filthy rich."

"He sells bathtubs?"

"And French champagne."

"That sounds heavenly. Soaking in a tub and drinking champagne at the same time."

"They don't drink the champagne. They bathe in it."

"I beg your pardon?"

"They bathe in champagne."

"But…it's so…expensive."

Colt laughed. "That's the point."

"It's wasteful."

"That's even better."

"It's odd."

"Might feel nice."

Elizabeth was surprised at his comment. Was this the same uptight, task-minded man she'd begged more than three and a half weeks ago to take her to the Klondike?

For the next two days, Champagne Charlie and his crew stayed a hundred yards ahead. Elizabeth glimpsed him through the scrub pines, a tall and talkative man, yellow sombrero slung on his blond head. He glanced once in a while in her direction, but since there were hundreds of travelers between them, it was impossible to introduce themselves. Besides, Champagne Charlie intimidated her. And she was too exhausted from the daily grind of walking, lifting, washing, soaking, eating, cleaning and making several trips back and forth through the forest.

"It's here," Colt said to her the next morning. He stopped on a slope of wild grass and pointed through two poplars.

"What?" Elizabeth pulled her sheepskin jacket tighter around her.

"The lake we're going to navigate."

She leaned in beside him. The water below, as smooth as a glass marble, glimmered against the Yukon sky. Dozens of handmade rafts and boats bobbed on its surface.

She smiled. Colt pressed his hand on her shoulder and pointed beyond the lake, partway up a mountain.

"Look there," he whispered.

His warm breath tickled the side of her neck. "Where?"

His dark cheek brushed her ear. "There."

She turned her face and almost grazed her lips along his sheepskin collar. His jaw, rough from three days' growth of beard, smelled pleasant.

"What are we looking at?" Then suddenly she saw it. "Ohh…" A herd of two hundred caribou was making its way across a river, beyond the hundreds of stampeders in the valley. Dozens and dozens of brown shiny coats, topped with antlers, floated through the water and leaped to the other side.

She had barely begun to admire it when a disturbance erupted.

Murmurs of shock rippled through the crowd. Elizabeth straightened to attention. Her hearing pricked.

Unknown voices carried the messages up the slope.

"My God. He's hurt!"

"How bad?"

"Stabbed him right through the bone!"

"Losing a lot of blood!"

Elizabeth pushed her way through the crowd, Colt right beside her. "Who's hurt?" she asked strangers. "What is it?"

Colt braced his arm around her shoulder, giving her strength, but the blow came swiftly.

"Champagne Charlie, miss. They're cuttin' off his leg."

Chapter Twelve

The saws were already out and lined up along the river-bank when Colt and Elizabeth reached the chaotic scene. The Yukon wind blew through her hair. It dried her perspiration but did nothing for her pounding heart.

"Don't cut it off," Elizabeth hollered, fear taking hold. She and Colt shoved their way among the men.

Champagne Charlie had been impaled on a branch from a fallen tree, the branch protruding from the river he'd tried to cross. The three-inch shaft was still stuck in the femur bone of his right thigh. He'd been there roughly twenty minutes while his panic-stricken crew had rushed around for help. Charlie himself was guzzling a bottle of rye, pale as a polar bear as blood trickled down the back of his bare, broken leg. Someone had had the sense to hack off his purple pant leg so they could get a better view. From the front, his white leg looked normal, but from the back it was pierced by a hunk of wood.

"Help me through the crowd," she whispered to Colt. "And then, by God, find that red trunk."

"What are you going to do?"

"I don't know." She willed herself to remain calm. "But whatever happens, the medical saws in my trunk are a lot cleaner than those."

"What do you know, lady?" one of Charlie's crew asked.

"I was a—a helper to my grandmother. I'm a midwife," she lied, pushing her shoulders against a bystander till she was standing knee deep in the water beside Charlie. Icy liquid filled her boots and weighted down her skirts. Her pulse kept pounding.

"Charlie, hello. I'm Liza and this here's my brother, Colt."

Charlie moaned and opened his groggy lids.

"I think I can help you."

"Don't pull it out." Charlie murmured. "If you pull it out...I'll bleed to death."

One of his men stepped forward, a big man with a belly, and leaned close to Charlie's face. "We gotta pull it out. Your leg might have to come with it."

"Give me a chance," Elizabeth pleaded, assessing Charlie and struggling to maintain control of her own rapid breathing. "I might be able to save it."

"You're a woman," said the big man. "You're more likely to throw up at the sight of—"

"You're wasting time." She noticed Charlie was shaking. She slid off her sheepskin jacket and thrust it over his shoulders. "I saw this procedure once—"

"Where?"

"I told you, my grandmother—"

"No offense, miss, but you don't look old enough to know—"

"Listen to her," said Colt. "They call my sister the Healer. She's got the touch of magic, they say."

Colt peered at Elizabeth with eyes wide. He didn't know what he was saying, either. Anything to make them listen.

"Magic hands," Colt repeated as Elizabeth's heart raced.

Charlie's lids opened. "Let her try. I need me…some special kind…of magic."

Colt whirled around and spotted Anderson behind him. The rest of the Mounties had stayed behind on the slope to guard their supplies and watch the crowd.

Colt instructed Anderson to find the trunk. Then with orders from Elizabeth, as gently as he could behind Charlie, Colt sawed through the branch to detach it from the tree. Charlie's men helped. Elizabeth kept the man himself calm. She ordered more whiskey. She was focused on Charlie and able to forget about her own fears.

"It's a good thing, Charlie," she said gently, "this water's so cold. It's slowing down the bleeding."

The man was beginning to shiver uncontrollably, even beneath her sheepskin jacket. She hadn't noticed she was trembling, too, until she felt the warmth of Colt's jacket when he pressed it around her.

The rest happened in a flurry. They carried Charlie and the three-foot stick to the riverbank and set him softly on his side, nestled on a pile of blankets. Anderson, along with another man, ran toward them with the red trunk.

Elizabeth popped the lid to reveal a treasure chest of tonics, sutures and instruments.

"Where'd you get this stuff?" Charlie's lead man asked.

"It belongs to Dr. Donovan Wellsley," Colt lied.

The young mail carrier hedged. "It doesn't belong to you. I may lose my job."

Elizabeth drew up a syringe of morphine. "He'd want us to use it. Donovan is a personal friend of mine. You can ask him yourself when we reach Dawson. He's two or three days behind us."

Colt crossed his arms in the path of the mailman, blocking his advance. "I guarantee you won't lose your job."

"We'll pay him triple what it's worth," said Charlie's man, the one with the big belly.

Half an hour later it was over. The leg was saved for now. The branch was out. Charlie slept. His shivering stopped. Elizabeth, wet and trembling with the cold, closed the trunk. She stepped away from Charlie as his men trembled in great relief. With rifles drawn, half of them were still protecting their champagne and bathtubs, while the other half guarded Charlie.

Colt pulled Elizabeth to her feet. He draped an arm around her quivering shoulders and cradled her. She pressed into the crux of his warm body.

Pacing through the crowd, he headed up the slope.

"Where are we going?" she asked.

"It's time someone took care of you."

Colt wanted to kiss her.

He wanted to swoop Elizabeth in his arms and soothe her, to kiss her temples and her throat and her mouth.

Yet he knew he never would. They were being watched by a hundred different faces as he walked her to a new spot on the sunny bank, joining the other Mounties who were just arriving. The Saint Bernard circled around them.

Colt huddled her around the newly built fire and ordered Tommy to rifle through her bag for dry clothes.

"You're wet, too," she said to Colt.

"I'll change after you."

Tommy returned and plopped her jeans and shirt on the log beside them. He left to give orders to the rest of the men to unpack for the day. They'd spend it here, overlooking the river and lakes, Champagne Charlie, his broken leg and his crew.

Colt swore beneath his breath. Elizabeth had been as brave using her bare hands, standing in frigid water, as any man he'd ever witnessed with a gun. Except now that it was over, she seemed to be in a state of nervous shock, unable to help herself.

Absently, she slid onto a log by the fire. He reached down and lifted her foot in the air. Her wet skirts flew down her leg, exposing a bare calf.

With her mind apparently still on the medical procedure she'd just finished, she gazed up at him. "What are you doing?"

He ripped off her wet sock and pulled on a dry one. "You're shivering so bad your lips are blue. You've got to get out of these clothes."

He removed the other sock, then forced her to pull on her pants. After she did, his fingers slid to her waist. He unbuttoned her skirts and yanked them down her hips.

"Hey!" She was finally aware he was trying to help her.

"Your skirt and petticoat are wet, too. What about your drawers?"

"They're fine!"

He relaxed. At least she had the energy to fight. He wasn't quite sure why she was shivering so much—the cold, or the strain of what she'd been through with Charlie.

"You're amazing," he said softly. And then came that urge to kiss her again.

But Anderson was watching as he and the packers were stacking their crates.

Rising to his feet, Colt tugged a blanket over her shoulders and went to get a fresh change of clothes for himself. The thought of kissing her never left him.

Who was this captivating woman who was teaching *him* what the true sense of duty meant?

"Champagne Charlie wants to see you."

Charlie's lead man lowered his rifle and walked toward Elizabeth. Temporary log huts dotted the banks behind him. The cabins were deserted by their original builders, now used on a first-come basis by weary travelers.

Elizabeth poised her hammer above the nail she was banging into one of three scows they were building to cross to Lake Bennett. The square, flat-bottomed boats would carry them and their supplies through the lakes that merged with the Yukon River and flowed toward Dawson City. Floating on water would be heaven compared to carrying everything on foot.

One and a half days had passed quickly by the water's edge. Around them, hordes of stampeders were chopping trees and whipsawing wood, building rafts and barges. Their horses had arrived, skinnier but in good shape. This morning, Colt had shaken the hands of the Chilkat packers, paid them and released them from a duty well done.

Elizabeth stared up at the messenger, who went by the name of Slim. He was in his forties, with a heavyset middle incongruous against the rigorous climb they'd just endured.

"What is it?" Her stomach flip-flopped. She adjusted her cowboy hat. "Does Charlie need more morphine?"

Colt, shirtless while he and Anderson sawed in the midday heat, came to join her.

"No morphine." Slim adjusted his suspenders. "The last shot you gave him worked fine. Wants to see you about somethin' else."

"Something wrong?"

"Didn't say."

"I'm coming," said Colt. He grabbed the shirt dangling over a stack of dried beans, and pushed one arm into his sleeve.

Elizabeth tried not to stare, but found herself gazing at Colt's naked chest. Broad muscles pulled across his shoulder blades. Slimmer ones flexed along his waist. Hours in the sun had already bronzed his skin.

As he did up the bottom buttons of his shirt, he turned at the crates and she caught the fine hue of his flesh from the front. His nipples, flat and brown, had deepened in the sun. The fine line of hair that traveled from his belly, skimmed the top of his pants and trailed below his belt, made her wonder what treasures lay there, as well.

He caught her looking.

Embarrassed to her bones, she glanced away and followed Charlie's messenger to his camp. Saint wagged his tail beside her, hitting the back of her skirt with every swish.

Charlie leaned forward in his makeshift cot when he spotted her coming. One of his men stuffed blankets behind his back. This allowed Charlie the dignity of sitting up, while he kept his broken leg propped on a cushion of sheepskin.

His toes were pink; circulation was fine. There was an eager spark in his eyes, and he moved with more energy. He'd turned a corner. He'd be all right as long as his wound didn't fester.

His dog team of white and speckled huskies sat obediently, untied, beneath the shade of a log hut.

"Mornin' Liza. Colt."

"Did you eat a good breakfast?" she asked.

"Bacon and eggs."

"Good." Eggs were rare and costly, but some of the travelers were transporting chickens.

"How's the leg?" Colt removed his hat and tapped Charlie's shoulder with it.

"The pain's leveling out. We're gonna head out in the morning."

"So soon?" asked Elizabeth. They were going, too, and desperately hoped that Donovan Wellsley wouldn't arrive before then. There was no telling what might happen if folks found out the red trunk didn't belong to him.

"No sense lying here," Charlie said weakly. "I've got enough men...to help me get to Dawson. I hear they got a good doctor there."

Was he speaking of Gerard?

Elizabeth perched on the crates of champagne and swung her dangling legs back and forth. Colt slid down beside her. She gave Saint a pat on the shoulders.

Charlie lit up a cigar, took a short puff and blew a ring of smoke at the pines that shaded him. He coughed and rested. "So, how many babies have you delivered?"

She startled. "Babies?"

"You said you were a midwife."

"Oh…yes. Seventeen." It was the truth.

Colt spun around in surprise.

"How many survived?"

"All but two."

Charlie whistled, barely audible. "That's very impressive."

"Not impressive enough. The two were born much too early."

"How many broken bones have you fixed before mine?"

Should she tell him the truth? Colt was watching her carefully.

"Two broken arms and one femur."

"All women?"

"Yes, sir."

"I also assisted in three hysterectomies."

"I'm not sure what that is."

"It's when—"

He dragged a hand into the air and waved her off. "Don't need to know, thanks."

She hushed. Why wasn't Colt saying anything? Shade from the pines slanted across his face. Not too long ago, he'd accused her of knowing only how to handle rashes and fevers.

Charlie rubbed his temples beneath his broad sombrero. His voice was still a bit weak. "What else have you done…for sick folks?"

This was the tipping point. She couldn't admit to anything more, or she'd risk disclosing she was a doctor, which would bring their assumed identities into question.

She shook her head, implying there was nothing more.

"What was the outcome…on the femur you fixed?"

"Same as yours. A permanent limp. But you have to watch for festering of the wound. You've got to have someone change that gauze daily. Cleanse the wound with that special tonic I gave you."

"I'll remember." Charlie's throat sounded raw. "What about you?"

"Beg your pardon?"

"What do you want in return, for what you did for me?"

"Well…I hadn't really thought…there's nothing that I want."

"Nothing?" Charlie turned to Colt in disbelief. Charlie winced softly, likely in pain. There was only so much morphine could do. "I've gotta say…I've never come across someone who wants nothing."

Colt cleared his throat. He braced his hand against one long leg, cowboy boots digging into dirt. "My sister's a good woman. Our folks always taught us to abide by the golden rule."

Charlie laughed gently. "The golden rule is a lot different in this neck of the woods than it is where you grew up. Here it actually *means* gold."

Elizabeth rose and brushed off her skirt. "Well, then, if there's nothing more, we'll be going."

"I'd like to give you a bathtub," said Champagne Charlie.

Her stomach tingled. She smiled and then broke into laughter at the very thought. "That's very kind of you. What a generous thought. But we can't carry a bathtub—"

"I'll have it delivered to you in Dawson."

"But…I hear they're worth a fortune."

Charlie mustered his strength. "You can use the tub tonight. We'll set it up in one of the cabins…wherever you say…and heat the champagne."

"Champagne? I couldn't bathe in—"

"Why not?"

She gulped. "I hear you charge five thousand dollars in gold for that privilege." Considering most working men earned a dollar a day, the figure was astronomical.

"There's a lot of folks in Dawson," he said weakly, "who don't know what to do with their riches. I help 'em decide."

"But five thousand dollars, sir, is a lot more than I could possibly accep—"

"I've got twelve tubs. One less won't kill me. The branch that impaled my leg might have."

She took a moment to savor the friendly gesture, then swallowed past the lump of appreciation in her throat. "A bath would be the most incredible gift I could ever imagine on a trip like this."

Charlie smiled so wide he showed a set of sturdy teeth. "We'll have it set up for eight o'clock. We'll heat up plain water and soap for the first run, and then, for the second, you can soak in champagne to your heart's content."

The man's generosity was overwhelming. Her smile took over, spreading into every muscle of her face.

Colt rose and removed his hat, looming over Charlie. "Sir, I must thank you on behalf of my sister. You sure know what makes a woman smile."

Charlie nodded. "I like that. I know what makes a woman smile." He motioned to the Saint Bernard. "I'd like to give you something, too, Colt."

Colt frowned. "Me?"

"You were there helpin' Liza the whole time."

Charlie nodded to Slim. Slim whistled to his team of huskies. A white one came running.

"I'd like you to have one of my best dogs. She's a lead."

Colt gaped from the gorgeous husky to Charlie, then back to the dog.

"She'll make a good companion to your Saint."

Colt laughed as Saint bounded toward his new friend. A dog like this back home might sell for ten bucks, but here on the trail, a pack dog was worth upward of five hundred.

"Her name's Eve."

"She's beautiful." Colt patted the mound of brilliant white fur. "And you're a very generous man."

"My ma taught me the golden rule, too."

Colt shook the gentleman's hand, and Elizabeth kissed his cheek. Charlie looked down at the ground, suddenly self-conscious, then gazed back up in time to see Colt's jaw tighten at the kiss.

"And just so you know," Charlie whispered, away from the others. "I'd bet every tub I own that you're not brother and sister."

Chapter Thirteen

The lantern was lit and the water was warm.

"Will you be all right, alone?" Colt asked Elizabeth as he walked her to a deserted log hut near the lake.

"I usually take my baths alone." She raised her eyebrows and hid a smile.

Colt rubbed his jaw back and forth, which told her he felt uneasy. He studied the sunlit lake instead of her. "Of course."

Elizabeth pulled at the towel dangling around her neck and pushed the cabin door wider to relish every detail. Although the sun still blazed in the sky, only one window allowed light to penetrate the cabin. The dimness was offset with a lantern flickering on the sawn log beside the tub, and three beeswax candles casting their warm glow on the steamy water.

Steam drizzled down the windowpane and welcomed her as she stepped inside.

Someone had placed a mat beside the claw-footed tub to ensure her feet wouldn't suffer from the cold. The tub was enormous—a six foot double slipper style with high backs on both ends.

Never, even as the privileged daughter of a cabinet minister, had Elizabeth seen or felt such luxury. It didn't matter that the cabin was cut from hacked logs, that the entire shack could easily fit inside the front hall of her family's mansion. It didn't matter that the workmanship in nailing and leveling wouldn't pass her father's approval even for an outdoor privy. She'd be undressing in absolute heaven.

Colt left and she undid the top button of her blouse.

"So I guess you got someone else to run your bath after all."

Startled by his voice, Elizabeth wheeled around. She hadn't realized he was still at the door. "Must you always tease?"

He noticed her open button, sliding his gaze from her eyes to her throat, to her fingers poised above her breastbone. "Not always."

His sultry mood penetrated hers. Her throat seemed to clamp. Both waited for the other to speak.

His voice rumbled. "Sorry, I—I've got to go."

"Thanks for the walk."

Carrying a towel of his own, he yanked it from around his shoulders. "One of Charlie's men is standing outside, about thirty feet away. I've ordered Anderson to stay guard, as well."

"Anderson, too?"

"Charlie's taken quite a shine to you."

"He's a gentleman. He won't try anything."

"Just in case." Colt looked down at her bosom. "You can be…very tempting."

Her lashes fluttered and she gazed down at her bag, which had been delivered by Charlie's men earlier.

"Do you think he'll keep his word and not say any-thing…about…about his suspicions?"

Colt shrugged. "Just keep insisting we *are* brother and sister."

"I suppose no one can prove otherwise."

"My men would take the secret to the grave."

She knew it in her heart, too. Every one of them treated Colt with utmost respect.

Colt grasped the doorknob. "I'll drop by and check on you after my own swim in the lake."

"How can you bathe in water so cold?"

"Necessity."

Elizabeth nodded. For the last four weeks, she'd heated water over a campfire and bathed from a bowl.

"Let me ask Charlie to heat up a tub of water for you and each of your men," Elizabeth suggested for the third time.

"Enjoy your bath." Colt declined again. "There'll be time enough for the rest of us when we reach Dawson."

At the lake, there were two areas cordoned off for bath-ing—one section for women, the other for men. She'd heard that the women's was protected by armed guards. At Elizabeth's request, Charlie hadn't spoken a word of her upcoming champagne bath to anyone but his trusted men and her brothers. Bathing was a private affair, and Eliza-beth would savor it more knowing she'd be undisturbed.

Colt pulled the door closed. "Keep your gun where you can get to it."

And he was gone.

There was no lock on the cabin door, but she propped a log against it. Nonetheless, she was at ease here.

It didn't take her long to strip. She set her holster down beside the lantern, tugged off her pants and pantaloons, and was soon down to her corset.

Unhooking the front stays, she released her breasts. Hot, moist air from the steamy tub encased her naked flesh. Her nipples tightened, her belly contracted. She sighed, found the bar of soap that doubled as her shampoo and sank into the water.

"Ahh…" Leaning back into warm liquid, she rested her shoulder blades against the tub.

Water dipped into the valley between her breasts, soothed the back of her knees, massaged her aching muscles and made her marvel at the joy of having a simple need met.

For ten minutes, she lay with her eyes closed, floating in paradise. Her thoughts turned to Colt and where he might be at this very moment. Was he naked, too?

Had his senses come alive, as hers had, at the feel of water pouring around her? Did he feel the energy, the human need to be soothed and touched and cleansed?

Did he think of her, lying here naked, as she thought of him? Wondering what his firm body looked like, might feel like beneath her wandering fingers. Beneath her belly and her hips.

She reached for the soap and lathered her breasts, wondering if given the chance, he'd care to see her fully unclothed. Imagining how his large, rough hands would grip her flesh.

Colt submerged his soapy head into the frigid water and gasped when he came back out. Icy mountain rivers fed these lakes.

Gooseflesh riddled his limbs. Blood pumped through his arteries, trying to keep him warm. Sensations surging through every part of his body invigorated his purpose for being on this trek, and sent him into a frenzy for the woman he'd left behind in the cabin.

Elizabeth. Elizabeth. Elizabeth.

To be with her would be torture so exquisite he wouldn't dare come up for air, for fear of never lying next to her again. *Not* to be with her when she was lying in a tub of heated water, exposing her slender body to the four walls of the shack, was a waste of goddamn beauty.

What spell had she cast on him?

He shook his wet head and strode out of the water, avoiding the other men using the lake.

Toweling himself in the middle of a Yukon evening, with the sun tipping against a snowy mountain peak and owls hooting in the trees above, would have to be enough beauty for Colt.

She wasn't his to claim. She wasn't his to even dream about. And yet, as he tugged into clean denim pants and shirt, then made his way back to her, he ached to crash through the cabin door and tell the world to go to hell, if only for a moment to hold her in his arms.

Elizabeth waited for sounds that Colt might be outside. She strained forward in the tub, hoping to hear the deep rumble of his voice, perhaps a round of laughter with Anderson, or a knock on the door and a word of caution to her.

Nothing came. No sounds of Colt. No knock.

She finished with her bathwater and tugged into a fresh blouse and skirt. She didn't bother putting on undergarments since she was getting back in, waiting as the water was hauled out in buckets and replaced with warm, golden champagne.

Rubbing her long wet hair with a towel, she sat on a log inside the shack and peered out the open door for a glimpse of Colt.

He didn't come.

She tried to stifle her disappointment. What on earth was she expecting?

The tub was almost full. Anderson checked the room and left, waiting for Charlie's team to finish pouring the buckets of bubbling alcohol.

This is insane, thought Elizabeth, gazing at the pretty bubbles of air rising from the bottom of the white porcelain to the steamy surface. *I'm about to step into the most expensive liquid in the world.* Imported from France. Enjoyed by royalty, by presidents and prime ministers, in ballrooms and boudoirs.

She stepped to the door to close it for the final time, and then looked up to see him sitting there at the edge of the lake, behind a wall of trees where no one else seemed to spot him.

Colt.

Her heart buckled. Her palms grew moist. Her lips trembled and her pulse galloped away with the wind.

Colt looked at her as though he was a hungry wolf and she his prey. He rose from where he was sitting. Likely, he could see her silhouette because of the lantern and candles sputtering behind her.

She didn't close the door. It was open a foot wide, just enough for his eyes. The moment stretched, too tense for words.

Knowing he was focused on her, she reached up with shaky hands, undid the buttons of her blouse, very slowly, and peeled away the fabric. It fell first from her naked shoulders, then her bare breasts. She captured his skewering gaze and let her blouse fall to the floor. His mouth parted in response. He kept walking toward her, his expression heated, his stride resolute.

Boldly, she tucked her thumb beneath the button of her waistband, flicked it and down came her skirt. She stood before him, fully undressed. The moist air of the cabin drifted over her bare skin, down her nipples, and rustled the triangle of hair that met her naked thighs.

She couldn't bear to look at him, couldn't bear if he walked away from her intimate offering. She'd die from humiliation. Seconds passed that seemed liked minutes. Was he walking back to camp? Would he have one more piece of ammunition against her, to tease her, to laugh about? How desperate she was to be sending him this invitation, apparently with no shame. With each pounding moment, she waited and waited and nothing….

With a sob, she reached for the door to close it.

But he was there before she could. Colt slid into the cabin, pressed the door closed behind him and lifted her chin.

"I could inhale you," he murmured, almost inaudible.

Her chest felt as though someone was gripping it with a vise. What should she do? What did she *wish* to do?

What she didn't want to do was talk. Explaining and excusing would ruin the whole thing. She wanted this man. It was as simple as that. As a physician, she believed that at this time of the month she was free from the possibility of conception. It was safe.

He seemed to sense the need for silence, too, for he said nothing. Their voices inside the cabin would carry to the outside, and Anderson would be at the door in an instant.

Colt kept his fingers on her chin, making her look at him looking at her.

Candlelight fluttered against the strong line of his cheek. His stubble was gone, and she detected the scent of shaving cream. His eyebrows rose in a dark slash above even darker eyes. He devoured her with his appetite for viewing—running his warm hands over her bare shoulder, grazing her arm with soft fingers, cupping the under part of her breast and gazing at it as if it was a model of beauty. He moaned and rubbed a thumb across her areola. She watched his lashes flick. He swallowed. When he thumbed her nipple, the sensation went straight to the midpoint between her thighs. He aroused her as no man ever had.

He slid his moist lips to her breast and kissed the tip. He tongued the nipple. Again, the connection between her breast and her private center seemed to explode. She was wet for him already, and they hadn't yet kissed.

She raised her face. Her nose brushed against his broad shoulder, her lips met his shirt. She inhaled deeply, loving the smell of him.

He worked his lips to the other breast, nibbling gently, then up her throat, at her ear, across her cheek, and finally, finally, to her mouth.

He plunged his fingers into her wet hair, cupped her head with a large hand and maneuvered her, naked, against the door. It was outrageous to be totally nude while he was fully clothed, but everything about this evening was outrageous.

Their lips met, dancing across each other, unsure and hovering. Then he gripped her firmly at the back of her bare waist, stepped closer so that he was pressed against her abdomen, his chest against her tumbling breasts. Uncertainty left him as his mouth grew possessive on hers, plunging and discovering and melding into one. He tongued her upper lip, she smiled into his mouth and circled his tongue with her own. He responded by lowering his hands from her back and waist to her bare bottom. He kneaded her flesh and pulled her closer and she ached for him to take her right there.

One of his hands moved from her bottom to the front of her thigh, and cupped her mound of hair.

She pulled away from his mouth and tried to slide out of his grasp to indicate they should slow their pace.

She was laughing, silently, and he uttered a sound of frustration when she stepped away completely. Smiling, she stood poised at the bathtub, where the fur matting tickled her clean feet.

In a teasing mood, he crossed his arms, leaned back against the wall to study her naked form and allowed a slow smile to pull at one corner of his mouth.

With good humor, she tilted her head back at him, as if to say, *You like what you see? Come and get it.*

He did just that, approaching her with open hands, trying to grab her waist.

She pulled away, wagging a finger and gazing pointedly at his belt buckle.

He nodded, understanding, and unbuckled it.

She took a tremulous breath. The hair rose on her arms. After he unbuttoned his pants, his hands rushed to his shirt. With eagerness, his fingers flew over the metal discs, but she stepped forward to slide the faded cotton off his wide shoulders, slowing him down by kissing his biceps and inner elbow and fingertips.

He tried to grab her again but she dodged him, insisting he stay put so she could admire his torso. Firelight from the lantern whispered an orange glow over his smooth muscles and highlighted the faint hairs. He was a primitive animal of sinew and flesh, interested in mating.

She would be with Colt tonight, she thought with a smile.

He tugged out of his pant legs, as if eager to unleash the erection he could no longer hide. And then he stood proudly, as nude as she, on the other end of the fur mat.

They enjoyed each other for a long minute, neither speaking nor touching, simply watching.

His body, hewed from power and virility, glistened with muscles and tendons in beautiful proportion. She loved how she had affected him, his rigid and large erection. Her gaze traveled up the hair to his belly button, then his chest, then eyes. A look of vulnerability shadowed his face but was gone in an instant. She basked in the pleasure she saw reflected in him when he gazed at her, from the points of her breasts to her tummy, to her thighs and calves.

His dark hair was still slightly damp from his dip in the lake, but the brisk temperature made his skin glow with health.

Standing there, she fought desire so strong she wondered if she would suffocate. Sighing with deep contentment, she turned toward the tub, the heated bubbles of gold, and stepped in. As she made herself comfortable, a heavenly warmth seeped into her calves, then thighs, then bottom. He watched her move and she wondered what he saw in her—simply the flesh of a woman who desired to make love to him, or a woman unsure of what their roles might be in the future, but who was dead certain she wanted him in her tub. Now.

His shape blocked the lantern light. The wisp of hair at his temples fluttered in a faint breeze that blew through a crack in the log wall. Sunlight poured through the square window behind him. Branches from an outside spruce tree tapped at the pane, the only sound in the room.

Colt stepped into the tub at other end. It was a tight fit, but he maneuvered his legs around hers. Rapture filled his face, likely, she thought, at the bubbly feel of the champagne, at the comforting warmth that cushioned him.

The golden liquid trailed up the valley of his breastbone and lapped against his chest.

With her feet and legs entwined with his, she slid forward and drizzled champagne across the breadth of his shoulders. He, in turn, yanked her by her upper arms and slid her even tighter, till she was but a kiss away. Cupping his hand, he poured champagne over her breast, mesmerized at the view, and then reached down to suckle the sweet liquid from her nipple.

She nearly melted with bliss. His hot tongue on her flesh, his warm breath lapping at the sweetness, the desire sparkling in his eyes, the concentration on his handsome face.

Could this be real?

She slid her slender legs past his waist, one on either side of him, till her feet rested on the tub behind him.

Her heart hammered against her ribs as he cupped her bottom, slid her toward him, and propped her on his lap.

His erection pressed against her backside, making her ache for him to slide it in.

But he didn't want to yet. He bent his head and with a light touch of his fingers, parted her center and kissed her there.

She tried to stifle her groan. He kissed deeper, to one side of her mound and then the other, then she felt the hot pressure of his moist tongue.

She cradled his head. Did he taste champagne? Did he taste her?

Wanting him to stop so that she could pleasure him, she found herself unable to pull away. He cinched his powerful arms around her slim waist and urged her to lie back in the warm bubbles, coaxing her to relax. She eased back into the liquid, engulfed in the warm splendor of champagne. He made her feel delicious.

He kissed and nibbled and tongued her. Using his thumb, he aroused her further, making her hips sway, making her muscles knot tight with hopes of sexual release, her stomach tense with restraint, until finally, the pressure culminated in a great release as he made love to her with his mouth.

Elizabeth held her breath, willing herself to make this moment last, to remember it always, aware of the dark and handsome officer she was with. She trembled in the bubbles. His wide hands spanned her lower back, beneath the surface of the liquid, as she floated in a sea of honey.

When the contractions subsided, he lifted his head and watched her. She gasped for air, satiated with sensual pleasure, smiling shyly at the man who made her heart pound.

Needing only a moment to revitalize, she unwrapped

her legs from his waist. She curled up on her haunches and then pressed her face forward, feeling warm champagne lapping around her dangling breasts as she approached him for another kiss.

Chapter Fourteen

It was a willing kiss between two lovers, lost in the excitement of their first interlude together, locked in each other's arms with their hearts drumming together.

She was something.

Colt wanted Elizabeth now with an urgent desire that blocked out all reasoning. He buried his face in the wet crook of her neck. Her breath was summer warm on his collarbone. She lavished his skin with light kisses and rushed to kiss his mouth. He savored her, kissed her upper lip, her nose, her eyelid, her brow, her forehead. Anything he could reach and sample. He cupped her breasts, tongued the nipples again and again, slurping the sweet taste of French champagne off the exquisite skin of a goddess.

He'd once vowed he wouldn't come near her, but she tempted him beyond his dreams. She was a giving, caring woman who approached life with both sleeves rolled up, willing to work hard and long until whatever needed doing was done.

Elizabeth, with the glossy brunette hair, whom he longed to see again in her natural blond.

He was careful to tread lightly, to move quietly in the water so as not to attract the attention of the guards outside. Above all else, Elizabeth's reputation had to be protected. This was his duty. His most precious duty yet.

Complicit in the deed, Elizabeth slid her lips to lightly bite his shoulder, then she crouched in the water, on all fours, and slid her head to his most private area.

The low rumble of affection at the back of his throat was difficult to suppress. Her mouth on him was instant pleasure. Leaning back against the tub, he squared his shoulders and succumbed to her touch. She grasped his shaft and licked the tip and he sagged back against the porcelain, unable to move even if he tried.

But mustering his strength, his resistance, he realized this wasn't how he wanted to spend himself. He wanted to join with her, to be inside of Elizabeth in the most intimate sense.

Growling with a pang of desire, he gripped her upper arms and urged her to sit up. When she looked deep into his eyes, he saw the tenderness there, the unspoken feeling of uncertainty and need rolled into one.

He wouldn't hurt her. He'd never hurt Elizabeth.

Turning her over in the warm champagne, he planted her on her hands and knees and approached her from behind. He rose from the bathwater on his knees himself, and she, gently, then urgently, pressed herself toward him, inviting him in.

He rubbed the tip of his shaft on her moistness. He reveled in the heat of her opening, then plunged inside.

The muscles of her creamy bare back moved with grace. Her waist nipped in at the sides, and the round swell of her hips drove him crazy.

The pumping of his movements made the champagne slosh around them, as though they were trapped in a large champagne glass, caught in the waves of love.

Their rocking was urgent and beautiful and he felt as though he'd been born to be with her for just this moment. He reached around her waist and gripped her between the thighs, sliding two fingers into her moistness, taking his time and urging her on, until slowly her muscles grew taut and she released, coming for the second time. The intimacy he felt making love to her etched itself into his heart.

Rock hard, he turned her around and sat her on his lap. This is how *he* wanted to come. Looking into her face, seeing the rush of heat to her cheeks and watching her lower lip shudder with unspoken feeling.

With his mouth on her budding nipple, he thrust his body up and down beneath her, and she rode him with mounting speed, making him delirious with want. Finally, he couldn't bear withholding any longer and allowed himself the joy of exploding inside of her.

The ache…the clutch of muscles…the heartfelt connection to this remarkable doctor. It went on and on and on.

"Elizabeth," he whispered, mumbled, uttered softly into her temple. The name he hadn't dared call her for eight long years.

The champagne inside the tub was cooling, and Colt knew they wouldn't have much more time together. It had kept them warm for roughly forty-five minutes, perhaps an hour, while they'd made love. The air inside the cabin dripped with hot steam. Towels lay crumpled on the floorboards beside them.

Damp tendrils of hair escaped the knot at the back of her head, accentuating the sharp pretty features of her face. Her cheeks, softly matted with drops of champagne, dimpled as she glanced from his damp chest to the fine hairs on his thighs.

He wanted this to last all night. He wanted to stay here with Elizabeth, admiring the way her breasts jiggled, how her pink nipples moved in synchronized beauty, and the gentle expression on her face as she sat back in the tub and stared at him with that subtle smile.

Reaching over to the log beside them, Colt lifted one of two unopened bottles of champagne. She gave him a nod to indicate she agreed, and he popped the cork.

It hit the ceiling with a smack and they stifled their laughter.

Someone knocked on the door. "Liza?" Anderson called.

She stiffened. "Yes?"

Feeling wicked, Colt handed her an empty glass and poured.

"Are you all right?" Anderson's voice came muffled through the door.

"Yes, I'm fine. I…I just opened a bottle of champagne."

Anderson's voice reverberated with laughter. "Well, then, cheers."

"Thank you."

When they heard his footsteps leave the door, Elizabeth brought the glass to her lips and sipped. She passed it to Colt and he sipped, too.

It tasted like her—sweet and expensive and of high social class.

He wondered who else had been her lover. Had there been more than one? A flood of jealousy rushed through him. But he had no claim on her future, let alone her past.

Positioning his shoulders against the tub, he lifted her soft foot and bit the arch. He kissed his way up her calf, across the bend of her knee, up her hips, the swell of her breast. His hand slid to her ribs and he pulled her closer, kneading her side with his hand, caressing her knee with his other. She ran her fingers across the back of his neck, at the soft tangle of hair that sat at the base of his spine. He murmured a wordless reply, feeling lucky to be with her, adrift from the turmoil and headaches that plagued them on the trail.

The taste of champagne was heady on his lips as he kissed her full on the mouth. The weeks of small intimacies they'd shared had culminated in this extraordinary moment. He wondered if he'd ever be the same.

"Liza, are you finished?" Anderson called to her through the door again.

"Two minutes!" Elizabeth pulled her long woolen stocking to the top of her thigh and dropped the hem of her skirt. It fell to her boots. Fully dressed, she glanced at Colt adjusting his holster across slim hips.

And now, the difficulty began.

She'd spoken more to Anderson during the lovemaking than to Colt himself. There was something comical in that, but very disappointing. She had so much she wanted to say and ask, to put right, to question and to hope....

When could she say it? They had to make the time. Perhaps on a walk this evening?

She lifted the wet towels off the floor. When her back was turned, Colt grabbed her by the waist and pulled her against him, encircling his long arms across her front, burying his face into her hair. His body felt firm against her softer one.

Anderson was right by the door; she could hear him shuffling, and so she and Colt said nothing. If his men discovered what he and Elizabeth had done in this cabin, they'd never look at their commander with the same regard. Although she didn't feel that Colt had compromised his duty or his work by getting involved with her, his men might think otherwise.

She hadn't compromised him, had she?

Elizabeth sighed, brought a loose hand up to caress the hair on Colt's wrist and hoped that they'd find the words to say later.

"I'm coming!" she hollered to Anderson.

Motioning to Colt to remain behind the door, she opened it. Even though it had to be nine-thirty in the evening, sunlight poured into the room. So did the evening chill.

She squinted in the light and handed Anderson a bottle of champagne. "I saved one for you fellas."

Anderson took it and grinned. "That's mighty kind of you."

"The least I could do."

"Thank you. I've never had champagne."

"I—I think you'll like it," she said, planting her hand halfway up the door slab, conscious that Colt was breathing on it six inches away.

"How was your bath?"

"Wonderful…a bit hot, though. I'd—I'd like to take a little walk by the lake to cool down."

"Let me put this away and I'll join—"

"No, thank you. I think—I think I see Vira and her brother making their way down there."

Anderson turned around to look. "Where?"

"Beneath the pines," she lied. "Perhaps you can go and get them for me while I flag Charlie's men to haul out the tub."

Anderson, trusting man that he was, left to do her bidding, adding to her guilt. She peered around the door and the trees, and with no one in sight, signaled to Colt.

"I'm leaving without being seen," he said gruffly, "in order to protect *you*. Not me."

He squeezed her hand in passing and that was supposed to do as her goodbye.

It wasn't enough. With a big, silent ache in her throat, she watched him stride up the grassy bank. He moved with precision, long legs sheathed in denim, cowboy boots hitting the ground beneath the weight of solid muscles.

Colt didn't look her way again.

"The time we spent together was unbelievable," Colt whispered to Elizabeth on the trail.

A thrill of expectation skittered up her spine.

She squeezed his waist, felt the rock-hard muscles and smiled up at him. "You made me feel things…I've never known before."

A touch of humor pulled at his lips. "You don't say."

"Must you always tease?"

"I must."

It had taken them nearly an hour to settle things at the camp and find a moment alone. They'd left the Mounties sampling champagne and had made the excuse they wanted to check on Champagne Charlie before he fell asleep. The man was fine, and didn't seem any wiser on what had actually occurred in the cabin. Or, at least, he was discreet enough not to show it.

Daylight was dimmer beneath the canopy of aspens and firs she and Colt stood beneath. Her breath solidified in her throat as she looked up into his tanned face. His dark eyebrows gave his expression such depth.

"What do we do now?" he asked, more serious as he flicked his fingers across the hair at her ears. "I mean, you still have your path to go and I still have mine."

"That's true, Colt. I don't know what you think of me, now…obviously it wasn't my first time."

It had happened twice before with Gerard, in Toronto while she was studying far away from home. She'd been so lonely in a thriving city, aching to be held and touched by loving arms. How little she'd known Gerard back then.

"Shhh," murmured Colt. "I think…I think you are the most beautiful woman who's ever walked into my life. If I thought for one moment I was your equal…"

Hot tears stung her eyes. "You are *more* than my equal, Colt. But there are such complications to overcome."

Could they be together? How would this work day to day? Could he accept her as a working doctor? But she was slated to practice in the Klondike, and he was obligated to guard her father, far away. Each were on missions they believed in with every beat of their hearts.

He had allowed her—even helped her—give medical care to Charlie, but how far was Colt willing to go when her identity was out in the open? Would he stand by her side proudly then?

And her Uncle Sebastian—what of that complication?

Having been with Colt, having made love to him, she knew instinctively that his days as a young pickpocket hadn't tainted him in any way. Perhaps it had made him stronger, more skilled as a Mountie to counter thieves.

She chose to trust him.

"Colt? Is that you?" Tommy's voice carried through the trees and startled them.

Colt dropped his arms and stepped away from her so quickly she barely had time to register the voice.

She blushed with embarrassment. In the deepest part of her heart, she knew Colt wished to protect her reputation as the virginal woman everyone thought her to be.

In any case, no patient, male or female, would come to her for help if her character was in question.

Yet, Colt's quick withdrawal made her turn away in turmoil.

She should be honored that he'd protect her in this fashion. Proud that he was putting her reputation before his own pleasure. Pleased that the strong, dutiful Mountie who guarded her father was also guarding her.

But she was also uncomfortable. It was she who'd undressed in front of him, she who'd pushed him to choose between a naked woman and his own duties. Could any man resist such a willing woman in this wilderness?

"You two comin' back? We've got an early start in the morning." Tommy caught up to them.

"Yeah, we better go," said Colt. "We don't want to stick around in case Wellsley shows up."

Elizabeth nodded and headed back. She stepped in front of the men on the narrow footpath and ducked her head beneath branches. She told herself that what she felt for Colt, the tender feelings she couldn't suppress, he was feeling, too.

She had to believe in herself and Colt.

Unfortunately, they never had the opportunity to speak alone again that evening.

She tossed and turned in the tent, unable to face him. She listened for hours as Tommy snored. Colt was unusually silent.

Morning sunshine greeted her and lifted her spirits. Colt touched the brim of his cowboy hat in amused greeting at breakfast.

The scene at the lake was a madhouse. Folks scurried to get their craft in the water, some herding half a dozen goats onto their rafts. One enterprising fellow had roped together his sheep as if they were a dog team. The sheep didn't seem to mind. No one else, Elizabeth noted, had the gumption to attempt to bring horses, as Colt had insisted.

He was remarkable in his determination. Witnessing him, she believed anything was possible when a person set their mind to it.

In the light of day, their situation seemed brighter. They'd be spending the next week together, wouldn't they? She and Colt would sort out whatever they had to, together for seven whole days.

Seven whole days!

Racing to begin, Elizabeth smiled as the saloon girls dropped by to say they'd be heading out within the hour themselves.

"Champagne Charlie has one remarkable business," drawled Belle. "A woman could get caught up in his luxuries."

"Sure could." Colt winked at Elizabeth when no one could see.

"You have a hankerin' for those sort of things? Champagne baths?" Belle asked her.

"Sure. Don't all women?"

Belle laughed. "I wasn't sure if a fine woman like yourself…"

"In a lot of ways, I'm no different than you."

Belle smiled and when Elizabeth extended her hand to wish her well, Belle hugged her instead.

"There's something about your sister that I like," she said to Colt. "Farewell. See you on the water." She waved to the other Mounties who were attracted by the low-cut nature of her blouse. "You fellas are welcome to join me and my ladies any time you wish."

The painted ladies giggled and waved.

Tommy removed his hat and nodded. "We'll keep that in mind."

Buxton cooed. "Bye, ladies."

Anderson looked up from the apricot crates he was unloading on a scow. "Holler if you need us!"

"Sure will, sweetie!" Belle adjusted her shiny red hat. "Remember now…we want two boxes of sausages and three of apricots when we get to Dawson!"

Will and Eddie marched over and kissed a couple of the girls on the cheeks.

Elizabeth thought it sweet, if rather forward, but blushed when she caught Colt glancing her way in amusement. Was he thinking of all the deeds they'd done in the tub last night?

She continued packing. Her unspoken duty was to fold the tents. She'd gotten quite good at it. Thirty minutes into it she spotted Vira and Frank floating by on their own raft.

Elizabeth pretended not to notice them, but Frank called out.

"It was nice to meet you, Liza! We'll see you on the water!"

With a hand pressed to her waist, Elizabeth waved back. "Godspeed!"

So much had happened on this trip. So many folks she was coming to know. So much confusion about who she was and what she was doing with her life.

Champagne Charlie added one more twist as he and his men floated by. They'd built him a bed made of sheepskin, tucked into one of the porcelain tubs. His broken leg was raised to help the circulation, and he looked in fine spirits as he waved to her and Colt.

Elizabeth was relieved to see Charlie heading out. The sooner he made it to a hospital—no matter how uncivilized the conditions—the better off he'd be.

"Fine mornin' for a swim," Charlie joked.

"No swimming for you," said Elizabeth. "Slim, do you have your morphine syringes all ready to go?"

"Yes, ma'am."

"And remember to cleanse his wound like I showed you!"

"Yes, ma'am."

"Don't let him sit for more than two hours in one position!"

"Yes, ma'am."

"You know what, Colt?" Charlie shouted just before disappearing behind a bend in the lake. "That *sister* of yours worries too much!"

The obvious way he said sister made Elizabeth glance away with a heated flush. Had Charlie's men seen or heard anything last night at the cabin and reported to him?

No. He couldn't know.

"See you in Dawson. Save me ten crates of those apricots!" Charlie waved and disappeared.

Minutes later, Elizabeth and the Mounties joined the fifty or so other boats on the lake and pushed off with their three scows.

They were divided in the same way they slept in the tents. She, Colt and Tommy on one, along with Amelia, one black mare and two dogs. Buxton and Anderson on another, taking two mares, and Will and Eddie on the third with the last two horses.

Four of the horses, and the mule, had calmly climbed on board, but the two mares traveling with Buxton and Anderson had the skitters. The Mounties planned to stop and exercise the animals every few hours.

Fortunately, with the current in their favor they wouldn't have to paddle hard. From here the lake would empty into smaller lakes, then the Yukon River, and finally to the Klondike River and Dawson. The sun's warm rays bounced off the emerald-colored water. Pine trees lined the mountains. Gulls cawed overhead, ducks squawked in the river, and the lake teemed with fish.

With Colt beside her, Elizabeth felt as though she could tackle the world.

"Hey, there," called one of the young Mounties who transported the mail.

He wore a fur cap this chilly morning. Her red trunk sat prominently aboard his flat-bottomed scow.

"Mornin'," Tommy called. "Mighty big load you're carrying."

"Looks like more than you came with," said Colt.

"It's all the mail from the winter," called the carrier.

Elizabeth's nerves fluttered. What did he just say? He'd said something similar before, but it hadn't sunk in.

"You mean…you don't usually carry this amount?"

He shook his bearded face at her. "One of the barges was blocked up with ice on Lake Bennett. The ice broke up at the end 'a May, and this was the first chance we could get to it."

Her mouth dropped open.

Colt, dipping his oar into the water, noticed her reaction. He furrowed his brow, not comprehending.

The heat drained out of her. Last winter?

Frantically, she scrutinized the sacks of mail. They sat in bags of canvas, labeled according to the town they'd come from. She read the names: Fort Edmonton, Toronto, Halifax…and finally, to her horror, there it was. Vancouver.

She'd mailed it in November, thinking that…certainly not thinking of the ice…she'd thought messengers could still get through.

But seeing the trail herself, she knew now they couldn't possibly get to Dawson without the benefit of the built-in roads, the only roads the stampeders had—*the waterways*.

Gerard hadn't received her letter.

Blazes. She gulped down her fears. He must think they were still engaged.

Chapter Fifteen

"Still engaged?" Incredulous, Colt replied to what Elizabeth had revealed to him the minute they had hit the shoreline and found time alone.

"He must think so."

While the rest of the Mountie team was taking lunch on the banks of a small lake, they'd used the excuse of walking the dogs. Buxton was visible through the trees, grooming the horses. Saint and Eve pounced at each other beside Elizabeth, rolling through the grass and fallen leaves.

Queasy at the news herself, Elizabeth stopped beside a spruce so tall she couldn't see its top. She plucked nervously at the fragrant needles. She wanted to be frank with Colt.

He crossed his muscled arms across his chest. His holster swayed as he studied her.

"That means…I've compromised you in ways I hadn't intended."

The emotional upheaval she was feeling was reflected in the lean cut of his face. His lips parted. His gaze penetrated hers. He seemed shocked at the turn of events.

"But I'll tell Gerard," she insisted. She could still feel the warm burn of Colt's kisses on her breast. "I'll tell him in person I no longer wish to marry him."

"Your father hired me to deliver you to Dawson. To him."

"My father no longer controls my life."

Colt frowned. He adjusted his cowboy hat. "Does he control mine?"

"No…no of course not…"

Colt viewed the dogs. His Adam's apple bobbed up and down. "Are you so sure? Not in my private life, maybe, but in my profession. And where you're concerned, on this trip, private and profession are rolled into one."

"You can say what you will, but I'm no longer interested in being with Gerard."

Colt touched her chin. "I'm interested in being with you."

A warm glow spread through her.

"But I never should have brought you along."

Her optimism faded. "How can you say that…after the night we…"

"It's precisely why. We're heading into dangerous territory. Up till now, we were traveling alongside hundreds of other folks. This trail's different. These woods are filled with people carrying guns and taking the law into their own hands. They'd kill to get to you. If anything happened—"

"We could argue about that till the sun sets…which it never does around here. Or, we can deal with things the way they are. Deal with Gerard when we get to Dawson."

"Gerard again." Colt's eyes narrowed. He rubbed his

temple. "What does he have to do with the Mishenko claim?"

Startled, Elizabeth stepped back beneath a branch. It was the first time Colt had expressed suspicions about Gerard.

"Are you really going to be totally honest with me, Elizabeth, or only when it suits you?"

Ouch. She watched Saint nipping at Eve's heels and tried not to let Colt's question dig into her. This was an emotional time for both of them. Last night had happened unexpectedly. Never in a million years when she'd left Vancouver would she have predicted they'd have these kind of feelings for each other.

And what exactly were those feelings?

Emotion gathered in her throat.

They'd shared a night of lovemaking, but the problem was they hadn't been able to speak a word during their time together or afterward. And now...

"Unfounded rumors about Gerard could hurt his practice," she offered softly. "It would be unfair to ruin his reputation if he had nothing to do with this." She pushed on a branch and it ricocheted up and down. The scent of spruce drifted upward. "Quite frankly, I don't know how he's tied into the Mishenko claim, or Uncle Sebastian, but I believe he was involved in some way. I trust you and only you with this information."

Saint bounded around her feet. She picked up a stick and tossed it, playing fetch. "How about an honest answer for me?"

Colt rubbed his neck, staring at her, then crouched down to pat Eve. The dogs' ears pricked up at the sight of a hare. They yelped and tore off after it.

"Would you have come to me on your own, if I hadn't…hadn't tempted you the way I had last night?"

"Elizabeth…"

"Please tell me. Your answer matters to me."

Colt rose and shoved his hands into his pockets. His voice was a caress. *"Elizabeth…"*

She waited but he said no more.

"That's answer enough."

She ducked beneath the trees and strode toward shore, feeling stupid that she'd exposed her feelings when all he really wanted was…

Colt overtook her. He grabbed her by the waist and knocked her down to a bed of needles.

"What are you doing?" She yanked and pulled, but he held her arms above her head and locked her wrists with a powerful grip.

Elizabeth squirmed beneath him. He sat boldly on top of her. She tried to knee him. He tried to kiss her.

His rough touch sent a shiver of arousal through her. Misty gray eyes burned into her flesh.

"I wanted to kick that door down," he whispered hoarsely in the forest. "I wanted to claw it open with my bare hands. I imagined you naked in that water and it drove me insane. Last night was the most incredible night I've ever had…and I don't regret a minute."

She relaxed beneath his grasp.

"Aren't you going to say anything?"

Her body craved his hands, but words wedged in her throat.

"Elizabeth?"

"I didn't know…I didn't know it could be this way with you…that you could make me feel like this…."

His mouth came down hard on hers. Instinctively, her chest came up to greet his. Colt let her hands go and they curled up around his neck. He flattened his body against hers and pulled her into the circle of his hold, sensual and rock hard against her thighs.

A soft gasp escaped her as he nuzzled her throat. Clawing at her buttons, he undid the top two, exposing her rosy corset and burying his face in her cleavage. She ached to be with him again. United as a couple.

"Someone might see us," she said.

"They might," he groaned, not stopping for a second.

The thrill of getting caught made her shiver. They were doing something illicit, something lovers did who couldn't get enough of each other.

Grasping at the buttons of his shirt, she nearly tore them open. When they came undone, the fabric dipped along her ribs and concealed her own exposure.

"You're something to behold," he whispered, gazing at her pink nipples. "Doctor Elizabeth Langley."

Then he was lost in the splendor of her breasts, kissing the tips and the tender flesh that squeezed from the sides of her corset. His tongue roved her skin and she longed for him to bury himself in her.

They didn't have time. They couldn't waste a second. *Someone might see*.

Clawing at her ankles, Colt grabbed her foot, then her calf, her knee, and wove his fingers up to the middle of her thighs. With a quick slide of his fingers, he was inside her pantaloons and touching her, there in the private spot he'd held last night.

"What are you doing to me?" he growled.

"Everything you want."

He smiled into her mouth as he kissed her, teasing her with his tongue, circling hers, and at the same time pressing his fingers deeper.

When she was close to the brink, when she thought she couldn't take it anymore and didn't care who might stumble across and see them, he pulled his fingers out and pushed his body in.

He was still wearing his pants. His buttons were undone, enough to slide his enormous erection into her roused body.

"A perfect fit," she moaned.

"Hmm," he replied, biting her neck, the back of her ear, and thrusting inside of her as if he couldn't get enough.

Their muscles released at the same time. Waves of passion crashed through her, over and over, joined with Colt, the man she never wanted to part with.

He went rigid above her, clenching every muscle, groaning softly in ecstasy and savoring every last drop.

When he collapsed on top of her, he laughed softly into her ear.

"You're very good at your duties," she teased gently. And kissed him tenderly on the lips.

"Elizabeth and I will be splitting from the rest of you tomorrow. First thing in the morning." Colt made the big announcement to his men two evenings later as they made camp on the Yukon River.

As his men and Elizabeth digested the news, two rafts surged past on the rushing waters. Colt gave the folks a friendly wave, although he and his men kept their hands in close proximity to the guns flanking their hips. Every day or two they would encounter a roadhouse along the shore serving warm coffee, fresh biscuits and bowls of steaming canned vegetables. Travelers were passing the word along about thieves and con men on the trail ahead. Unfortunately with no particular details, it was all rumor.

Tommy looked up at Colt from the salmon he was frying at the fire. Two rabbits Buxton had snared were roasting over the coals.

Buxton listened as he patted a mare. Will stopped sorting through the tin plates. Eddie held seven forks in the air. Anderson looked over from his log as he scraped mud off his shoe. Elizabeth was placing apricots into a tin bowl she'd set on a chopped log. She tilted her head to listen but wouldn't look at Colt.

His growing feelings for her were threatening to overtake him. He found himself taking chances, snatching kisses and heated looks and God forbid...*even more*...when he thought no one was looking.

But the time had come to temper himself. He'd almost gone out of control where she was concerned, but last night he'd slept solid for the first time in a long while and was seeing clearly again.

He was the commander here. He gave the orders. He had to protect her, and had a mission to accomplish that was bigger than the two of them. That mission had to take priority, not his soft feelings for Elizabeth.

He wanted her. There was no doubt in his mind. Whether he could have her—for more than one night— was another question. It hounded him and forced him to consider all the possibilities, good and bad.

No matter what she said, she was still engaged to Gerard, and that bothered the hell out of Colt. And no matter what *he* said, he still worked for her father. It didn't matter how many times Colt made love to her, none of this would change until they got to Dawson City and worked things out.

If they could.

If she'd have him, or even want him when she got back to her grandfather's side.

A deeper fear, one that nagged at Colt when he watched her silently working at the campsite—pretty face concentrating on her tasks, supine body flexing and stretching beneath curving muscles—rooted and wouldn't let go.

Rosalyn had left him. The minute she'd had the chance with someone better, she'd left him.

Given the chance with someone more her equal, would Elizabeth do the same? Maybe she'd see that Gerard was the better man, after all. Maybe her father did know best.

And what was Colt supposed to do with a doctor? How could he add meaning to her life when what she wanted professionally was so foreign to him, he didn't know how he'd fit in?

Tommy flipped the fish frying in his pan. "I thought you wouldn't leave us till after we shot the rapids at Miles Canyon. Past that point is where most of the crimes are occurring."

Will set the plates on Elizabeth's log. "No-man's-land between the town of Whitehorse and Dawson City."

"We're only a day away from the rapids," said Colt. "I don't want to take the chance with Elizabeth. I promised her father."

Tommy nodded. "Fair enough."

Buxton led two mares to fresh grass. "We'll unload the apricots and sausages off your scow right now. That'll leave you with just your personal things. Hardly worth stealing."

"We'll need two mares," said Colt.

Anderson piped up. "The roan and the black one are the calmest."

Colt nodded. "Fine." He turned to face her. "Elizabeth? What do you say? Ready to split up?"

"That's fine, Colt. I'm...I'm sorry you have to make a detour on my behalf."

Her apology was certainly different than how she'd approached him at the beginning of the journey. But in their four and a half weeks together, he'd come to know a lot more about her and why she wanted so desperately to reach Dawson—to be beyond her father's reach, to do as she pleased in her own medical practice, treating all patients alike, male and female.

She was damn good at what she did.

"You'll be in command, Tommy."

Tommy gave Colt a nod.

After dinner, the men rearranged the crates on the scows. Colt and Elizabeth's held little more than necessities.

Sounds on the river drew Colt's attention. The men's posture changed. They stiffened and took notice, hands dropping to holsters. All day long, Colt had been on edge. At every snap of a twig, he'd been jumpy. Twice, he'd pulled out his six-shooter. False alarm every time.

"It's you! Oh, it's you!" Vira Mishenko, her brother, Frank, and six men traveling with them docked their rafts below the Mounties'.

"Mind if we join you?" Frank hollered.

His men looked to Colt. He gave the okay.

"Company would be nice." Anderson secured their ropes to shore.

Vira stepped off on firm ground, surrounded by purple fireweed and thick cotton grasses. Elizabeth rubbed her hands on her skirt, adjusted her holster, and with a timid smile greeted the woman. Their friendship was fragile, Colt realized, and he wondered how long it would last when Vira discovered who they were. Who Elizabeth was.

Two hours later when everyone had filled themselves on wild salmon from the icy Yukon, they sat around the fire and discussed their tales. The six men traveling with Vira and Frank, railway workers from Seattle, excused themselves for a smoke down by the river.

"We saw a moose," said Vira.

"And vultures," said her brother. "They were feeding on dead mice."

"Did you…see Dr. Wellsley?" Elizabeth asked.

Vira shook her head. "No. I guess he's still lagging behind."

Elizabeth sighed with relief. Colt deduced what she must be thinking—that Wellsley hadn't been able to contradict her story about the red trunk to either the mail carriers or Champagne Charlie.

"Any word of the Thornbottoms?" Vira asked.

"Someone yesterday told us that Theodore broke down and hired a packer. Apparently, he's able to afford more than he was letting on."

Vira smiled and sipped her tea. "Ivan used to be like that. Cheap in the present so we'd have something in the future."

Elizabeth shifted her legs by the crackling fire. The softness in her face glowed in the evening sun.

Vira continued. "When we lost the claim we were penniless. I took to doing folks' laundry, and he tried for months to find steady work."

"Was he successful?" asked Colt.

"No." She looked at the others and regret flashed across her dark features. "*Yes*...yes he was. He worked hard on my behalf. He hated that I had to wash other men's clothes, but I wanted to contribute."

Elizabeth lowered her gaze to her hands.

"In the end, he didn't have to be so cheap. I wish he would have spent every penny, because now he's gone."

"But he left you with a little bit, then," said Elizabeth. "He probably would have liked that, knowing he provided something for you."

Vira smiled gently. "It was enough to pay my way back to San Francisco. And return with help."

Colt watched Elizabeth pull in a hard breath. This couldn't be easy on her, sympathizing with a woman who'd been left broke by her uncle.

Elizabeth leaned forward anxiously, looking as though she wanted to do more for her. "Another apricot?"

"If you give them all to me, you won't have anything left to sell."

"Go on," Elizabeth nudged. "We've got tons more." She giggled. "Literally. I'll have another, too."

The women ate the fruit as they stared quietly into the fire. The Mounties were just getting up to prepare their bedrolls when more visitors approached from the river.

Colt rose, uneasy, and splayed his hand over his gun. Tommy, Buxton and Anderson did the same.

"Howdy! Howdy, folks!" A hefty man, dressed in a fur-trimmed coat for the chilly evening, paddled his canoe from twenty yards away. Another man, broader and heavier, but more serious and many years younger, paddled with him.

When they got closer, Anderson slid his hand off his gun. Colt kept his grip steady on his weapon. Innocent looks didn't count in this neck of the woods. Even if the man was wearing a clerical collar beneath his duster.

Vira jumped up abruptly. "We must be going."

"But," said Elizabeth, "I thought we could camp together for the night."

"My brother wants to get in two more hours on the water."

Frank rose and they said goodbye. The railway men followed. As they boarded their scows, they nodded to the bearded clergyman who waited, paddling on the spot, for the seconds it took to clear the shoreline.

Vira's brother nodded at the newcomers and introduced himself. "Frank Kolya and my sister—"

"Vira," she said simply, avoiding the men in the canoe and quickly rowing away.

Colt waited for the clergyman and his partner to disembark. The two men ignored the multitude of crates marked Apricots and Sausages at the shoreline, walked right past them. That was odd, thought Colt. Most folks made a comment on the unusual fruit.

"Canoe is a strange way to travel," said Colt. "Where's all your gear?"

"We're not coming from the mountains." The clergyman scratched his brown beard. "We live in Whitehorse. We travel up and down the river, spreading the word of the Lord." He spoke with great clarity.

Elizabeth held out her hand. "Pleased to meet you, Reverend."

He smiled and politely took her slender hand in his burly one. He made his round of handshakes to the incognito Mounties, and finally planted himself in front of Colt.

"And you are?" the stranger asked.

"Colton Blade."

"Pleased to meet you. Nice that you're traveling together as a family." His eyes flickered with intelligence. He seemed especially intrigued at Colt's cool demeanor. But maybe this was natural for a preacher, to be attracted to the hardened men who didn't appear to be believers. Not that Colt didn't believe in the Almighty, only that he didn't necessarily believe in preachers.

Preachers who wore guns.

But wasn't that essential in these parts? He made Elizabeth wear a gun, and she was doctor.

Maybe he was being too hard-nosed. With all eyes upon him, he reached out and shook the hand the man was offering.

"I'm Reverend Yates. Just Yates is fine. No need for anything fancy. Now, where you folks from?"

Chapter Sixteen

~~~~~~~∾∾∾∾∾~~~~~~~

Should he overtake them at gunpoint? Pierce Rawlins contemplated his decision. The pulse in his temple beat with excitement.

Standing around him in the never-ending sunlight, the Blade family stoked the campfire and recounted tales of their harsh journey. They'd been talking for an hour. Rawlins didn't give a shit how difficult their trek had been. He was focused on the cache of treasure. He avoided staring directly at the crates of apricots and sausages stacked six high and ten deep on the scows. Rawlins rubbed his phony beard and savored the sweet, peachy aroma drifting his way.

Jefferson—alias Jones—sat beside him on empty crates. He hadn't shaved for a week, which was enough to change his usual appearance. He stared at the pretty wench, Liza. She didn't have much to say, but the way the fire framed her meaty curves was enough to hold the brute's attention.

Her serious brother, Colton, eyed Rawlins again from

across the fire. In turn, Rawlins offered his pack of chewing tobacco.

Colt waved his hand in refusal. "Don't touch the stuff. Bad for the teeth, Reverend."

"You're a wise man."

The two red-haired brothers, however, accepted.

Beneath his breath, Rawlins swore softly in delight. These brothers—ranchers they said—were clever. The way Colt was assessing his every move made Rawlins quiver. He pinched a wad of tobacco between his fingers, slipped it in his mouth, rolled the bitter spit on his tongue.

Had Colt heard of his cleverness on the trail? How much he'd been able to steal?

Did Colt think he could outsmart Rawlins?

Ha!

This young rancher was no match for a man of his caliber, who'd been living off this land for two years and knew every watering hole and set of rapids between Whitehorse and Dawson City. But the man could certainly try.

Dammit, Rawlins wished Colt would.

The brothers were well armed. Leather holsters, well oiled, squeaked with the weight of expensive guns. Hell, even Liza had a revolver slung on her lush hips. Rawlins drew in a breath of sweet evening air. A woman with a gun. Well, now, how intoxicating was that?

But what to do about his decision? Apricots would be hard to pass off as belonging to Rawlins. He hadn't seen or smelled the foreign fruit for two solid years, not since the last time he'd been south. Folks on the trail would ask where he got them. They'd get suspicious. It was the same reason he stayed away from Champagne Charlie and his tubs. Too hard to get rid of rare merchandise undetected.

Rawlins sold invisible things. He *was* invisible.

Sausages would be easier to dispose of. The apricots would be nearly impossible…dammit…but they'd bring in a goddamn fortune.

How was it possible to lust after succulent fruit?

Nah…he should leave well enough alone. Risk was one thing, but this would be suicide.

No apricots. He stared at the lovely shape of Liza's bosom as she poured coffee, wondering what she looked like beneath the lace. He gritted his teeth and tried to squelch the fever of desire. Could he take the succulent woman instead?

He knew one thing for sure as he stared at Colt's solemn face. To get to her, Rawlins had to get past the brother. A little battle with this clever fellow might be thrilling. Hell, maybe Rawlins would take the apricots *and* her.

"Thank you for the coffee, miss." He gave her his most charming smile.

"It's my pleasure, Reverend. How is it you came to be here?"

Elizabeth took note of Colt's silent directives and sat next to him beside the fire. From the tight way he crossed his arms and his penetrating stare at the reverend and his sidekick, a giant man introduced as Jones, she sensed Colt didn't trust them.

But then, Colt never trusted anyone.

She tried to sit back and enjoy the evening. She was growing accustomed to the continuous daylight, and marveled at how much activity she, Colt, and the rest of the team could squeeze into the extra-long days.

"My people come from the prairies." The reverend

sipped his coffee. "Small town a hundred miles north of Regina."

Colt rubbed his jaw. "All that way. What brought you here?"

"Gold. What else?"

"How many claims have you staked?" asked Colt.

A muscle tightened in the reverend's jaw. "None. I'm here for the sake of stampeders. Not the gold itself."

"Mighty big of you to come all this way on behalf of…folks like us."

The reverend eyed Colt.

"Heathens need direction."

"You callin' us heathens?" asked Tommy.

The reverend scoffed. "No, sir. You look like abiding citizens. I mean the heathens gold fever creates of men, naturally."

The Mounties stared at him. Elizabeth thought he had an interesting manner of speaking. He enunciated every syllable.

Colt cleared his throat. "Jones, where are you from?"

Jones eased into his seating. "British Columbia." The voice was a deep boom. He was a strange-looking character. His face looked like a hammer. The nose bulbous with a flat tip, lips pushed back, a clump of hair at the back of his neck falling into the shape of a hammer's claw.

"What part?"

"Victoria."

"What brought you here?"

"Same thing. Gold at first. Now I've found…more meanin' workin' with the reverend, here."

"Let me ask you this." The reverend leaned in close to Colt. "This question always tells me immediately what's in a person's soul. Who's the most interesting person you've met on the trail so far?"

Elizabeth smiled. The clergyman had a fascinating insight. He spoke as though educated.

"You first," he said to her. "Since you seem to have an answer."

"A man named Champagne Charlie."

"Ah, yes. Women seem to enjoy his bathtubs."

"Ever met him?" asked Colt.

The reverend skipped a beat. "Nope."

Colt frowned.

Tommy stirred his coffee. "The most interesting gal I met…maybe I shouldn't say…."

"Go ahead." The reverend put his lips to his coffee.

"A bunch of saloon girls. One who goes by the name of Belle Moon."

Reverend Yates laughed. "That's honest enough. They sound like women I need to talk to. Were they behind or ahead of you on the journey?"

"Likely a day or so behind."

"I met a group of college men," said Anderson.

The reverend barely looked at Anderson, as though he wasn't interested. "You don't say."

"They were robbed blind of their haul of coffee beans and tea bags. They're studying economics at the Vancouver university and thought they'd make a fortune here. But they're going home defeated."

"That's too bad."

"Said they were robbed by a fellow pretending to be a dentist."

"Dentist?" The reverend glanced at his fellow Jones, and planted a huge hand on his tin mug of coffee. "Guess

you can't trust anyone. I want you folks to be careful."
He riveted their attention with his intensity. "You folks
mind if Jones and I camp here for the night? Decent
folks like us can protect ourselves if we stick together."

Colt blinked at Elizabeth. "Sure. That clear spot down
by the river looks good."

Yates stared at the distant spot. "I was thinking closer
to the fire."

"There's more room for you down by the river."

The reverend nodded. "Sure. Good enough. Thank
you kindly."

Colt eased back onto the log with a powerful shift of
his long legs, next to Elizabeth. "Now, you see. I find that
dentist intriguing."

"Really?"

"Don't you, Reverend? I mean, the man hasn't got a
clue about what folks really think of him."

The big man's smile faded.

"He exalts himself to a high position, pretends to be
a respectable dentist. It's artificial."

"Maybe he's a well-schooled man."

"Maybe. Or maybe he's not schooled at all. Just
someone who likes *pretending* he's smart."

The reverend let out a howl of laughter. "Now I've really
got to know. Who's the most interesting person you met?"

"You," said Colt.

A strange expression crossed the reverend's bold
features. A combination of pride and uncertainty. "Me?
How's that?"

"Well, take for instance your birch-bark canoe. You've
been up and down the Whitehorse rapids, yet I don't see
any scratches."

The reverend pointed a bulky finger toward the river, making a point. "That's a new canoe you're looking at. My original one got smashed on those rapids."

Colt nodded. "Ah, that would explain it. Then how about that big wad of chewing tobacco? Will and Eddie ran out of their cigarillos two weeks ago."

"My followers keep me in good supply."

Colt blinked. "Your followers."

"Yeah."

"Where'd you build your church?"

The reverend grinned at Jones. Jones threw his hands into the air and chuckled.

Saint and Eve walked by and the reverend pulled them in to pat them. "Good boy. Good boy." He scratched Eve behind the ears. "You're a nice dog, too. Good dog." The mutts basked in the attention.

Colt was eyeing Yates strangely. "You've got a church, don't you? I mean…all those followers need someplace to go."

"It's this side of Dawson."

"What's the altar look like?"

With a huff of frustration, the reverend stood up and shoved his hands into his pockets. He rocked back and forth on his big square boots. "You know, it's men like you…who make my work the most meaningful."

Colt grinned. Back down, thought Elizabeth. Colt was getting under the reverend's skin.

"Don't you believe in the church?" the holy man asked.

Colt scratched his bristled cheek. "I'm a man who's seeking answers."

"Maybe I can help you. First, though, you've got to be willing to yield."

"Yield?"

"Show some humbleness. Like your sister here."

"Colt always was the loudmouth of the bunch." Elizabeth tried to temper the situation with humor.

If this man was truly a minister, then God help them for being rude. On the other hand, if Rawlins was a conniving criminal, then God help them for getting him all riled up.

The reverend smiled coldly, causing Elizabeth to tense. "Your brother's smart. He'll make a good businessman when you get to Dawson."

Colt leaped toward the fire and tossed the remaining drops of his coffee into the flames. Water droplets sizzled. "Reverend, did you have much schooling?"

Reverend Yates answered slowly. He patted Saint again. "No one's bothered to ask me that before. Four years studying economics in college. Didn't use it much, though. I wound up as a reporter for the *Vancouver Times.*" He smiled and it sent a shiver through Elizabeth. "Now look at me."

Pierce Rawlins anticipated a fight. Looked forward to it. Imagined how surprised his prey would be when he pulled out his gun. He listened to his own deep breathing while lying on top of his bedroll. The sky glistened in a navy-blue twilight. Not too far away, pretending to sleep, Jefferson stared at him from beneath a clump of scrawny pines. The dogs were quiet and didn't bother them, as Rawlins was hoping. Boulders shielded them from the Blade family. Away from the fire, Rawlins was chilled bone deep.

That son of a bitch wouldn't share his camp.

The Yukon River roared by, and the mesmerizing scent

of apricots filled the breeze. Rawlins heard his men call from their hidden spots. Some chirped like crickets, others called like birds.

Rawlins cupped his hand over his mouth and, as an owl might, hooted three times.

A distant hoot came in response.

His plans were in place.

His chest rose and fell in a surge of anticipation.

He'd never attempted something like this before. Tonight would be his first.

Colt waited for them. With his hand on the trigger of his gun beneath his wool blanket, he waited for the thud of footsteps. Would they come? Or was Colt wrong about the reverend?

In the twilight hours, birds called and owls hooted. Colt stared at the stars in the dimly lit sky, then turned on his hip and watched Elizabeth lying four feet away on the same side of the fire.

He'd ordered her and the rest of his men to sleep with guns drawn, fully clothed. Tommy mumbled and shifted beyond the fire. The other men, twenty feet away, were silent. Perhaps sleeping. Perhaps listening. Buxton was down by the river, secretly on watch.

Elizabeth, lids closed, pulled the blanket up and curled her body toward the heat of the fire.

Orange flames reflected off her face. Firelight licked at her mouth, caressed her chin, fluttered across the velvet down of her cheeks. She worked her shoulder muscles into the warmth of the blanket. Long, silky hair fell across her arm. He wished he could brush it back for her and tuck her cold shoulder into the hollow of his own.

She haunted him.

She made him wish he could protect her always. Memories of that night came hurling back to him as he lay studying the way her hips swelled beneath the wool. Warmth seeped into his pores. He almost sensed the warm champagne dipping around his body, and remembered how her bare flesh had come alive beneath his kiss.

Questions echoed into the windswept night. Would they be together again? Had it been a cruel twist of fate to allow him the pleasure of her touch, only to deprive him forever when they reached Dawson?

She had to believe in him. To hell with Gerard. To hell with her father and grandfather.

And while he was at it, to hell with Rosalyn, too.

Elizabeth stirred.

"Wait for me," Colt whispered.

"Hmm?" Her eyelids fluttered but didn't open.

"Wait for me, Elizabeth. Give me a chance when we reach Dawson."

She mumbled dreamily and pulled the blanket tighter with both hands. He studied those hands, reminded of how they'd felt upon him, hot and possessive, yet so gentle.

He watched the flames cast soft shadows on her profile, her forehead and nose, the upsweep of her rosy lips. She was indeed a beautiful woman.

Then he heard it.

He jolted to attention.

Footsteps rushed them. Where were the dogs? The dogs!

"Ambush!" Colt leaped to his feet, guns drawn. The Mounties roared to life as Colt swung toward the trees.

The criminals wore bandannas on their faces. A shadowy figure aimed a barrel at him, but Colt blasted first. The stranger hit the ground, likely dead.

Tommy and Anderson fought off five intruders with their fists. Will and Eddie pounded against another six men.

Buxton was supposed to be on guard. Frantic, Colt wheeled around to look for him. The dogs barked from behind the trees. Where was Buxton? *Where was Buxton?*

Colt pivoted to protect Elizabeth.

Too late.

"Well, well, well." The reverend held a six-shooter to her head.

Her lips parted. She panted softly and turned her glistening eyes to Colt.

Every ounce of blood drained from his face. His heart beat with a fury.

"Leave her alone."

"Your sister's hard to resist."

His voice pounded from his throat. "Leave her alone."

"She's smart, too. I like that in a woman."

"Leave her alone!"

The reverend cocked the trigger. "If you ease back slow, real slow, I won't find it necessary to blow her head off."

"If you think," said Colt with a deadly calm, "I'm going to let you leave with her, you're gravely mistaken."

Elizabeth swallowed hard and didn't take her soft eyes off Colt.

Yates snickered. Colt's temple throbbed with rage. His muscles clenched, aching to snap the man in two. The dogs growled at Yates but weren't trained to attack.

"That's mighty fine talk for someone who's surrounded." He glanced to the slumped man beneath the tree. "Violence?" His face snapped back to Colt. *"You harmed my men?"*

Holy hell. This man was insane. He was the one holding the *gun* to Elizabeth's head.

"Where's my *brother?*" Colt screamed, a new tremor of fear rolling through him. "What the hell did you do with Buxton?"

A twig snapped behind Yates, he turned around in alarm, dragging Elizabeth with him. It was Buxton with his revolver cocked at the criminal's face.

"How's that feel, Reverend?" Buxton snarled. His hat was gone and his hair messed up, as if he'd been slugged in the head. "How's it feel on that end of the gun?"

In the split-second opening, Colt dived for Elizabeth. Buxton cocked the trigger but—thank the Lord—didn't pull it at Yates, thus accidentally her. When Colt came crashing down on her, Buxton swung at Yates full force. but was caught from behind by Jones, who'd grabbed Buxton by his hair. Now Buxton had to fight off both Yates and Jones.

On top of Elizabeth, Colt tried to grab for Yates's legs, but there was no clear winner when a gun fired into the air.

Tommy had shot another thief.

"To the river!" Yates called to his men. "To the river, *now!*"

They retreated, unable to snatch Elizabeth. Thank God, Colt still had her.

"Are you all right?" As the other Mounties raced behind the gang to the river, Colt turned his attention to her, trembling beneath him. He tipped her chin.

Lying in a pile of spruce needles, as she had once before, Colt recalled, Elizabeth nodded, still panting.

"Are you?"

He nodded back.

He rose to his feet and turned to help her, but she'd already leaped up and was brushing off her skirts. She raced to the two fallen men, pulled down the bandannas and checked the pulse at their throats. Both dead.

Colt could tell just by looking.

Saint and Eve circled around Colt and Elizabeth, whimpering and likely wondering what the hell was going on. Elizabeth followed the dogs, patting and murmuring to them. Colt was glad for the interaction, for Elizabeth to get her mind off the two dead criminals.

Tommy and Anderson returned up the slope, followed by Buxton, Will and Eddie.

"They got away with the food," said Tommy.

"They took it all?" asked Colt. "Sausages and apricots?"

"Both scows."

Colt sighed and hitched a hand to his waist.

Elizabeth glanced from Tommy to Colt. Her pale expression changed to one of dawning realization. "Wait a minute. Wait just one minute." She brushed spruce needles off her arm and stepped back to assess the Mounties. "You weren't running very fast after them."

She turned and glared at Colt and he felt the twinge of guilt creeping into his face.

Her accusation echoed through the pine trees and the early-morning sunshine. "You wanted them to ambush us. Didn't you?"

Chapter Seventeen

Elizabeth listened to the breeze rustling through the pines above them as she waited for her answer. The Yukon River, thirty yards wide, the color of a turquoise jewel, gushed beyond Colt's shoulders. When the dogs raced past them, a hundred startled swallows hiding in the shrubs lifted their wings and soared to the sky. The Mounties, six tall statues chiseled from rock, lifted their faces to the birds and the sun.

Colt placed his hands on his hips and found her gaze. His forehead was smeared with the dirt and sweat he'd accumulated in fighting off Yates.

"That's why we came. We need them to lead us to their hideout."

Her lips trembled. The fight was over for now, and she was safe, so why was she shivering? "You goaded him to do it. You taunted him at dinner. You told him he was full of himself."

"Yes, I did, and he enjoyed it."

"Why would you taunt a lunatic? He might have killed one of us."

"We had our eyes on him. He's deliberate. He's educated. He knows what he's doing, and he's got this scheme down pat."

"But he nearly," she whispered, "got away with me."

The light in his eyes flickered. "I never would have let that happen."

"But things can turn so quickly."

"Elizabeth." Colt rubbed his stubby jaw. The button below the collar of his shirt was torn. One seam on his broad shoulder was ripped. Gentleness came out in his tone as he gripped her by the shoulders. "I never would have let that happen. And neither would my men. I gave orders for everyone to watch out for you."

Colt nodded to the others and the men sprang to their duties, clearing the camp as if given a silent command.

"It's true." Tommy doused the fire with a pail of water. "Colt said you were top priority. That's why he said he was going to take you away, just before the thieves showed up—remember?"

Buxton groaned, and she stepped out of Colt's warm reach.

"Can I have a look at you?" she asked Buxton. His head had to be throbbing.

Buxton slumped onto a log and bent over, allowing her to examine him. His demeanor was far different from how he'd treated her when they'd first met.

She parted the hair above his left ear. He flinched. A lump the size of an apple greeted her.

"Easy does it." She worked her fingers through the rest of his scalp, trying to be gentle. "You've got one big lump. But the skin's not broken. No broken skull bones, either."

"The son of a bitch is gonna pay."

"Did you get a good look at him?" asked Colt.

Buxton sighed. "Never saw him. He came up from behind."

"Look for a man who's left-handed," she said.

Colt nodded in agreement. "If he came up from behind and hit you on the left side, he had to be left-handed."

Elizabeth soaked a washcloth in a pail of cool river water and applied it to Buxton's lump.

Colt kicked dirt onto the remaining embers. The other Mounties packed axes and pots as quickly as they could. Saint and Eve whimpered at Buxton's feet. Despite his own discomfort, he petted the dogs. Buxton always hovered around the various animals, large and small, she noted, ensuring they were fed and comfortable.

"That's why Yates befriended the dogs," said Colt. "So they wouldn't bark when he ambushed us."

Elizabeth held the compress to Buxton's head. Colt had observed many details about Yates, while she'd noticed so little.

She could barely look as Colt went over to the dead men and checked their pockets. Nothing of significance. A pocketknife. Some cash. A broken cigarette. He removed their guns and ordered them buried on the spot. Will and Anderson grabbed shovels and took to digging.

"We'll need another set of rafts," Colt told Tommy and Ed. "There'll be folks passing through shortly, I'm sure. We've got enough cash to make an offer they can't refuse. Leave them some nails. It'll be easy for them to build more, but we can't spare the time."

The apricots and sausages were gone, just as the Mounties had hoped, Elizabeth realized. Fortunately, they could replace the scows.

Tommy and Ed tore off for the shore.

Colt unhitched two mares, and on his way to the river, strode past Buxton and Elizabeth.

"I think we were set up."

Buxton recoiled beneath her fingers. "By who?"

Elizabeth dipped the cloth in cool water again and re-adjusted it on his lump, ignoring the chill of the morning air over her blouse and shoulders.

Colt patted the restless black mare. She settled beneath his firm touch. "Frank and his sister, Vira."

Elizabeth gasped softly. She rubbed her cheek with her free hand. "Now you've really lost me. How can you tie them into this?"

"They arrived just before Yates. Did either of you notice Vira's reaction to him?"

They shook their heads, no.

"She saw him coming, turned as white as a ghost and sped the other way as soon as she could."

"But she introduced herself," said Elizabeth.

"From ten yards away, floating downstream."

"She didn't give her last name," said Buxton, squinting as he thought of it. "Because Yates already knew it."

"I don't know." Elizabeth frowned, unable to believe it. "I don't know about that theory…."

She removed Buxton's washcloth and took a peek at the lump. It was going down.

She squinted into sunshine, at the silhouette of Colt's rigid shoulders. "How are you planning on catching this man?"

"We'll follow his trail, between Whitehorse and Dawson City."

"That's hundreds of miles."

"The current on the Yukon River runs between seven and ten miles an hour. If we include the added speed of our own paddling, but subtract for rest breaks…in fifty hours we can still cover five hundred miles."

"Three days to Dawson City."

"Yup."

"He's got the crates," said Buxton. "We don't know where he's gonna ditch the stuff, but he'll be traveling slower due to the weight."

Elizabeth removed the cloth and lowered it to her skirts. "Go ahead," she said to Buxton. "Do your packing. I'll bring the compress along and we'll use it on and off throughout the day."

Buxton rose and went to collect his things.

She patted Colt's mare. "What makes you think Yates is going all the way to Dawson?"

Colt handed the reins to one of his approaching men, Tommy, and went to unhitch two more mares. "Because he told me," Colt said over his shoulder.

Elizabeth raced to pack her bags. "When?"

"Not in so many words. But it was clear. He said his church is in Dawson."

She kneeled on her bedroll and rolled up her blanket. "That's pretty vague."

"To me, it's clear as day. He's enticing us to follow."

She glanced up as Colt led the horses past. The ground beneath her knees shook. "Why would he do that?"

"Boredom."

When she sat back on her haunches, incredulous, her hair spilled from her clasp. "Boredom?"

"He wants a run for his money. He's smart and is itching to show us how much."

"Then maybe he's more crazy than any of us thought."
She eyed Colt, standing tall with his Stetson, defiance radiating from every pore. She trembled at the thought of where all of this would lead them. "Or maybe you are."

Colt was a man who knew what he wanted. And he wanted two things. To deliver Yates to justice.

And to hold Elizabeth in his arms again.

The roar of the Whitehorse rapids ahead rushed past Colt's ears. On their scow, Colt, Buxton and Elizabeth paddled like hell to control their craft. The mule and two horses standing toward the back had finally settled into the rhythm. Saint and Eve lay quietly beside them, looking like monstrous sleeping dogs. Beyond them, the mountains were getting farther apart and flatter.

The Mounties had bought two rafts from passing strangers eager to make some cash. Tommy and Anderson were directly behind them on one. Will and Ed followed on another. Three boats in total.

With muscles taut beneath his shirt in the midday sun, Colt gripped his oar. Elizabeth, beside him in long skirts and sleeves rolled to her elbows, was damp with spray. Perspiration ran down her temples. Determination was set in her eyes.

He'd never seen a woman work so damn hard. They'd spent three hours paddling to get to these great rapids, just outside the town of Whitehorse. Along the way, they'd asked everyone they'd met the same question.

"Has a large bearded man, a reverend going by the name of Yates, passed by? He's hauling a ton of apricots."

"No, sir. No one by that description. No apricots."

Colt concentrated on paddling. They were rushing

through a canyon. Jagged basalt cliffs formed a gray wall on either side of them. Water as clear and blue and emerald as he'd ever witnessed, pounded beneath the planks of the raft. His boots vibrated.

Clouds had been filling with moisture for the past hour, and a sudden shower overtook them. Strangely, the sun was still shining on the other side of them. When he looked up above the canyon, a double rainbow arched the sky, one layered beneath the other. He gasped at the beauty, then nearly fell in awe when a triple rainbow burst through the distant mountains. Under other circumstances, Colt would think the scenery was sent from heaven. This minute, however, he feared the waters would swallow them whole.

"Stop. Stop, stop, stop!" Colt back-paddled and eased them to shore. Tommy, Anderson, Will and Eddie followed Colt's lead. "We'll drop off the horses here," he told them.

A roadhouse was nestled on the banks. A dozen men waited at the docks and pulled them in. Obviously, this was a rest stop before shooting the rapids. Canyon City, one man said.

"Need a pilot?" men called.

"No, thanks. We can guide our own craft."

"They're big rapids, mister."

"We rode a few already."

"But these ones are monsters."

"So I hear. We need you to take the animals, though. I understand you got a path that runs above the rapids, all the way to town. How much?"

From Whitehorse, it was still roughly two and a half days to Dawson City by river, and they needed their rafts to get there. There were no civilized roads to ride the horses over the boulders. The mares couldn't carry the weight, anyway.

They settled on a price and agreed to pick up the animals in Whitehorse at the end of the day. Elizabeth took the time to change the cold compress on Buxton's head.

"Ready?" Colt asked her thirty minutes later.

"Ready." She grabbed her oar and knelt on the left side of the raft. Buxton did the same behind her. Colt took the right. Saint and Eve settled in behind.

Elizabeth hunkered down, her oil slicker clinging to her back. Colt gave her a gentle smile. At one time, he'd used the word delicate to describe her. Now he couldn't think of a stronger woman he'd want at his side.

Buxton gave his nod.

Colt shoved off and they careened down Miles Canyon.

Folks lined the cliffs, one hundred feet above them. They vied for a spot between the thick growth of willows, spruce and pine, to watch yet another scow attempting the impossible.

"Avoid the island!" they called.

"Slow down!"

"Bless you all!"

Some whistled in amazement.

In a blur, Colt noticed the trams lining either side of the cliffs. Hired guides were rolling wooden cars, filled with people's belongings, toward town.

"Oh, my God," Colt whispered, looking straight ahead.

Beyond an island barrier in the middle of the canyon, gushing white streams of water, dozens of rapids, were shooting up from the basin. The rapids looked like galloping white horses, their thick creamy manes flowing behind their shoulders. True to legend, the vision of these rapids, by the first white men who'd ever seen them, was how the town of Whitehorse got its name. Galloping white horses.

"Brace yourselves," Colt hollered above the water thundering around them.

He gripped his oar, planted his knees on the planks and careened down the valley.

Half of the scow submerged. Ice water soaked his knees. He thought they were done for. But then the raft kicked up and over the white foam, and again, and then they found their balance.

"Yee-ha..." Colt turned his head and laughed along with Elizabeth. Her skin glowed with the same thrill he felt.

A man could get used to this kind of freedom, battling nature, a willing partner by his side. They'd conquered the impassable rapids. Was this how his father felt, chasing across the continent for half his life?

The rapids fell behind them, and smooth, heavenly water took them another mile into Whitehorse. It was a tent town on a small plain on the banks of the Yukon River. Cliffs rose above the tents, and a mountain range beyond that. The town had sprung up as a transportation hub, a meeting ground on the river. They docked their craft and Colt, Elizabeth, Tommy, Buxton, Anderson, Will and Eddie headed up the banks.

It was back to solid footing beneath their boots. With a hand at her slender waist, Colt helped Elizabeth up the slope. She removed her oil slicker, no longer needing it to protect her from the rapids. Her long brunette hair had come undone from its clasp, her cheeks were taut with the excitement of their adventure, her eyes alive with spirit.

The land beneath his boots was secure, but he, as a man, was not.

He'd never felt more unsure of himself than when he looked into Elizabeth's searching eyes. What could he provide for her, that her father and Gerard could not?

The next morning when the team rose and packed yet again, Elizabeth was wearing a new pair of denim jeans.

Colt smiled as soon as he noticed them. During their evening in Whitehorse, when they'd caught up to their horses, and investigated for word of apricots or ministers that never came, she'd somehow bought a new pair of pants.

She'd risen early to fish and had caught a salmon in the river. Buxton seemed to be feeling better, and was caring for the horses.

As Elizabeth fried breakfast at the campfire, Colt admired the curves in her jeans. The denim hugged her behind, making him remember how the gentle swell of her hips felt beneath his hand. How soft her thighs were, how willing she'd been to mold into his naked body.

Her shirt—his shirt, the blue one he'd given her in Skagway—was tucked neatly into the waist of her jeans, and a wide leather belt cinched the narrow span below her ribs. Her bosom, held tight in place by her corset, filled his shirt to overflowing.

Colt was amazed at Elizabeth's transformation. He wondered if Gerard and her grandfather would recognize her.

Two days later, with dozens of blisters and bruises between them, and his sore muscles worked raw, the team of seven finally arrived in Dawson City, on the Klondike River.

There'd been no sight of the Reverend Yates, no sign of sausages or apricots and no stories about a crime ring headed by reverends, dentists, or anyone else.

Had Colt slipped up? What was he missing? Why hadn't he seen or heard anything along the trail?

"They're close." Colt, flanked by Elizabeth and his brothers, strode down the main street of Dawson City minutes after they arrived. "I can feel it. They're here."

"You go by feeling a lot." Elizabeth had to nearly run to keep up to his pace. "For a man I once thought had no feeling whatsoever, you go by feeling a lot."

Colt thought about what she said. It was true, he decided, for looking at her, dressed in her scuffed jeans, her dark braid messed from the wind, his *feeling* was that he shouldn't lead her straight to the hospital and into Gerard's arms.

"You sure you want to go there first? Wouldn't you rather meet your grandfather? Or find us…yourself…a hotel room to wash up in?"

"That would take hours. I want to do this now."

Colt nodded softly. He sure as hell didn't look any better than she did, dirt streaking his pants, his rumpled shirt in bad need of ironing.

Colt stopped on the crowded boardwalk beneath a sign marked Gold Nuggets Bought Here. A lineup of working men, caked in mud but laughing and telling jokes, stood in the doorway heaving and barely holding up sacks and pails of various sizes. Gold? That much gold in Dawson?

"You men go on ahead," said Colt to his team. "Check into the nearest hotel. Ask around about Yates. I'll join you soon."

"You sure?" Buxton peered from Colt to Elizabeth.

"Yeah. When I get back, we'll go to the Mountie outpost together."

Will and Anderson grinned. Tommy sighed, pushing back his Stetson. Buxton and Eddie took off their hats. They all knew what this meant. It was time to reveal who they really were. No more secrets.

The men strode down the boardwalk, walking lighter than they had in days, thought Colt. They walked past a saloon and barbershop, and headed toward a large woodframe building on the southwest corner, Dawson Digs Hotel.

Colt swung around to gaze at the rolling landscape beyond the town limits. He pointed to a sprawling log cabin. "There's the hospital."

He started walking, pressing his hand into the small of her back, enjoying the warmth of her blouse, but Elizabeth stopped.

"Colt, I want you to know…"

She fanned her face from the morning heat. Sunshine poured down on her brown cowboy hat and created soft shadows on her cheeks. Her lips, chapped red from the sun, were parted. Even the turn of her earlobe was beautiful.

She struggled to find words. "It's not over between us."

She said it more like a question than a statement.

He lifted her chin and stroked her cheek. He wanted to hold her close and reassure her…or maybe he wanted her to do that for him. In either case, he couldn't make or accept any promises until they faced what they had to.

"I don't want it to be," he whispered.

Two men dressed in banker's clothes eyed Elizabeth as they passed. The way they craned their necks, you'd think they'd never seen a woman before.

Colt placed his hand at the back of her warm neck, and they walked into the hospital.

The small windows didn't let in a lot of light. And that was one thing Dawson had an abundance of—daylight. Twelve narrow cots, ten of them filled with men of various ages with various illnesses, lined the walls.

It wasn't difficult to spot Gerard Thornton.

He was the tall, thin and black-haired surgeon sitting near the far wall, unwrapping gauze from a patient's head. The injured man also had a broken arm, set in a splint. Thornton finished with the unwrapping and peered at the stitches. He murmured something to the patient, and then got up to wash his hands at a washstand in the corner.

Elizabeth pulled in a deep breath beside Colt. Her boots stopped on the plank floor, making a scuffing sound.

Thornton glanced in their direction. He blinked. Then he closed his eyes once more and refocused on Elizabeth. His face was an impassive block of ice, as if he couldn't comprehend what he was seeing.

"Elizabeth?"

Colt crossed his arms, bracing himself for the reunion, and stole a glance at Elizabeth.

She smiled at Thornton. Colt's heart thudded.

"Hello, Gerard," she said softly. She removed her cowboy hat and went to greet him.

When Thornton hugged her, Colt wanted to fade into the floor.

He reminded himself she was being polite. That she'd written a letter to Thornton he had yet to see.

Unable to stomach it, Colt turned away from the scene, noting two other doctors, young men, attending to patients. At a desk by the front door where Colt stood, he noticed a stack of mail.

It had arrived.

And then Elizabeth was suddenly there, too. She peered at the stack that Colt was staring at and reached for the cream-colored envelope addressed to Thornton.

"That just came two minutes ago." Thornton grinned. "We haven't had mail for half a year. I had to finish up with that patient first." He frowned at her hair. "Why did you dye it? Where did you come from? Who brought you?"

Thornton's gaze finally settled on Colt. "Ah, I see. Sergeant Hunter."

In all the weeks Colt had yearned to hear his true name called, it didn't feel right coming from Thornton's mouth.

Colt gave him a curt nod.

Elizabeth removed the letter from the pile. "I'm here now, so I'll take the letter back."

"But I'd like to read it." He caught her hand, but was distracted by the blisters. Thornton glanced at her dirty jeans. "You need to wash."

Elizabeth swallowed. A look of shame crossed her

face. "When I wrote this letter months ago…I—I thought you'd receive it before I got here."

A messenger boy came through the front door, delivering a two-page newspaper.

"Thanks, Haden." Gerard pulled a nickel from his pocket and gave it to the boy. "Why don't you go on down to the Land Claims Office and tell Mr. Langley his granddaughter's here."

"Yes, sir." The young boy tore off.

Gerard turned back to Elizabeth. "Start from the beginning, Elizabeth. Tell me how you got here. And please give me the letter."

He held out his hand.

Give it to him, thought Colt. *Give the man the letter.*

But seconds ticked by. Elizabeth didn't move.

Give him the letter.

Colt tried not to let it hurt. He tried to understand Elizabeth, and why she found it necessary to take the letter back, to tuck it into the satchel she'd brought with her.

She'd seen Gerard. She'd felt his arms. She'd seen his smile. Which meant she'd changed her mind about all the things she and Colt had discovered about each other on the trail, he thought numbly.

Chapter Eighteen

Elizabeth couldn't do it. Not here. Not like this. The two other young doctors, not to mention several of the patients, were staring at Gerard. She didn't have the heart to break the news in such a public place.

Is that what Colt expected of her? To shatter Gerard Thornton?

She didn't get an opportunity to think more of it, for two men burst through the hospital doors.

Champagne Charlie's men.

Colt descended on them first, followed by Elizabeth.

"Where is he?" Colt asked the grief-stricken man they'd come to know as Slim. "What happened to him?"

Slim was out of breath, holding his side. "He's comin'. Get ready." He panted, gazing around Colt's shoulders. "Is there a doctor here?"

Gerard stepped forward. "That would be me."

Slim nodded at Elizabeth. "I see you met the midwife."

Gerard squinted down at her and she witnessed the

doubt in his eyes. It was something she'd seen in his expression from the first time she'd told him she wanted to be a surgeon.

Female physicians helping other females were tolerable. Midwifes were tolerable. But a female surgeon...didn't impress Gerard.

Six more men burst through the doors into the log shelter. The last two carried Charlie on a homemade canvas stretcher. He was pale and unconscious.

Elizabeth rushed to his side, picked up his wrist and felt for a pulse. It was rapid and weak. But it was there.

With her own pulse racing, she moved quickly. She washed her hands, picked up the nearest stethoscope, settled Charlie into a cot and questioned Slim on his condition.

"He fell asleep last night and hasn't come out of it," said Slim. "Up till then, things were goin' well."

"Let me check his heartbeat." Gerard pushed his way in and took over.

Colt watched from the foot of the bed, arms crossed, not speaking. *Lord, he hadn't said one word since they'd arrived. Not one. What was going through his mind?*

Elizabeth didn't think she could take any more strain between the men, and then her grandfather waltzed in.

"Elizabeth," he hollered, breathless at the door. Short, round and gray-haired, he was a sight for sore eyes. Her heart opened up to him.

"Elizabeth! Come here, girl! I won't believe it's you till you come here!"

She smiled at her grandfather. "I'm busy, Grandpa, please. This man needs help first."

"But Gerard's there—"

"Grandpa, *please* understand. I'll be right with you."

She turned away to tend to Charlie. She tore off the bloody bandage on his thigh, ignoring Gerard's look of dismay. She asked Colt to lift the injured limb and placed Charlie on his side so she could get a good look at the wound, at the back of his leg.

Colt helped without question. Gerard stared at the two of them. But as soon as he caught sight of the festering wound, he cursed and was at her side in a flash.

"Who could do this?" He winced at the redness.

Elizabeth was already soaking the wound with cleansing tonic. It wasn't full of pus. Not yet. The redness was just beginning, so maybe they still had a chance to save the limb. But Charlie was unconscious and that worried her.

"This leg should have come off," said Gerard. "He obviously got care from someone on the trail. Who on earth would be so cruel to avoid the inevitable?"

"Me," Elizabeth said softly. She looked up at Colt.

His dark features softened. He tilted his head at her and shook it slightly, as though trying to disagree with Gerard's assessment. But there couldn't be any disagreement with a festering wound. If the festering spread through his bones, he'd lose a lot more than one leg. He'd lose his life.

"I did it," she confirmed, shame and doubt rising through her, as they always seemed to around Gerard.

Gerard's mouth fell open.

"It was me who helped this man three days ago. Blame me for anything that happens."

Colt stood in the background. He was ill at ease in the hospital, uncomfortable in the natural territory of Elizabeth and Thornton. Colt knew how to survive in the woods, on the trail of crooks and criminals, but not here, surrounded by injuries he knew nothing about.

"How did Elizabeth get here?" Mr. Langley stood next to Colt in the single-room hospital. The old man wasn't looking at the activity bustling around Charlie, but he spoke in a condescending tone. Colt was, after, all, hired help.

Colt leaned against a wooden pillar. "I brought her."

"You?"

"And my men. Six of us altogether."

"Six men and one woman?"

"That's right, sir."

"And her father knew of this?"

"Yes, sir."

"Why has she come?"

"That's something you have to ask her."

The stocky man pivoted his face from the floor to Colt's solemn gaze. Colt felt the man's pulsing anger. It was rising up his neck and staining his gray whiskered cheeks.

The old man said no more. As things calmed down around Champagne Charlie, when he'd been given syringes full of medicines, had his wound scraped and mended and bandaged up again and God knew what else, Colt was shuffled to the sidelines. He was losing control of everything, and couldn't do a damn thing about it. He was forgotten by Elizabeth, shunned by Gerard; he'd been an insult to her grandfather, and a total failure at finding Yates.

After five weeks of protecting her, Colt found it difficult to leave Elizabeth's side. But she had to lead her life in the hospital. She had to help Champagne Charlie as best she could, settle things with Gerard and her grandfather, while Colt's own pressing duties called to him.

An hour and a half later, Colt had bathed and shaved at the hotel, and had made it to Mountie headquarters with his men.

Commissioner York, the commander of the entire Yukon, shook Colt's hand. The men stood outside the outpost cabins. They were admiring the horses Colt had delivered in the corral. While Colt's men discussed their journey with three Yukon constables, the commander spoke to Colt.

"By God, those mares are something. I've never seen such healthy horses come through here."

"You can thank my men for that. They took good care of the animals. Especially Buxton. I mean Luke." There was no need for the phony names any longer.

"We're mighty obliged. Of the forty men I've got here, we only have twenty horses between us."

"So what have you heard of this Yates man?"

The commissioner chewed on a peppermint stick. "He goes by a lot of names. Never heard Yates before. Darwin is one. Kipling is another. To add to your list of careers, he's also passed himself off as a playwright, and twice as a lawyer."

"You say you saw some apricots last night?"

"Yeah, but we couldn't trace them any further than the two men in the bar. Said they were sold a crate of whiskey and a crate of apricots down by Bonanza Creek. I've known these men for years. They're drunks. They're not thieves."

The apricots were in the area, though. Yates must have a lot of men at his disposal.

Colt hitched his boot on the bottom of the fence rail. Sunshine warmed his cheeks. "Maybe my men should have taken Yates out when we had the chance. I wanted to track all of them down. Instead, I might get no one."

"It's always a hard decision to make."

"Why do you think he disguises himself in such educated roles?"

"Wants to make a point. That he's smart and we're stupid."

"Hmm." Colt pondered the list of professions. What was he missing? Something was here. A piece of the puzzle staring him in the face. He *felt* it, just as Elizabeth had once said. Colt went by feeling a lot, and his gut was telling him now. The puzzle piece was *here*.

"Come on," said the commissioner. "I'll show you around town. Mind if I try out one of your mares?"

"They could use the exercise. Say, show me where they dig the gold. And show me where the rich folks live."

Elizabeth had once thought she'd have more freedom in the Klondike but she had less. She was trapped no matter which way she turned. Gerard was insisting she treat only women. Her grandfather wouldn't talk to her about anything significant. And her fragile relationship with Colt had come to a dead stop. They were thrust back into a situation that demanded each stay in their place.

"Why does that man give you such power?" Gerard asked Elizabeth the following morning while she sat at Charlie's bedside. Gerard looked tired. Dark shadows rimmed his eyes.

He was referring to Slim. The faithful friend wouldn't

leave Charlie's bedside all night, shotgun in hand no matter what the doctors said about leaving it by the door. Slim wouldn't allow anyone but Elizabeth to administer morphine and cleanse the wound.

"He trusts me, Gerard. Is that so hard to understand?"

"But what did you do on the trail? The leg is almost—"

"I *saved* his leg." She drew her strength and faced him squarely. "I *saved* his leg, Gerard. And it looks like it's going to be all right. As long as we watch over him and keep applying the poultices. The wound is draining, and the redness is subsiding."

"Right," said Gerard, unable to look at her.

At her grandpa's cabin late last night, Elizabeth had a hip bath, washed her hair and ironed her clothes. She hadn't explained the small details yet to Gerard about her trip with Colt and her "brothers," but Grandpa knew them all.

He'd listened but hadn't responded. He was as silent as he always was with her when something displeased him.

Gerard left Charlie's beside to tend to another patient. Slim sidled next to her.

"What's this rumor I hear about your brothers?"

Elizabeth's heart quickened. "Are they all right? What's—"

"They're fine. But they're walking around in red uniforms."

A smile came to her readily. "You don't say."

"They're not your brothers?"

She shook her head.

Slim grinned. "Well, I'll be danged. Charlie's not gonna believe it. Are you a midwife?"

Elizabeth smiled and drew her shoulders together

proudly. "I'm a doctor. I studied medicine for five years at a college in Toronto. I'm Dr. Elizabeth Langley."

"Well, I'll be danged." Slim held out his hand and she shook it, one of the most touching moments of her journey. "Charlie's not gonna believe it."

Tears escaped her, happy ones, as she laughed along with Slim. When Gerard looked over from the other end of the beds, he rose to join them. Maybe he'd understand, thought Elizabeth. Maybe this time he'd congratulate her on saving Charlie's leg, on being as strong as she was.

But he had no smile as he approached. "May I speak with you outside? John and Marcus will keep an eye on Charlie." He nodded at the young doctors.

"Sure," she said, slipping away from Slim and into the bright outdoors. The streets of Dawson were busy with folks hurrying by the shops, others hauling wheelbarrows full of shovels, one man unlocking the door to a saloon.

Gerard had removed his surgical frock, which revealed a handsome wool suit. They hadn't gotten but five paces when he asked her.

"What happened to the lovely woman I left behind?"

Her smile and her pleasant experience with Slim left. "You've answered your own question. You left her behind."

"She was supposed to wait for me."

"You never asked me to wait. You told me."

"Then maybe I should ask you now. There's a preacher in town. Let's wed and return to Vancouver. I don't much like this place. We'll go back to your father and the social class where a woman like you belongs."

"I've had a lot of time to think about things on this trip. One of things I discovered is that I like this place."

"Here? This wilderness?"

"It's God's country."

"It's godforsaken country."

"You seemed to enjoy it. As long as I didn't join you."

"That's because it's no place for a woman. Dammit, Elizabeth, you have no idea..." He lowered his voice. "They've got a stretch of cabins on the last street in town. Filled with painted women."

Elizabeth steeled herself. "I saw a triple rainbow in Whitehorse. I saw a herd of caribou floating across a river. We saw whales, and I met folks I'd never be able to say hello to if I lived beneath my father's roof. Beneath *your* roof."

Gerard peered at her with lost respect. "Are you listening?"

"They have painted women in Vancouver, too."

Gerard glanced down at his hands, at a loss for words.

"There's another reason I'm here, Gerard."

He looked up and sighed.

"I'd like to know. How were you involved with Uncle Sebastian's claim?"

Watching her, he rubbed his wool suit. "What are you talking about?"

"My uncle told me it wasn't rightfully his. He told me you knew that."

Gerard scoffed. "So you think I shared in your uncle's mistaken numbers?"

"I don't know what to think of you anymore."

Gerard hedged. He didn't answer. She grabbed him by the arm and demanded, "I came a long way to hear the truth. Either you tell me, or I'll get the Mounties to ask."

With an angry yank, he removed his arm from her

hold. "He told me that he made a mistake. *I* had nothing to do with it. He came to me for advice after that fellow—that Mishenko fellow—was killed in that awful fight."

"What advice did you give him?"

"That if it was recorded on paper, in the Land Claims Office, it was his."

"And why cause a scandal with your potential in-laws?"

Gerard sighed.

Elizabeth remained steadfast. "It was my dream to come to the Klondike with my grandfather. It was supposed to be me, but you took the opportunity for yourself."

"You're a selfish woman."

Elizabeth unbuckled her satchel and found the envelope she'd been so careful to save him from. "This is for you."

"Ah, the letter you so willingly give and take."

"You can have it now."

"What does it say?"

"That we're through."

"Grandpa? Are you home?" It was the following evening. Elizabeth was returning to his cabin after hours spent at the hospital.

She stumbled in the cramped doorway, and nearly fell over the red leather trunk that had been delivered yesterday.

"Grandpa?"

"I'm here, child," he called from the kitchen. A lantern lit the room, but not nearly enough to illuminate the dark corners. A cast-iron stove sputtered along one log wall, taking away the early-evening chill.

Grandpa came out with bread rolls and a can of corn.

Something was still frying in the kitchen, she could hear the snap and sizzle, the smell of ham or bacon. Or was it beef?

"You shouldn't have come."

"I had to."

"Why?"

"Because Grandma would have wanted me to."

His round shoulders stiffened. "I was married to my Elizabeth for forty-one years. Don't presume to tell me what she would have wanted." He smacked the table with his palm. "The sooner you keep your tongue in check, the better off we'll all be. Now you get your things together, and marry that man."

"Which man are you talking about?"

"Is that your way of talkin' smart?"

"No, Grandpa. But at least we're talking."

With an uneasy hand, Elizabeth set the plates that he'd stacked on the pine table. "Do you really want me to leave?"

He grumbled something and went back into the kitchen. She heard the frying pan sizzling louder.

He returned with two empty tin cups and a bowl of sugar.

Perhaps if she explained things the way she saw them, her grandfather would understand. "I can handle more than you know, Grandpa. That man that you saw in the hospital…Charlie…had a terrible accident. He broke his leg on the trail. I set it for him."

Silent, Grandpa trudged into the kitchen again and returned with a pot of coffee. He poured.

Elizabeth rubbed the table, trying to find the gentle words she'd been seeking for years. "I…I learned in college what I could have done for Grandma."

His gnarled old hands stopped pouring. He set the coffee aside, crossed his arms, but didn't look at her.

"She'd be pleased to know that we have medicine to strengthen the heart. Or ease the suffering."

He didn't say a word.

"You know what else I learned in college? I learned to put faith in my own skills. And I learned that some men are like Gerard." It was difficult to talk past the lump in her throat. "They give false hope to women like me, pretending I'm a partner at their side when at every opportunity they're given, they step in front and leave me behind. That's what he did when he volunteered to bring you here. It was my idea, Grandpa. I wanted to come to the Klondike."

His old eyes flashed. "Your idea?"

"Yes."

She took a moment to gather her thoughts.

"Grandpa? You want to know a secret? Sickness and illness terrify me, too. But now, I have the skills to help." He moaned, but she kept going, fighting off the tears that threatened to spill. "I know you loved Grandma for forty-one years," she said as gently as she knew how. "But I loved her, too."

He was crying, then. He turned around and walked into the kitchen, shoulders quaking with his sobs, and she understood he didn't want to speak of it again.

Ten minutes later, her grandfather came out holding a pan of fried sausages. He'd recovered. A calm expression had softened his face. "Here. Bought these yesterday. Haven't had sausages for nearly two years."

Elizabeth looked down at the brown patties and began to laugh, releasing her tension.

"What's so funny? Don't you like them?"

"I've been eating the same ones for five weeks straight."

"These are the ones you told me about?"

"Yes. Where'd you get them?"

"Fellow that supplies me with paper. At the Land Claims Office."

"We'll have to tell Colt."

Grandpa peered over her shoulder at the window.

"I think you can tell him yourself."

Startled, Elizabeth wheeled around to see a blur of a figure pass by the window. Colt?

There was a loud knock on the door. Grandpa didn't budge, so she rose. She reached around the red trunk, opened the door and peered out.

Colt stood there in full Mountie uniform.

She could barely breathe. With a broad Mountie Stetson angled across his darkly handsome face, his hair trimmed and his cheeks smooth from a recent shave, Colt peered down at her softly. There was an elegance in his stance, in the way his broad shoulders filled his scarlet uniform. Dark breeches clung to his legs, and tall brown boots came nearly to his knees. A holster diagonally crossed his chest, openly declaring he wore a gun and was unafraid to use it.

Caught up in so many different emotions, Elizabeth was entranced by the change in his appearance. He looked serious and dutiful. It brought back the wall that used to divide them in Vancouver. He was her father's bodyguard, she the minister's daughter.

"Hello, Elizabeth."

"Hello, Colt."

His warm gaze traveled across her face. "You dyed your hair back to your natural color."

Her hand shot nervously to her braided loop. "I had

difficulty finding the right tint. Belle Moon located it for me."

He nodded slowly, as if grasping everything she was saying and not saying. His eyes traveled to her new burgundy-colored blouse and sweeping black skirt.

She had an urge to explain. "The clothes I took on the trail are now as thin as rags."

"May I come in?"

Pressing her palm on the door slab, she opened it wide. "Oh, yes. Sorry. Yes, of course."

"I'm here on business." Colt nodded to her grandfather, who seemed to be fascinated at the communication going on between her and Colt.

She hoped her grandfather would bite his tongue, and that whatever he was thinking would go unspoken.

Her grandfather rose from his chair. "What is it?"

"If you have the time right now, sir, I'd like you to open the Land Claims Office for me. I'd like to take a look at the ledgers from last year. I'm interested in the documentation of Sebastian Langley's claim."

She knew her grandfather was already aware of the discrepancy of the claim, because her father had asked him to check into it.

"I'd like to go, too," she said.

Colt nodded. The night they'd shared, drenched in champagne, burned vivid in her mind.

Did he still feel it, too? The want.

"Elizabeth?" said her grandfather.

With a little jolt, she glanced to see him already standing at her side, dressed in a wool coat and hat.

She donned her sheepskin jacket—and her brown cowboy hat because she wasn't in the mood for a tight bonnet. She doubted she'd ever wear a bonnet again. Hats were more practical to shield the sun, and fan away the dust and flies.

The office was two streets over. Grandpa took out his set of keys and let them in.

An hour later, the three of them were still reading the ledgers. Elizabeth pulled out a rolled parchment from her satchel. She untied the ribbon and set it on the counter in front of Colt.

"The deed to your uncle's claim," he said. "You had it with you all this time."

"I also have Aunt Rose's letter of permission to give you." She removed the document and gave it to Colt, since he was the Mountie official.

Elizabeth studied the ledger, the columns of names and numbers. "It's all how Uncle Sebastian said it would be. His claim, five hundred feet wide by two thousand feet long, three hundred yards downstream from Bonanza Creek."

Grandpa was finding it difficult to believe. "They're still mining that claim. It's hauling in a lot of gold."

"I know."

"I can't believe my son, Sebastian, did this. When your father asked me to check into it, I found no proof."

Elizabeth explained. "Uncle Sebastian initially believed it was rightfully his. He told me he sampled the ground first, scraping the dirt to see if it had gold potential, before recording his claim. When he struck gold and raced here to record it, Mishenko was already in line arguing that it was his. Uncle Sebastian believed Mishenko had jumped the claim after watching him sample it. Later, when Mishenko died, Uncle Sebastian found a post dated with Mishenko's name, buried in the dirt. He'd been telling the truth. But he was dead, so Uncle Sebastian kept his mouth shut."

"From what I hear," said Colt, "claim disputes are common."

"Happens all the time," said Grandpa. "Mishenko's word against his. I remember the commotion. And I believed my son."

"You can still believe in him. He wants to make this right. He wants the claim to go to Mishenko's widow."

Colt removed a sheet of paper with a list of names. "Mr. Langley, would you mind pointing out these other claims?"

"What's that?" asked Elizabeth.

"The superintendent took me on a tour of the area yesterday. He pointed out some of the miners who've struck it rich. I'd like to see how their claims were recorded."

"Sure," said Grandpa. "Let's see what you've got there."

Elizabeth glanced at the list but the names meant nothing to her. Webster McGraw, Al Billins, Slade Turner, Wilhelm Schpiel, Norton Dunn, Clay Hewett, Pierce Rawlins, Jack Lake, Micki Horton…

"No women on this list?"

"They're irrelevant for what I'm checking."

After an hour, they found most of the names. "I'll have to come back when I have more time." Colt nudged Elizabeth. "Let's go talk to Vira Mishenko before she goes to bed."

"You've seen her?" asked Elizabeth.

He nodded. "She's staying at the hotel. I told Tommy and two men from the outpost to join us at ten. In case she's got something to do with Reverend Yates, we'll need extra guns."

"Yates? Who's Yates?" asked Grandpa.

Elizabeth tucked the deed back into her satchel, next to her pistol. "The man who stole the sausages."

Grandpa rubbed the back of his wrinkled neck. "I'm confused."

Colt marched to the door and said his thanks. "We'll explain it when we get back."

Elizabeth gave her grandfather a kiss on the cheek. With a hand to her trembling stomach, she left with Colt. After five long weeks of arguing about who was responsible for the death of Ivan Mishenko, Elizabeth was about to face his widow and find out.

Chapter Nineteen

With jittery nerves, Elizabeth strode beside Colt along the boardwalk. Tommy and two other Mounties marched behind them. In the cool evening breeze, with the sun slanting against the rooftops, her skirts rustled against Colt's boots. Black skirt against black breeches.

Elizabeth tilted her gaze past his broad red sleeve to his firmly set face. She had lots to tell him about Gerard and her new decisions, but that could all wait for the more critical matters they had to deal with.

"Have you discovered anything more about Yates?" she asked.

Colt maneuvered her past a young couple and their toddler as they were opening a restaurant door to enter. It was wonderful to see a child, thought Elizabeth. There were so few of them here.

"I can't quite pin it down." Colt angled his chest to squeeze behind her as she slid through a crowd gathered at the bank. "What do a reporter and a playwright have in common?"

She thought about it. "I don't know. What?"

"That's what I'm trying to figure out. Those are two of the identities Yates has used."

"You think that's the missing puzzle piece? A connection between those two phony jobs?"

"Might be. Also, did you notice when he speaks, he enunciates every word?"

"I thought it unusual, too."

"He's careful about words. That's why I think if we figure out what these two professions have in common…"

"Your idea's far-fetched."

"Maybe."

"A playwright and a reporter. They have words in common. That's what."

"Exactly. Words. That's what I keep telling myself. Words." He touched her hand and they crossed the street. "But where does that get us?"

"No place I can see."

Pushing their way past the crowd of men at the hotel doors, they entered, bounded up the stairs and knocked on suite number three. Colt signaled for the three other Mounties to wait at the end of the hall.

Frank opened up. At the sight of Colt standing there in police uniform, flanked by Elizabeth with her new hair color and clean clothes, Frank seemed taken aback. He lifted his eyebrows and glanced into the room at his sister, Vira, seated on a chair by the bed.

The six Seattle railway workers who'd been traveling with them were seated around a table playing poker and drinking whiskey.

Vira, looking stunned, stood up and came to the door. She peered down at Colt's uniform.

"What's this?"

"I'm a member of the Mounted Police." Colt removed his hat.

She swallowed nervously and looked to Elizabeth. "Something we did wrong?"

Elizabeth toyed with the strap on her satchel. "We've come to ask you some questions, Vira."

Vira glanced up at Elizabeth's golden hair, and Elizabeth felt the heat of embarrassment at having lied to this woman for so long. They had a friendship, thought Elizabeth, based on lies.

"First, we should tell you we're not brother and sister. And I'm not a midwife but a doctor."

Stunned, Frank looked at Vira, as if deciding what to do. After a long moment, he nodded at them. "Come into the parlor. Want a drink?"

"No, thanks." Colt stepped in and nodded to the poker players. The men froze in surprise and speechlessly watched them until they'd stepped into the side room.

After they were seated on firm chairs, Colt planted his boots on the carpet and leaned forward. "We were part of a team of Mounties traveling from Vancouver. We're after a group of men who've been robbing people blind on the trail. Reverend Yates, remember?"

Vira inhaled sharply. Her eyes flew to her brother.

"Yes, go on."

Colt took ten minutes to explain the situation. Elizabeth was grateful to have him seated next to her, speaking so calmly when she couldn't stop fiddling from her bout of nerves.

After taking it in, Frank settled back into his chair. Vira

turned pale. She took a hankie from her sleeve and rubbed her nose.

"I believe you know Reverend Yates," Colt said to her.

Vira sniffed. "I've never met the reverend."

"It's odd how the two of you took off as soon as you saw him."

Vira shuffled on the seat and looked at the floor. Her brother poured himself a whiskey from the bottle behind him.

"Vira," said Elizabeth softly. "I'm sorry that I deceived you. I didn't know I'd be meeting you on the trail."

"What do you mean, meeting me?"

"Sebastian Langley was my uncle."

Vira let out a soft gasp.

Frank lowered his whiskey. "The man who robbed her husband."

"That…that might be true. We just came from the Land Claims Office, and that might be true. The gold claim might belong to you."

A look of confusion came over Vira.

"But before any of this is settled, we need to know how you're connected to Reverend Yates."

Vira began to weep. "I've never met him. But I have seen that man who was with him. The big one with the mean eyes."

"Jones?"

"I don't know his name. When Ivan lost the claim, he couldn't find work to support us. He turned to the reverend for work."

"Your husband was part of the crime ring?"

"I didn't know it at first. When I found out what he was doing in order to make ends meet, I begged Ivan to leave them. But that…that animal who accompanies the reverend…he's the one my husband fought with in the hotel that night."

"About what?"

"Ivan told me he was going to meet with a man who was part of the gang. My husband described Jones to me. Ivan said he was going to tell him he no longer wanted to be part of them." Vira pressed her hankie to her nose. "I guess Jones went mad. He pummeled Ivan to death."

With mounting tension, Colt and Tommy walked Elizabeth home. Vira's disclosure had been unbelievable. But it made sense, thought Colt. She couldn't disclose the truth last year to investigators because her husband had been involved with criminals. It was her brother, Frank, who'd convinced her to return to Dawson City and seek help. Vira herself hadn't done anything wrong, and she deserved to see justice.

"Elizabeth," said Colt, "if you were rich, how would you spend your money?"

She strode briskly beside him. She was still pale, shaken up by the meeting with Vira. "What sort of question is that?"

"Would you become reclusive?"

"Maybe. If folks bothered me enough."

"Would you become flamboyant?"

"No."

"You're not that kind of person, though."

"Lots of people react in different ways to many different things. What are you getting at?"

"What kind of person Yates might be, since he's rich."

"Oh."

They reached Elizabeth's cabin. She slid the key from her satchel and opened the door. When Colt noticed the red trunk inside, something hammered inside his brain.

He laughed softly. "That's it."

She pulled in her shoulders, slender and beautiful in the fading sunlight. Trees whispered on the other side of them. Grasses growing below the front porch rustled in the wind.

"What's *it?*"

Colt touched the broad brim of his Mountie Stetson and nodded toward her door. "Your trunk." His voice raced, his breathing pounded. "Do you remember when we disembarked from the ship at Skagway?"

"Yes."

"Do you remember all the different packages that were loaded for mail delivery on top of your trunk?"

She frowned. "Two hatboxes. A banjo. And…"

"And a dictionary. Remember? Two full volumes of the English Dictionary."

She tilted her face in the light. Shadows dipped around her eyelashes. She smiled in sudden amazement. "Words."

"Exactly. What a reporter and a playwright have in common. Yates is well-read and well educated. That dictionary was ordered by him. I'm sure of it."

"So if you find the dictionary—"

"The package has his name printed right on it. Yates's real name."

"Or someone who holds mail for him."

"Yes. And an address."

The thrill of discovery drummed through him. Elizabeth, flushed and radiant, kept smiling.

"Stay here with your grandfather," he ordered, falling

into full command mode. "We've got to find the mail carriers. And wait for me, Elizabeth. Wait for me."

Elizabeth had settled into bed, exhausted from the day, but still excited at Colt's breakthrough, when she heard the knock on the door. She heard her grandfather roll out of his bed in the parlor. He unbolted the door, but she didn't hear anything more.

"Grandpa?" she called.

Footsteps sounded on the floor planks. Elizabeth sprang out of bed, slid her robe off the hook and dashed into the parlor. "Grandpa, is it Colt?" she asked eagerly. Her bathrobe flew behind her as she raced out on tiptoes. Did he find the address?"

"Good evening," said Yates, holding a gun.

Her blood turned cold. Her bare feet stuck to the cool floor.

The man was huge. He was clean shaven this time. Short dark hair. Still had an ugly face and ugly grin.

Trying to remain calm, drawing on her medical training, she glanced behind him. Grandpa was lying on the sofa, limp, eyes closed. Frantic, she started to race to his side.

Yates shoved the barrel of his gun into her ribs.

She froze.

"Don't worry about him. Pack your clothes."

"Why?"

He sniffed through his nose. "We saw you going in to visit Vira Mishenko."

"So?" Elizabeth's heart squeezed up to her throat. Grandpa was breathing. Thank the Lord. She watched the gentle rise and fall of his chest. They'd hit him over the head and knocked him out. She grasped for an explanation he might fall for. "I know Vira from the trip. She…she wanted to share a recipe."

Yates cocked the trigger. "Do you think I'm stupid?"

Fear rumbled through her, the likes of which she'd never felt before. Fear for herself and grandpa, but also fear for Colt. Where was he? Had some harm come to him? She winced at the thought, then hesitated, not knowing what to do.

Yates laughed softly, without humor. "It seems I outsmarted your *brother,* anyway. When he discovers you're missing, Sergeant Colton Hunter will know who got the best of him."

An hour later, anger raged through Colt. The bastard had taken her.

Helping her grandfather sit up, Colt extracted as much information from the old man as he could, but there was nothing more he could piece together. *Stay calm,* Cold told himself. *Stay calm for the sake of Elizabeth.*

Pierce Rawlins had already cleared out his cabin. His men were gone. As were most of his food supplies, clothes and ammunition, and most of his books. He was gone for good and didn't plan on coming back.

Where the hell had he taken Elizabeth? Colt no longer cared about the criminal gang. He didn't care about apricots or sausages or gold claims. He cared solely about Elizabeth, a kind-hearted doctor trapped in the middle of something he'd started.

Colt ordered another constable to sit with Langley while he talked it over with Tommy outside. The other Mounties—the four brothers who'd traveled with him on the journey—were still on their mission somewhere in the wilderness, trying to track Rawlins within a fifty-mile radius. They'd been gone for days.

"Rawlins has to be here someplace," Colt said to Tommy. The breeze rustled at the sleeve of his uniform. His neck grew chilled. "They can't get far without horses. They've got a few between them, but not many." He strode back and forth from willow trees to aspens, willing himself to figure this out. Then the idea struck. "The river."

"But which way?" called Tommy, also in uniform, splaying a hand on his holster. "Which river?"

"Follow me." Colt raced to the horses, directing the other Mounties he'd brought with him. "The rivers are the fastest passageways out of the Yukon. We'll ride to the junction of the Klondike and Yukon Rivers." Two dozen Mounties dressed in full scarlet uniform thundered behind Colt, all the horsepower and manpower they could muster in the middle of the night. He prayed Elizabeth would still be with Rawlins if—when—they found him.

Blue twilight glinted above the trees. The muscles of his mare strained beneath Colt's thighs as he pressed forward. He couldn't lose Elizabeth. He couldn't live without her.

They raced out of town, over the hills, through the dips of the valley, beyond the slopes of Bonanza Creek, site of the richest veins of the Klondike.

The slopes, once filled with gold, sat in ruins as they galloped through. Most of the hills had been hacked and gutted from men clawing through them, looking for riches. Wooden sluice boxes coiled through the landscape. Hundreds of tents filled with sleeping miners dotted the hills. Some men came out when they heard the hooves pounding, many of them sleeping in the same dirty clothes in which they worked. Gravel beds of the Klondike, that yielded nuggets the size of fists, whizzed past Colt and his men. Colt was racing toward the bigger river, the one that roared from here to Skagway to the ships and to freedom.

Breathless, they stopped one hundred yards away from the juncture of the Yukon River to avoid being heard. Colt dismounted, signaling his men to do the same. He had yet to see anything suspicious.

It was three in the morning, and the forest was lit in an eerie midnight blue. Maybe Colt was wrong. Maybe there was nobody here. He turned his cheek to the cool wind and listened to the night birds call. He smelled the dew on the grass and the moss growing near the banks of the Yukon.

And then the sizzle of a burning fire. His pulse sped. A campfire.

Creeping closer to the river's edge, he spotted the damned faces. Rawlins bent over poking at the fire with a stick, his beast of a sidekick, Jefferson, smoking beside him. When Colt saw Elizabeth dressed in her nightrobe leaning against a log, he moaned.

A twig snapped above Colt. A blasted bird. He froze. Jefferson looked up from the campfire into the forest. Elizabeth reached for her satchel.

"Hey," Colt heard Jefferson say to her. "What are you doing?"

"I'm cold," she said.

Rawlins, heavyset and clean shaven, removed his coat. "Here, take this."

She hesitated, then took it from him and placed it over her shoulders, concealing most of her upper body.

Hold on, Elizabeth, thought Colt. *Keep warm, conserve your strength and hold on just a minute longer.*

Along the river's edge, Rawlins's men were loading the scows. There were roughly two dozen criminals to overtake. But they had an equal number of Mounties.

Colt took his time watching while masked by the forest. Barely breathing, he took another step closer to the fire.

When he saw Tommy across the way, five yards from Rawlins, Colt gave the signal. His dropped his arm and his men moved.

Guns drawn, Colt lunged for Jefferson. Tommy lunged for Rawlins. Neither man could shoot for fear of hitting Elizabeth.

Elizabeth screamed. She jumped flat to the ground, out of the way. Criminals raced from the river to help their boss. Mounties swarmed the scows. Guns fired.

Colt got in a good punch to Jefferson's jaw, but another man tackled him from behind, allowing Jefferson to smash Colt's face with his fist.

His jaw crunched. Then Colt heard a gunshot. Jefferson clutched his shoulder and fell to the ground.

Colt whirled to look at Elizabeth. With her nightrobe strewn about her bare legs, she held her pistol firmly anchored above her knees.

"Good shot," Colt told her. She looked tired and scared, swollen circles beneath her eyes. He wanted to hold her, but Tommy and another Mountie beat him there, coming to her aid. Her eyes were riveted on Colt and for a split second, they silently said hello in this soft manner.

Then Colt, gripping his revolver, chased after Rawlins.

As heavy as he was, Rawlins leaped to a scow. Colt ran as hard and fast as he could, the wind whipping at his ears as he raced one hundred feet through the bush. He leaped to the raft with all his might. He made it, and bounced onto Rawlins's scow. The raft rocked beneath their boots. Both men balanced their weight, shifting to face each other.

Rawlins had dropped his gun on the hurdle, and now Colt faced him squarely, panting in the wind. Small sacks of what looked like gold dust scattered at Rawlins's feet. Gold glittered in the moonlight.

"You're a failure, Rawlins."

"My men are going to kill you. Shoot him!" he hollered into the blueish-black sky.

His hollow voice echoed off the trees lining the river.

"There's no one there. Look around."

Pale and breathless, Rawlins slowly turned his broad head to scan the shore.

The dozens of Mounties had apprehended his men. Handcuffs were pulled out, wrists snapped tight, wounded men taken into custody.

"You're on your own, Rawlins."

Rawlins dived for the gold dust. He grabbed a handful and threw it into Colt's eyes. Colt teared up at the stinging pain. Temporarily blinded, he blinked and stumbled backward.

Rawlins tried to escape and jumped for the river, but as his face hit the water, Colt slammed a leg on top of the man's hips and stopped him. Sliding his handcuffs from his shoulder harness, Colt shackled the man's wrists.

Colt blew out a big breath of exhilaration. He wiped the gold dust from his eyes with the sleeve of his uniform.

"You're under arrest, Rawlins. For murder, attempted murder, kidnapping and armed robbery."

With a heave, Colt dragged him fully back onto the scow, flat on his face. Colt rolled Rawlins over to look at him. Scattered gold dust poured into a small pile beside his head and water that splashed on board carried it away through the cracks between the logs. Thousands of dollars sinking to the bottom of the Yukon, gold he'd made from selling stolen goods.

"You fooled a lot of people, pretending you were a recluse because you struck it rich. But I couldn't find your name in the Land Claims Office. You had a lot of money from the robberies, and you explained it away by saying you'd struck gold. Worked for a long time."

With a scowl, Rawlins spit beside Colt's boot. His hair was encrusted with wet gold dust.

"For a man who loves words, you're not using many," said Colt.

"I'll hire the best lawyers."

"You can hire anyone you want. You're still going to prison."

Chapter Twenty

Hours later, Elizabeth still felt as though an arrow had pierced her heart. She'd almost lost her grandfather, and she'd almost lost Colt.

With a sigh, she removed the hairbrush from her overnight bag and placed it on the hotel's bedside table. She unpacked her blouse and skirt and tucked them neatly on top of her red trunk. She'd need her clothes for her temporary stay at the hotel. Grandpa was in the hospital, recovering from a concussion, and she didn't feel safe staying in his cabin alone.

Colt was still finishing with Rawlins at the NWMP post, trying to extract more information. While hugging her quickly on the shoreline Colt had told her that he'd find her as soon as he could, for he had plenty to say.

She had so much to say to him, too. How could she thank the man for helping her find her strength?

Mounties from the outpost had delivered her here to the hotel, but there was no sign of Colt. No sign of Tommy or Anderson, Buxton, Will or Eddie, either. Those weren't even their real names, yet she had to hear their rightful names through rumor, as everyone else in Dawson had. She'd also heard that her brothers had left on a small mission to capture the rest of the Pierce Rawlins gang.

Now that Colt's duties were done, and all loose ends tied up, he was supposed to head back to Vancouver. Without her.

"Godspeed," she whispered to herself.

Someone knocked on the door.

"Who is it?"

"Special delivery, ma'am."

It wasn't Colt's voice. She pressed her face to the door. "What is it?"

The man behind the door panted. "It's mighty…heavy…please…open."

"Not until you say who you are and what it is."

"Ma'am…it's a bathtub…"

Champagne Charlie!

With a whirl, Elizabeth opened the door. The white porcelain tub gleamed in the lamplight. It was carried by two of Charlie's men she recognized from the trip.

"Come in, come in."

Slim poked his head around the door. "Charlie woke up an hour ago. He's gonna be all right. He wanted to make sure you got this."

"But I'll only be staying a few days here. It might be best to deliver it to my Grandpa's cabin."

"You know Charlie. He wants you to have use out of it now. We'll come back to move it whenever you like."

She smiled. "Then please, put it right over here by the fire."

* * *

Elizabeth finished bathing and stepped out of the fancy tub. Steam clung to the air. Wrapped in a towel, standing by the crackling fireplace, she unhitched the lid on her red leather trunk. Standing over it, she gave the top shelf, loaded with gauze and bottles, a good yank. When it came loose, she placed it on the floor beside the armoire. She did the same with the drawer beneath, until finally she spotted what she was looking for at the bottom of the trunk.

Fresh new clothing.

It was time for a new start in this wild new town.

Pulling out the cream silk dress, her Sunday best, she was startled by a knock on the door. Who could that be? Champagne Charlie himself?

She rose and pressed her face to the pine. "Yes?"

"It's me, Elizabeth."

Colt.

The sound of his voice made her insides rumble. She was thrilled, but… "I'm not decent."

"Good. Neither am I."

"I mean…I'm not…you know what I mean. Could you please come back a little later?"

"Open up before I kick this door in."

"Don't be so foolish."

"Step away from the door."

"Come on, now, Colt, let's be civilized. Come back in an hour or—"

The door rattled with a blow.

She yelped and stepped aside.

He gave it another kick and she, livid that he was ruining her door, slid to the latch and unlocked it.

"Are you crazy?" She clung to the towel that threatened to slide down her body.

"Crazy and miserable."

She took in the full view of him. He was dressed in the rugged jeans she'd come to know so well on their journey. She'd returned his blue shirt and he was wearing it now, pressed neatly, the collar crisp against his throat, the sleeves ironed at the corner of his shoulders.

"Miserable, huh?" She peered at his body with fresh concern. "You must be bruised from the fight. Your fist? Your leg?"

"My heart," he said softly.

Her own trembled at the words.

"Listen, Colt, there's something you've got to know. I'm not going back to Vancouver. I'm not going back to my father's. I'm not going back to the life I used to lead. The Klondike speaks to me, and I'm staying here for a while."

"It speaks to you?" A smile ruffled his lips. "Speaks to you?" He laughed. "How poetic." And then he marched in as though he'd rented the place.

Glancing at the tub and fireplace, he wheeled around. Lord, he filled the space as no one else could. "I know why my father did it."

"Did what?"

"Chased the gold. Chased the silver."

"Why?"

"It wasn't the gold or the silver. He did it for the journey. For the adventure. That's what filled him. That's what filled *me* on this trip."

So he'd felt it, as well.

"Champagne Charlie came to."

"So I heard."

Colt turned toward the water. His guns were slung low on his hips. His dark gaze lingered on the tub. "Yeah, I guess you have."

"What can I do for you, Colt?" She clutched her towel. Heat from the fire reached her bare arms. Her hair, still damp and heavy from her bath, clung to her shoulder blades. Her calves, rubbed raw from scrubbing so hard with soap, tingled.

His smoky gray eyes worked their way up her body. He took in her bare legs, the cotton towel, her bare shoulders, long loose hair nearly dipping to her waist. He studied her throat, then the gentle fingers that held up her towel.

When he spoke, firelight skimmed his throat. "What can you do for me? Let's see now…"

She swallowed at the handsome turn of his cheek. But she wouldn't be coaxed into anything she didn't want—

"I stopped by the hospital to check on your grandfather. He's fine," he added immediately to her look of concern. "I also saw an envelope in the waste bin by Gerard's desk."

She slid a hand down her arm, wondering what he was getting at.

"You gave him the letter," said Colt.

She gasped softly, insulted. "Gerard threw it in the garbage? How could he be so cal—"

With a mischievous set to his lips, Colt stepped closer and yanked at the bottom of her towel.

Appalled at his forwardness, she ran behind the tub. "How dare you."

He followed her and she sprinted around the other side.

"Don't come any closer. If you think all you have to do is yank at my clothing and I'll come running—"

He laughed. Then with a lunge, he gave the bottom of her towel another yank. She saw it coming and with an exclamation of alarm, used both hands and gave him a hard shove.

Her towel dropped to the floor at the same time Colt fell back into the water. Both events caused his eyes to open wide.

Colt was soaked. Elizabeth laughed. It started at the back of her throat and worked its way louder. He was quite the picture sitting in the tub, cowboy boots dry and dangling over the edge, thighs and crotch and shirt plastered to his wet skin.

With a laugh, he turned and eased his body into the water, making himself comfortable. He kept his boots up on the rim. "I hope you're not going to charge me five thousand dollars for this."

Still naked and liking the feel of it, Elizabeth sat on the bed and kept laughing.

His eyes roved over her, settling on her breasts. "This is the second time in my life that I've been fully clothed and you've been fully naked."

She sprawled out on the bed, lying flat on her belly, as dry and warm and bare as she was at birth. Her face was buried in the soft blanket and she smiled. She peeked out at him from the corner of her eye.

His gaze followed the trail of her golden skin, over her behind and legs.

"Elizabeth Langley, I've been in love with you ever since I can remember."

Warmth seeped into her, as gentle and soft as feathers on a chick. *"Oh..."*

"I believe that's why I was never able to say your name. Once I said it, I knew I'd have to make you mine."

Overcome with feeling, Elizabeth pulled in a short breath. The shades were drawn and firelight danced across the ceiling. She listened to the sound of the coals hissing behind Colt. His cheeks, mottled red from the fire, dimpled as he watched her. Strands of black hair fell across his forehead.

"The Klondike needs Mounties," he said. "I'm thinking of staying."

"What about being bodyguard to my father?"

"Tommy's going back. He's filled in for me before. He'd like the full-time responsibility. He can handle it."

She rose slowly and pulled out a white lace stocking from her pile of fresh clothing.

"Yes, I believe he can."

"What are you doing?" he murmured.

"I'm getting dressed for dinner."

He watched her, reveling in the sight of her nakedness. She pulled the white lace up to her right thigh, and reached for the other silk stocking.

Silk on her legs, smooth and warm, was something she hadn't experienced in weeks.

Her bare breasts dangled over her as she pulled on the silk. Colt didn't take his eyes off her. Just looking at the desire in his eyes made her stomach quiver and her heart pound. It was wonderful to hear him say these lovely things. She didn't want the moment to end.

She anchored her corset around her waist, tugging the

small straps over her shoulders and pulling on the stays at her bosom.

Next came the arm-length cream silk gloves. They were truly extravagant and reached to her underarms. The final treasure was her spiked leather shoes. Brown leather straps so dainty, she'd ruin them in a day on the trail. But these weren't meant for the trail. These shoes were made for lovemaking.

When he had a good view of her, speechless now, the glint of animal instinct in his eyes, Elizabeth went to him. She held out her hand and he took it. Rising from the tub, he stepped onto a mat, dripping wet. She slipped into his arms.

The kiss was gentle and warm. Then their hunger got the best of them and the kisses turned feverish.

Breaking away, she needed to say a few things to him, too, while she could still think straight.

"You're the first man to show respect for me as a doctor."

"It took a long time, though, didn't it?"

She smiled, naked, resting on his wet hip. "It did, you brute."

Then she grew serious. "But because of your lead, others have followed. Champagne Charlie listened to your opinion when you told him I had magic hands. Buxton allowed me to take care of his lump. Even Grandpa...notices something about the way you honor me."

Colt grazed his long fingers down her arm. "I've loved you forever, Elizabeth. I'd like you to be my bride. I'd like to stay in Dawson with you. I'd like to raise a family, if that's what you want."

Filling with bliss, she moaned and kissed his throat.

His beautiful wet throat. She'd held her tears in check. "I think I've always loved the dark and silent Mountie at my father's side."

When Elizabeth had packed her cream silk gown in Vancouver, storing it beneath the medical supplies of a forbidden red trunk, she had no idea she'd be using it in the Klondike. As a wedding gown.

Now, as she pulled the soft, rustling fabric over her head in her grandfather's cabin, she turned so that Milly Thornbottom could do up the dozen buttons at the back.

Mrs. Thornbottom clasped her hands together and beamed at Elizabeth. "You look so beautiful!"

Elizabeth smiled at the woman's robust expression. She felt beautiful, and couldn't wait to see Colt.

"I can't believe you're a doctor! And I can't believe you're not Colt's sister!"

Elizabeth joined in the women's laughter.

A week had passed since they'd arrested Rawlins and Jefferson. The wounded one had a broken arm from her bullet, but he was healing nicely, chained to the hospital bed. As soon as he recovered, he'd join his good friend Rawlins behind bars, where they'd spend a couple of decades.

Her beloved Mountie "brothers," she'd heard from her grandfather, had arrived back in town late last night. They'd captured eighty-eight men in their raids. Rawlins's gang had fully infiltrated the Klondike and his captive had been stunning. Colt would likely get promoted.

The Thornbottoms had arrived two days ago, along with Dr. Wellsley. Elizabeth hadn't seen Donovan yet, but she'd likely bump into him at the hospital. Gerard hadn't taken the news of her wedding very well, but in time, this, too, would pass. Vira Mishenko had been thrilled to receive the deed for her gold claim. She'd told Elizabeth she wanted to become a schoolteacher. The Klondike was in dire need of teachers.

Elizabeth placed the sprig of wild roses in her hair, lingering over the wonderful scent. She adjusted her beautiful lace train—which Belle Moon had provided—and packed her pistol in her satchel.

"Ready."

When Elizabeth walked out of the cabin to join her grandpa and make their way to the chapel, he took a good long look at her. The old man's eyes welled with tears. He said nothing, which was his nature, but he held his arm out for her now—he had asked to walk her down the aisle.

And that said everything.

Saint and Eve bounded up the grass ahead of them.

Milly, the only bridesmaid, walked alongside her mother and father. The Thornbottoms from Montana.

Tommy would be the only groomsman. The other Mounties had just made it back from nabbing Rawlins's gang.

The chapel sat nestled on a hilly slope. A field of green surrounded the one-room log cabin with hues so rich it hurt the eyes to look. Jade grasses, turquoise rivers, dark forest pine. A field of violet fireweed added color, as did the prickly rose growing at the chapel doors.

The building was tiny, but it was clean, the wood pews varnished with care, and the altar filled with the scent of wild grasses and flowers that the townswomen had swept it with this morning.

Sixty men and fourteen women turned their heads

when Milly walked down the aisle. Elizabeth followed proudly on her grandpa's sleeve, to join her groom.

"Hello," Colt mouthed softly. Dressed in a newly pressed red uniform, he stood at attention and placed his hand over hers as she took his elbow.

She nearly burst with emotion.

Tommy, also in uniform, stood tall beside his friend.

The town was lucky to have a minister. Elizabeth wondered how he got here, being so old and the town so new. Had he shot those rapids, too? Bent over with age, with seventy-odd years of wisdom, Reverend Murphy kept the ceremony short and lively.

Happiness filled her as she and Colt were whisked to the dance hall for the reception.

After the meal was eaten, the toasts were said and the dancing started, Elizabeth and Colt had a moment alone.

Colt leaned his dark head next to hers. She inhaled, never able to get enough of the scent of him.

"Would you like to say hello to your brothers?" Colt was teasing, and she smiled back.

"I'd like to thank them for what they did."

He brought her over to the Mountie table and she sat across from Tommy, Buxton, Anderson, Will and Eddie. They were all in uniform, clean-shaven, handsome men who would always tug at her heart.

"You look good without your beard, Anderson."

Anderson, sandy brown hair trimmed around his ears, grinned and held out his hand. "Don't tempt me, Elizabeth. You're already spoken for."

She smiled, putting her hand in his, then pulling him into a hug.

"The name's Dylan Wayburn," he said. "From Edmonton. Pleased to meet you."

Tears sprang to her eyes. "Hi, Dylan."

She moved on to the auburn-haired cooks. Gone were the muttonchop whiskers and beards. The tall one, as tall as a giraffe, whom she'd known as Will, wrapped his arms around her.

"John MacGyver. My brother Travis."

Not Will and Eddie, but John and Travis.

"Where you from?" she asked.

"Originally, the east coast. Nova Scotia. We're stationed in Regina. Both married."

She stepped back in surprise. "Married?"

"With children," said Colt. "Two kids apiece."

"I've got sons," said John. He pointed to his brother. "He's got daughters."

"How wonderful. Your wives must miss you horribly."

They nodded. "We're headed back tomorrow."

Tomorrow? Already? Lord, they were strong men. Elizabeth would be sorry to see them go. Tommy was next. She kissed him on the cheek. "You'll take good care of my father, won't you?"

"Yes, ma'am."

"And you'll take a letter back for me?"

"Of course."

The final man in line, standing beside Colt, was Buxton. With a quivering sigh, she extended her hand and he shook it. The scar beneath his left eye tugged as he gave her the closest thing to a smile she'd seen yet.

"My brother, Luke," said Colt. "Buxton is his middle name."

Elizabeth placed a hand on her stomach and inhaled.

"Is it true, Luke, what Colt has told me? You two truly are brothers?"

"Yes, ma'am," said Luke. "I'm three years older."

She stared in awe and disbelief at the dark features, the powerful stances of both men. Colt raised his eyebrow. "Were we good? Did we fool you?"

She laughed softly. "That's why Luke got away with talking to you the way he did."

Now that she thought back, Colt *had* referred to Buxton as his brother on occasion, but she thought it had been part of the plan.

She'd met such wonderful men on this journey. She'd never forget her brothers, blood or no.

Colt ran his hand through the hair at his temple. "He's the older brother I told you about. Who knocked the sense into me and Tommy when we were younger."

"Ah, I see." When they were petty thieves.

"Luke's a veterinary surgeon."

Elizabeth's gown swirled about her thighs. Her corset dug into her ribs.

The surprises never ended. "What do you mean?"

"I trained in Toronto," said Luke. "To care for animals."

Elizabeth stared from one brother to the other. They had the same dark pigment in their skin, the same intense eyebrows, the same dark hair. Luke's jagged scar concealed the similarities. The scar had thrown her. Plus the shaggy hair Luke had grown that was now trimmed.

"That's why you were always interested in the horses," she said. "And the dogs. And the mule."

Colt laughed. The accordion players began just then, and Colt pulled her away from his men.

"Are any of you staying here?" she called over her shoulder. "In the Klondike?"

Buxton and Anderson—or should she say *Luke and Dylan*—nodded. She'd have at least two friends, then. Brothers to her, always.

Colt pulled her to the dance floor. A guitar and a piano added to the sounds of the orchestra. He pressed his head to hers and ran his warm hands up the back of her silk gown.

"Do you know how long I've dreamed of this?"

"Couldn't have been more than five weeks."

He smiled. "Longer."

She understood what Colt was trying to say. That their hearts were woven together, that their paths had always crossed, that they were meant to be wedded.

She looked around at the amazing choices she'd been given. She wouldn't miss the luxuries of an old life that was never hers.

"I want to thank you, Colt."

He cupped his hand at the back of her waist. "Why?"

"Folks have been showing up at the hospital all week. Men. Asking for me. They come in with broken fingers. Lacerations. Medical problems that might need surgery."

"All I do is recommend the best doctor I know."

"I love you," she whispered.

He brushed his lips on hers and she knew they'd have an exciting night ahead of them. They'd take their time. They'd make love the entire week he'd booked them at the hotel. Fireplace, bathtubs, clean sheets and candles.

Then, they'd build their own cabin in Dawson.

She was lost in the circle of his arms and the gentle beat of the music when Colt pulled away slightly. He looked beyond her shoulders and nodded to someone.

Elizabeth lifted the side of her wedding gown, turned to see who it was and smiled at the unexpected guest seated at the table nearby.

"Champagne Charlie," she whispered. "How do you do?"

She slid to his side and sat down. Colt sat beside her, holding her hand.

"Much better." Charlie tipped his yellow sombrero. His face was full of color and vigor. His crutches were propped beside him. Slim was at the door. "I wanted to say thank you in person, before the two of you disappeared."

"You're most welcome, Charlie. I'm glad to see you on your feet."

"Is there anything I can do for you?"

She smiled and shook her head. "You've done enough. Nothing more. Please."

Charlie tipped back on his chair and shook his head at Colt. "I never met anyone who wanted nothing." He winked. "I *knew* you weren't brother and sister."

Colt grinned. Charlie got up on his crutches and joined his friends at the door.

Colt looped his arm around her waist. "Well, Mrs. Hunter—"

"Doctor Hunter," she corrected.

He kissed her cheek, and a flush of excitement danced up her spine. "Let's stay in the Yukon, then, and see where the wind blows us, Doctor Hunter."

* * * * *

Author's Note

The height of the Klondike Gold Rush occurred between the years of 1897-1899. For Americans and Canadians, the Yukon was one of the last frontiers.

The border between Alaska and Yukon Territory had never been clearly defined. It came into dispute between the Americans and Canadians when the massive goldstrike was discovered in Canada along the Klondike River close to Dawson City. The dispute was settled peacefully, and the border was defined and guarded at the top of the mountain peaks by the North-West Mounted Police.

I had the privilege of traveling to the Yukon and Alaska to research this book, to savor the wild beauty, touch the ice-cold rivers, and inhale pure, fresh air. I was stunned by the jagged terrain and rough waters the stampeders had to cross to get from Alaska to the Yukon, and tried to capture some of that difficulty in this novel. Only one of every three stampeders who set out for the Yukon made it. Many of these hardy people were eccentric characters. I hope you enjoy Klondike Doctor, the first novel in my new series about the Klondike Gold Rush. To see photographs of the area, please visit my website at www.katebridges.com.

Mediterranean Nights

Join the guests and crew of Alexandra's Dream,
*the newest luxury ship to set sail on the
romantic Mediterranean, as they experience
the glamorous world of cruising.*

*A new Harlequin continuity series
begins in June 2007 with
FROM RUSSIA, WITH LOVE
by Ingrid Weaver*

*Marina Artamova books a cabin on the luxurious
cruise ship* Alexandra's Dream, *when she finds
out that her orphaned nephew and his adoptive
father are aboard. She's determined to be reunited
with the boy…but the romantic ambience of the ship
and her undeniable attraction to a man she considers
her enemy are about to interfere with her quest!*

Turn the page for a sneak preview!

Piraeus, Greece

"THERE SHE IS, Stefan. *Alexandra's Dream*." David Anderson squatted beside his new son and pointed at the dark blue hull that towered above the pier. The cruise ship was a majestic sight, twelve decks high and as long as a city block. A circle of silver and gold stars, the logo of the Liberty Cruise Line, gleamed from the swept-back smokestack. Like some legendary sea creature born for the water, the ship emanated power from every sleek curve—even at rest it held the promise of motion. "That's going to be our home for the next ten days."

The child beside him remained silent, his cheeks working in and out as he sucked furiously on his thumb. Hair so blond it appeared white ruffled against his forehead in the harbor breeze. The baby-sweet scent unique to the very young mingled with the tang of the sea.

"Ship," David said. "Uh, *parakhod*."

From beneath his bangs, Stefan looked at the *Alexandra's Dream*. Although he didn't release his thumb, the corners of his mouth tightened with the beginning of a smile.

David grinned. That was Stefan's first smile this afternoon, one of only two since they had left the orphanage yesterday. It was probably because of the boat—according to the orphanage staff, the boy loved boats, which was the main reason David had decided to book this cruise. Then again, there was a strong possibility the smile could have been a reaction to David's attempt at pocket-dictionary Russian. Whatever the cause, it was a good start.

The liaison from the adoption agency had claimed that Stefan had been taught some English, but David had yet to see evidence of it. David continued to speak, positive his son would understand his tone even if he couldn't grasp the words. "This is her maiden voyage. Her first trip, just like this is our first trip, and that makes it special." He motioned toward the stage that had been set up on the pier beneath the ship's bow. "That's why everyone's celebrating."

The ship's official christening ceremony had been held the day before and had been a closed affair, with only the cruise-line executives and VIP guests invited, but the stage hadn't yet been disassembled. Banners bearing the blue and white of the Greek flag of the ship's owner, as well as the Liberty circle of stars logo, draped the edges of the platform. In the center, a group of musicians and a dance troupe dressed in traditional white folk costumes performed for the benefit of the *Alexandra's Dream*'s first passengers. Their audience was in a festive mood, snapping their fingers in time to the music while the dancers twirled and wove through their steps.

David bobbed his head to the rhythm of the mandolins. They were playing a folk tune that seemed vaguely familiar, possibly from a movie he'd seen. He hummed a few notes. "Catchy melody, isn't it?"

Stefan turned his gaze on David. His eyes were a striking shade of blue, as cool and pale as a winter horizon and far too solemn for a child not yet five. Still, the smile that hovered at the corners of his mouth persisted. He moved his head with the music, mirroring David's motion.

David gave a silent cheer at the interaction. Hopefully, this cruise would provide countless opportunities for more. "Hey, good for you," he said. "Do you like the music?"

The child's eyes sparked. He withdrew his thumb with a pop. *"Moozika!"*

"Music. Right!" David held out his hand. "Come on, let's go closer so we can watch the dancers."

Stefan grasped David's hand quickly, as if he feared it would be withdrawn. In an instant his budding smile was replaced by a look close to panic.

Did he remember the car accident that had killed his parents? It would be a mercy if he didn't. As far as David knew, Stefan had never spoken of it to anyone. Whatever he had seen had made him run so far from the crash that the police hadn't found him until the next day. The event had traumatized him to the extent that he hadn't uttered a word until his fifth week at the orphanage. Even now he seldom talked.

David sat back on his heels and brushed the hair from Stefan's forehead. That solemn, too-old gaze locked with his, and for an instant, David felt as if he looked back in time at an image of himself thirty years ago.

He didn't need to speak the same language to understand exactly how this boy felt. He knew what it meant to be alone and powerless among strangers, trying to be brave and tough but wishing with every fiber of his being for a place to belong, to be safe, and most of all for someone to love him....

He knew in his heart he would be a good parent to Stefan. It was why he had never considered halting the adoption process after Ellie had left him. He hadn't balked when he'd learned of the recent claim by Stefan's spinster aunt, either; the absentee relative had shown up too late for her case to be considered. The adoption was meant to be. He and this child already shared a bond that went deeper than paperwork or legalities.

A seagull screeched overhead, making Stefan start and press closer to David.

"That's my boy," David murmured. He swallowed hard, struck by the simple truth of what he had just said.

That's my *boy.*

"I CAN'T BE PATIENT, RUDOLPH. I'm not going to stand by and watch my nephew get ripped from his country and his roots to live on the other side of the world."

Rudolph hissed out a slow breath. "Marina, I don't like the sound of that. What are you planning?"

"I'm going to talk some sense into this American kidnapper."

"No. Absolutely not. No offence, but diplomacy is not your strong suit."

"Diplomacy be damned. Their ship's due to sail at five o'clock."

"Then you wouldn't have an opportunity to speak with him even if his lawyer agreed to a meeting."

"I'll have ten days of opportunities, Rudolph, since I plan to be on board that ship."

* * * * *

*Follow Marina and David as they join forces
to uncover the reason behind little Stefan's
unusual silence, and the secret behind the
death of his parents....*

Look for From Russia, With Love
*by Ingrid Weaver
in stores June 2007.*

HARLEQUIN®

Mediterranean NIGHTS™

Tycoon Elias Stamos is launching his newest luxury cruise ship from his home port in Greece. But someone from his past is eager to expose old secrets and to see the Stamos empire crumble.

Mediterranean Nights
launches in June 2007 with...

FROM RUSSIA, WITH LOVE
by *Ingrid Weaver*

Join the guests and crew of *Alexandra's Dream* as they are drawn into a world of glamour, romance and intrigue in this new 12-book series.

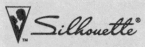

Silhouette®

Romantic
SUSPENSE

**Sparked by Danger,
Fueled by Passion.**

*This month and every month look for
four new heart-racing romances
set against a backdrop of suspense!*

Available in June 2007

Shelter from the Storm
by **RaeAnne Thayne**

A Little Bit Guilty
(Midnight Secrets miniseries)
by **Jenna Mills**

Mob Mistress
by **Sheri WhiteFeather**

A Serial Affair
by **Natalie Dunbar**

Available wherever you buy books!

HARLEQUIN®
SuperRomance®

Acclaimed author
Brenda Novak
returns to Dundee, Idaho, with

COULDA BEEN A COWBOY

After gaining custody of his infant son,
professional athlete Tyson Garnier hopes to escape
the media and find some privacy in Dundee, Idaho.
He also finds Dakota Brown. But is she ready for the
potential drama that comes with him?

Also watch for:

BLAME IT ON THE DOG by Amy Frazier
(Singles...with Kids)

HIS PERFECT WOMAN by Kay Stockham

DAD FOR LIFE by Helen Brenna
(A Little Secret)

MR. IRRESISTIBLE by Karina Bliss

WANTED MAN by Ellen K. Hartman

Available June 2007 wherever Harlequin books are sold!

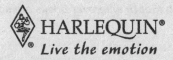

HARLEQUIN®
Live the emotion

REQUEST YOUR FREE BOOKS!

 **Harlequin® Historical**
Historical Romantic Adventure!

2 FREE NOVELS PLUS 2 **FREE GIFTS!**

YES! Please send me 2 FREE Harlequin® Historical novels and my 2 FREE gifts. After receiving them, if I don't wish to receive any more books, I can return the shipping statement marked "cancel." If I don't cancel, I will receive 6 brand-new novels every month and be billed just $4.69 per book in the U.S., or $5.24 per book in Canada, plus 25¢ shipping and handling per book and applicable taxes, if any*. That's a savings of close to 15% off the cover price! I understand that accepting the 2 free books and gifts places me under no obligation to buy anything. I can always return a shipment and cancel at any time. Even if I never buy another book from Harlequin, the two free books and gifts are mine to keep forever.

246 HDN EEWW   349 HDN EEW9

Name	(PLEASE PRINT)	
Address		Apt. #
City	State/Prov.	Zip/Postal Code

Signature (if under 18, a parent or guardian must sign)

Mail to the **Harlequin Reader Service®**:
IN U.S.A.: P.O. Box 1867, Buffalo, NY 14240-1867
IN CANADA: P.O. Box 609, Fort Erie, Ontario L2A 5X3

Not valid to current Harlequin Historical subscribers.

Want to try two free books from another line?
Call 1-800-873-8635 or visit www.morefreebooks.com.

* Terms and prices subject to change without notice. NY residents add applicable sales tax. Canadian residents will be charged applicable provincial taxes and GST. This offer is limited to one order per household. All orders subject to approval. Credit or debit balances in a customer's account(s) may be offset by any other outstanding balance owed by or to the customer. Please allow 4 to 6 weeks for delivery.

Your Privacy: Harlequin is committed to protecting your privacy. Our Privacy Policy is available online at www.eHarlequin.com or upon request from the Reader Service. From time to time we make our lists of customers available to reputable firms who may have a product or service of interest to you. If you would prefer we not share your name and address, please check here. ☐

COMING NEXT MONTH FROM

HARLEQUIN®
HISTORICAL

- **THE PREACHER'S DAUGHTER**
  by **Cheryl St. John**
  (Western)
  Lorabeth Holdridge is a bright butterfly, struggling to break out of
  her suffocating cocoon—will Benjamin be the man to help her?

- **McCAVETT'S BRIDE**
  by **Carol Finch**
  (Western)
  Ex-lawman Jack wanted a quiet life and a restful companion, so
  he sent for a mail-order bride. What he got was Pru—heiress,
  suffragette and all-around firebrand!

- **ROGUE'S WIDOW, GENTLEMAN'S WIFE**
  by **Helen Dickson**
  (Victorian)
  Christopher Claybourne is back—for his title, his revenge and,
  most importantly, for his bride!

- **TEMPTED BY INNOCENCE**
  by **Lyn Randal**
  (Tudor)
  Diego Castillo had vowed his life to God, but Celeste's purity
  could be his downfall....